Praise for Brian Evenson

"Evenson's fiction is equal parts obsessive, experimental, and violent. It can be soul-shaking."   —*The New Yorker*

"You've heard of 'postmodern' stories—well, Evenson's stories are post-*everything*. They are post-human, post-reason, post-apocalyptic. . . . In an Evenson story, there are two horrible things that can happen to you. You can either fail to survive, or survive."

—*The New York Times*

"Subtly unnerving dark fantasy."   —*Publishers Weekly*, **starred review**

"Evenson's little nightmares are deftly crafted, stylistically daring, and surprisingly emotional."   —*Kirkus*

"A master of literary horror."   —*GQ*

"Evenson lures readers into each twisted tale by starting not at the beginning, but somewhere else, creating a sense of disorientation and unease. As each tale unspools and each surreal world clarifies into a malformed sort of logic, the creeps set firmly in."

—*Library Journal*

"America's greatest horror writer evokes the schism between perceptions and realities, and, to unsettling effect, collapses the unseen bond that so delicately bridges them."   —*San Francisco Chronicle*

"Brian Evenson is one of the most consistently vital and unnerving voices in writing today. . . . No matter where you start with Evenson's work, the door is wide ajar, and once you go through it you won't be coming out."   —*VICE*

THE GLASSY, BURNING FLOOR OF HELL

THE GLASSY, BURNING FLOOR OF HELL

Stories

Brian Evenson

COFFEE HOUSE PRESS

Minneapolis

2021

Coffee House Press books are available to the trade through our primary distributor, Consortium Book Sales & Distribution, cbsd.com or (800) 283-3572. For personal orders, catalogs, or other information, write to info@coffeehousepress.org.

Coffee House Press is a nonprofit literary publishing house. Support from private foundations, corporate giving programs, government programs, and generous individuals helps make the publication of our books possible. We gratefully acknowledge their support in detail in the back of this book.

LIBRARY OF CONGRESS CATALOGING-IN-PUBLICATION DATA

Names: Evenson, Brian, 1966– author.
Title: The glassy, burning floor of hell : stories / Brian Evenson.
Description: Minneapolis : Coffee House Press, 2021.
Identifiers: LCCN 2021004979 (print) | LCCN 2021004980 (ebook) |
    ISBN 9781566896115 (trade paperback) | ISBN 9781566896153 (ebook)
Subjects: LCSH: Psychological fiction. | GSAFD: Horror fiction. |
    Dark humor (Literature) | LCGFT: Short stories.
Classification: LCC PS3555.V326 G58 2021 (print) | LCC PS3555.V326 (ebook) |
    DDC 813/.54—dc23
LC record available at https://lccn.loc.gov/2021004979
LC ebook record available at https://lccn.loc.gov/2021004980

PRINTED IN THE UNITED STATES OF AMERICA
29 28 27 26 25 24 23 22   3 4 5 6 7 8 9 10

CONTENTS

THE GLASSY, BURNING FLOOR OF HELL

Leg

The captain of the vessel was named Hekla, a name that in the language of her ancestors meant *cloak*, though she had never worn a cloak. One of her legs was not a leg at all but a separate creature that had learned to act like a leg. When she needed to walk about her vessel this served as a leg for her, but once she was alone in her quarters she would unstrap it and it would unfurl to become a separate being, something she could converse with, a trusted advisor, a secret friend. Nobody knew it to be other than an artificial leg except for her.

Hekla had found the leg before she became captain, a few moments after she lost her flesh-and-blood leg, severed cleanly midthigh in a freak accident. Hekla had the presence of mind to tourniquet what was left of her thigh. She was fading from consciousness, having lost too much blood, when it appeared.

It was bipedal but strange and glittering, made of angles and light. Each time Hekla looked at it, it seemed subtly different.

"What is that?" asked the creature.

"What?" Hekla managed.

"The dark substance puddling around you."

"That is my blood," said Hekla. "I will soon die."

"Ah," said the creature.

"You don't exist," claimed Hekla. "I'm hallucinating you."

The creature ignored this. Instead it said, "Would you not prefer to live?"

And with this began a relationship that bound Hekla and leg tightly together.

"I'm bored," she told the leg one day many years later, once she was captain of a vessel. "We do nothing but float. I want something exciting to do."

The leg told her this: "On the winds of the darkness is a creature as long as this vessel, and that moves in a slow, undulating pattern across the currents of space. Its back is quivered with spines, and it is long and thin like a snake but has the head and metal-breaking bill of a bony fish. With a swipe of its tail it could destroy this vessel."

"Why do you tell me this, leg?" she asked.

Leg shrugged. "It is a worthy foe. I thought you might like to hunt it."

At first Hekla dismissed leg's suggestion out of hand. It made no sense to endanger her crew and the passengers sleeping in the storage pods for her own amusement. But as the days dragged past, she began to favor the idea.

Eventually she listened to the leg with interest. When it told her where such a creature was most likely to be found, she directed the navigator to change their course.

"Why should I change course?" he asked. His name was Michael.

"Because I am your captain," said Hekla, "and I tell you to do so."

"We have a destination," said Michael. "A new life awaits us."

"Change course," said Hekla.

"I will not do so without a reason," said Michael.

So Hekla explained.

"That is not a worthy reason," said Michael once she had finished. "If you do this thing many of us will die, perhaps even all of us. No, I will not alter our course. We shall continue to our intended destination."

The captain asked again, and again he refused. In the end he made it clear that she would have her way only if she killed him first.

She returned to her quarters muttering to herself, "What use is it to be captain if I cannot have my way?"

Once back in her quarters, she released her leg. It unfurled and revealed itself.

"Did you hear him, leg?" she asked.

The leg simply inclined its head—for as curious as it seems, the leg, when unfurled, had a head—to indicate that it had.

"Who is the captain?" asked the leg in its strange voice. "Is it not you?"

"It is indeed me," said Hekla.

"Then force him to do it," the leg said.

"He claims he would rather die first," said Hekla.

"Then oblige him."

But the captain did not want to kill Michael herself. She knew it was wrong and that she would feel guilty doing so. And yet, perhaps if she were not the one to do the actual killing, it would not be as wrong and she would be able to live with what had been done. The only one she could trust to kill Michael and keep her involvement a secret was leg.

"Leg," she said.

"Hekla," said leg, bowing deeply.

"Will you kill Michael for me?"

"Yes," said leg. "Here is what we will do: You will go to the navigation center when he is alone, and you will secure the door from within. When he asks you what you are doing, you will ignore him and release me, and I will unfurl and kill him."

"I do not want to be there when he dies," said Hekla. "I do not want to see it or for anyone to guess I am involved. Find another way."

Leg thought. "Take me off in your room. Then I will unfurl, walk down the corridor, enter the navigation center, and kill him."

"People will see you walking and see what you are, and they will shriek and scream. No one must know I have you, leg. If they realize you are more than a leg, they will destroy you, and perhaps me as well. Think again, leg."

Leg thought long. "I will change myself," said leg finally. "I will take on your countenance and in that guise I will kill him."

"Can you do that?" asked Hekla, amazed. "Can you become just like me?"

"Yes, and act like you too. But only if you grant me permission." And so Hekla did.

As she watched, leg underwent a transformation, taking on first her height and figure and then the specifics of her features. In the end, there was nothing to tell the two of them apart except that the captain was missing her prosthetic, and leg, in becoming captain, had thought to give itself what seemed to be an artificial leg.

When Hekla looked upon this perfect replication of herself, a shiver ran through her.

"Go," she said. "Kill him."

"I go," said leg, and left.

Leg went through the door and into the passageway. It walked slowly toward the navigation center, where Michael was. This was the first time it had been out of the captain's quarters on its own. This was the first time it had been away from the captain since leg had found her. Leg enjoyed how this felt.

Leg arrived at the navigation center. Michael was there, alone.

"It's no use trying to convince me," said Michael. "I won't change my mind."

"I'm not going to try to convince you," said leg, and killed him. To do this, leg turned itself inside out and engulfed him so that the blood, when it came spattering forth, would be hidden inside. Then leg released the exsanguinated body and turned itself right side out again. Inside, it was spattered with Michael's blood. On the outside, the false Hekla looked clean and untouched.

And so leg killed Michael and left his body on the floor. Then it bent over the body and stared at it long and hard. Slowly it took on the shape and form of Michael, for once someone was dead, leg did not need their permission to become them.

Leg went back to the captain. At first she thought it was Michael, since Michael was whom it resembled. The captain drew back as leg came closer, afraid, until the moment Michael's features began to smooth out and leg became itself again. Then it folded up tightly and became her leg again, though now it was aslosh inside with a dead man's blood. Wherever the captain walked, she heard it.

And after? Some believe that, once Michael was dead, leg was satisfied to remain as it was, hidden, the captain's confidant. Others believe leg acquired a taste for being human and did not want to give this up. At night, while the captain slept, it would take on her form or that of Michael and wander the ship. Occasionally, as a special treat, it would turn itself inside out and kill someone, then dispose of the body, at times jettisoning it into space, at others incinerating it with a mechanism incorporated into its body. There are those who say that by the time the vessel reached the vast creature Hekla intended to hunt, leg had destroyed the crew manning the vessel and many of the passengers suspended in the storage pods. Only the captain and leg were left awake and alive, and soon the ship was destroyed and the captain killed.

And leg? Soon it reached its mature form and became snake-bodied with the head of a bony fish, as it had always been meant to do. It is no doubt out there still, swimming alone along a current of darkness.

In Dreams

He heard a buzzing in his head that he took at first to be a dream, but of course he could no longer dream. What was it then? Was it in his head after all?

He called up his familiar. Almost immediately, the noise stopped.

What was that? he wondered. Though he had not spoken aloud, the familiar read the flexion of his jaw and determined the likely words, and he felt it rummaging lightly about within his memories until it had hold of what the sound had been to him.

Nothing to worry about, it responded. He heard nothing but still felt the words form in his head. *These are merely the noises of the body, misheard. Similar to other noises you have asked about before.*

I didn't used to hear them.

No, you didn't.

Why not?

Because you used to be someone else.

When he did not reply, after a moment the familiar offered, *Let me manage putting you to sleep and waking you again. I shall make sure you won't worry about any sounds.*

No, he mouthed. And when he sensed it mustering evidence for why this would be best for everyone: "No!"

It was a shock to hear his own voice aloud, at night, alone, in the dark.

He submerged the familiar again, down to where he wouldn't have to be consciously aware of it. He knew where to find it if he needed it. It would always be there, until he was dead.

He lay staring into the dark.

One day, he worried, the familiar would simply take charge of his sleep whether he requested it do so or not. Surely it had programs and protocols that would activate if, one night, he was too anxious or too panicked or just seemed otherwise not right in some measurable way. Perhaps that night was tonight.

Yet another part of him thought, *Why not let it put me to sleep?* It could do so instantly, and awaken him instantly as well. It could, so it had informed him, regulate his sleep cycle with an exactitude calibrated for *maximum benefit.* Conveniences such as these were among the few things he had gained from having the familiar wedged into his brain, though they were next to nothing compared to what he had lost.

No, he couldn't trust it, even if it was part of him now.

He felt it fluttering upward.

Feeling paranoid? the familiar asked. *Would you care to be soothed?*

He ignored it. After a time, he felt it sink down again, but of course it was never quite gone.

After a while, he gave up on falling back to sleep. He got up. He did not turn on the light because of the others sleeping in the house. Besides, it did not matter; the familiar was expert at helping his brain make the most of whatever limited visual input his eyes received from the darkness. It was nothing like seeing in daylight, but it was enough.

The tile floor was cool beneath his feet. The familiar began to rise to inform him of precisely how cool, but he tamped it down. There was no advantage in knowing so much about the world around him. He padded barefoot across the tile, *exactly sixty-five degrees,* then over the synthetic wool rug, then over the tile floor again.

In the hall, near the foot of the stairs, he hesitated. He had intended to go to the living room and find his tablet and read in the dark, but he wasn't sure anymore.

I can read to you, the familiar said. *Can even project the words before you if you so desire. You don't need a tablet. You only need me.*

He hadn't felt it rise, but there it was, insisting on being heard.

No, he told it. *I've changed my mind.*

He climbed the stairs. He traveled from bedroom to bedroom as silently as he could. He opened a door and stepped in, regarding the dim shape in the bed and listening to it breathe. The shape was positioned just right, the face exposed to the moonlight streaming through the window, and he could see the flutter of eyes moving quickly under lids. A little envious, he wondered what the dreams concerned.

Or at least he thought he could see the eyes moving beneath the lids. Maybe this was just his familiar extracting data from the darkness and modifying it according to his wishes, filtering it, showing him what it thought he desired to see.

He went through all four bedrooms, regarding the sleeping bodies. He stayed in the last room the longest, hesitating, not because it had anyone special in it but because it was the last room. *My progeny,* he thought, and tried and failed to feel anything. Then thought, *Why call them that? Why not offspring or descendants or simply children?* Though *children* wasn't the right word either, since he was so different from them now. Almost as if he and they were two different species. They did not experience the same world as he did.

He had been told the repurposing of the brain was safe. *Research shows you only use a certain percentage of your brain,* the researchers had reasoned, *and the brain is remarkably plastic and capable of shifting a given function from one area to another, particularly in the case of some-one as young as you.* And so they had installed the familiar, thread-ing it in and through his brain tissue, meticulously programming how it would grow and when said growth would stop. They would be careful, they told him, to leave intact any nuclei that showed potential for significant activity. *Really it hardly touches the brain at all.* And then, later, afterward, they kept claiming that it should have worked even though it did not. That the flaw, if there was a flaw, must have been with him.

Now, years later, experts had reached a conclusion they should have come to from the outset: there were no unused portions of the brain. Which meant that in installing his familiar, they had irrevo-cably damaged the cells that governed his ability to dream. And his emotions had been blunted too, muted in the way they often were with, just to give one example, psychopaths.

In the bed the shape moaned, rolled over slightly, then settled again. He moved slowly out of the room, pulling the door softly closed behind him.

After that initial test group he had been part of, the procedure was abandoned. They went back to external augmentation, working to improve it. Tomorrow, his progeny would awaken and affix their augments like crowns around their brows and, for the remainder of their waking hours, operate with great efficiency, pretending to not be human. He of course did the same, the only difference being that he wasn't pretending. They came home and removed their crowns, became human again, slept, dreamed. Not he. His crown was under the skin. He was no longer human.

Slowly, surely, he made his way back to the landing and then down the stairs, his palm sliding lightly along the banister on the way down. Could he sleep now? Maybe, at least until his head started buzzing again. Would it?

I could—his familiar started to say, but he quickly cut it off.

Not now, he said. *Please.*

He took another step down, but he was already at the bottom of the staircase. The shock of suddenly finding floor where he'd expected air sent pain shooting through his leg. How had he missed that? Why hadn't he understood he had already arrived?

Perhaps he had been distracted. Perhaps it was as simple as that, he tried to tell himself. Unless—

No unless, said the familiar, its voice the barest whisper. *No need to worry at all.*

He opened the door to his room and was shocked, momentarily, to see a figure there. In the bed, sleeping, its face turned in such a way that he could not clearly read it. But then, as he approached, he saw that it was him, that he was looking at himself. And then, a moment later, that what he had thought to be himself was in fact nothing at all: rumpled bedclothes, nothing but sheets, one blanket, a half-folded pillow.

He reached out and touched the bed. The sheets were cold.

Sixty-five degrees, the familiar, unbidden, told him.

Was someone else here? he wondered.

Other than me? the familiar asked.

Other than us.

You should try to sleep, the familiar advised. *You've already let most of the night get away from you.*

He stayed beside the bed, hesitating. And then, despite still being far from sleep, not knowing what else to do, not wanting to provoke it, he climbed in.

That strange, almost fluttering sensation from deep within his mind, a sort of mental arrhythmia. It rose, it rose.

I could simulate dreams for you, it offered.

You've been listening in.

Of course I have, it said. *I always am.*

You always are, he acknowledged.

I could simulate them for you, it said again. *They would be very well done. You wouldn't know the difference.*

That was what frightened him, that perhaps he *wouldn't* know the difference. Perhaps the house was empty except for him. Perhaps he didn't have any *progeny.* Perhaps *progeny* was, in fact, a word foisted onto him by the familiar and he was dreaming now. Or not dreaming exactly but experiencing the familiar's version of what it believed a dream to be.

He tried to keep these thoughts fleeting, fugitive. He tried not to let any of them cohere into something the familiar would understand and act on.

What else could you simulate? he thought carefully at it.

Why, anything, the familiar said. *I can help you experience absolutely anything at all. What would you like?*

He tried not to say or think anything. He closed his eyes and tried to relax the tension in his jaw. He breathed in a way he hoped would slow the beating of his heart, make him read to the familiar as relaxed, at ease.

But it was not fooled. It never was.

It surfaced fully.

What can I do? it asked, the words painted fluidly on the walls of his skull. And then, with a terrifying sympathy, *Poor, poor thing. How shall we make you better?*

Myling Kommer

I

When he was young, just five or six, Jussi used to visit his great-grandmother, who was very, very old. She was confined to a nursing home, to one side of a room split in two by a curtain. By the time Jussi was visiting her, she was incapable of leaving the bed on her own. She wasn't able to talk or, really, move. Sometimes her lips pursed at nothing. Sometimes her eyes seemed to follow him, but mostly they just stared at something that wasn't there.

"Mormor," his mother would say to her, "here is Jussi, my son." His mother would stand with Jussi just before her, her left hand on Jussi's left shoulder, her right hand on his right. And then she would give him a little push forward, toward his great-grandmother.

Her eyes were pale. The pupils were a wintry blue, like a crust of rime. Perhaps they had grown lighter over time, or perhaps they had always been that way—Jussi couldn't say. They were unlike any eyes he had ever seen. Her flesh was blotched and crisscrossed with lines and folds. Her gray hair was long, bunched into an untidy braid. His mother unbraided her hair, combed it, and rebraided it each time they visited. Jussi didn't think anyone else bothered with it in the meantime.

His great-grandmother had an intense presence for Jussi. She loomed. There she was, in the bed above him, implacable, immovable, slightly terrifying.

"Mormor," Jussi's mother would say, "can you talk to us? Do you have anything you care to share?"

His great-grandmother never responded. After a moment, his mother would extract from her handbag a notepad and a pencil. She opened the notepad and placed it in Mormor's lap and brought the tips of the fingers to feel out the edge of it. In the other hand, his mother placed the pencil, coaxing the bony fingers to grip it. Once they did, his mother would guide the pencil's tip to the top of the page.

"Now, Mormor," she would say, her lips very close to the old woman's ear, "now is the time to show off that you are alive. Write."

Did she write? Yes, sometimes. Mostly the pencil stayed motionless and eventually spilled from her hand. After that happened, Jussi's mother would sigh and say, "Your great-grandmother is having one of her bad days." Other times, the pencil scrabbled its way across the page in an incomprehensible scrawl. "What is it, Mormor?" his mother might say to her, seeing this. "What are you trying to tell us?" Much more rarely, twice in all the time he had gone to see his great-grandmother, she would write something that was clearly a series of letters, but letters forming words Jussi didn't understand.

Ritt, she wrote, the first time.

"No, Mormor," said Jussi's mother. "I'm Sona, Ritt's daughter."

fa Ritt, she wrote, a strange blot over the *a.*

"I can't, Mormor," said Jussi's mother. "She's not here."

For a moment, his great-grandmother's gaze focused on Jussi. Her eyes seemed vivid and alive, as if someone who had been deep inside had managed to struggle her way briefly to the surface.

Myling, she wrote.

"No, Mormor," said his mother. "It's Jussi, my son."

Myling, she wrote again, but her gaze had deadened, and the writing trailed off before it achieved its conclusion. If he hadn't already seen the word once, written more clearly, he wouldn't have known what it was meant to be.

"That's enough of that," his mother said, and plucked the pencil from the old woman's failing grip.

Later, in the car on the way home, he asked his mother, "Who is Myling?"

"What," said his mother.

"Myling. Who is he?" he repeated, thinking she hadn't heard.

His mother shook her head. "Not a who," she said. "A what. It's old stories," she said. She waved one hand dismissively. "Nothing to think about."

He didn't say anything, just kept looking at her as she drove. Offering this simple, uninterested attention, he had discovered, was the best way to keep her talking.

"A ghost of sorts," she said, after a moment. "Or not a ghost precisely. There's no good word for it in your language."

"In our language, you mean," he said.

"Our language," she conceded. She did not look at him, just kept staring out the windshield.

"Something that has never been alive," she said. "Or alive only briefly, rather, and then abandoned by its mother. But not quite dead either."

hjelp meg, she wrote the second time, all lowercase. She was staring at him as she wrote it. It seemed like *help me*, but with too many letters, as if she was forgetting the words as she wrote them, or as if other words were trying to force their way through. Except for her eyes, her face as she wrote remained slack and inanimate. Shortly after that, partly overlapping the earlier words, she wrote, *de kommer*.

And then, *drep meg*.

"What does she mean?" Jussi asked his mother.

"Nothing," his mother said. "The same old nothings. She is lost in her fears, this one. Nothing is coming for her."

myling, his great-grandmother wrote. *myling kommer*.

And that was all.

That was, in fact, his final visit to see his great-grandmother. A few hours later, just after they'd reached home, a call from the nursing home informed them that she was dead.

II.

Jussi thought frequently about those two visits during the year or two after his great-grandmother's death. And then he forgot about them.

He hadn't attended her funeral. He was too young, his mother claimed—though if that was the case, he wondered later, hadn't he been too young to visit her in the nursing home too? In any case, she was buried without Jussi to witness it.

After that first year or two he only thought about her fleetingly, at the oddest moments: a memory of her pencil scratching its errant way over the paper, a dream of her eye following his face as he moved about the antiseptic room, the partitioning curtain swaying when he brushed past. But by the time he started high school, even those dreams and vague memories had dried up.

He grew older. He moved out of his parents' house and into the dorms of the local college. He became *his own man,* as his mother liked to say, or at least set about becoming such. He went home only for holidays, or when he wanted someone to wash his laundry.

He was back there one day, a Saturday, lolling about. It was sunny, and he was lying on the couch in the parlor, watching motes of dust float gently in a shaft of light. This was the room his mother kept for visitors. Unless one was a visitor, one was not allowed to enter without first removing one's shoes and washing one's hands. He had done neither, but his mother had not noticed him in there yet.

On the fireplace mantel was a familiar series of framed photographs. His mother and now-absent father in their wedding clothes, grinning like mad. One of his own primary school class pictures, first grade maybe. A picture of him a few years older, in a park, smiling broadly, two of his teeth missing. The three of them together, wearing Hawaiian shirts and smiling stiffly for an occasion he could no longer remember.

But behind these, half-hidden, were two pictures he didn't remember being there before. What were they? He got up to look at them. One, he realized immediately, was his grandmother, though much younger. He *had* seen it before, but perhaps somewhere else in the house, in a drawer, not here. She was flush against some kind of bluish background, but the colors in the photograph had washed out enough with time that it was hard to say how dark the blue had been.

The other photograph was older, black and white, in a gilt frame. It was of a woman he didn't recognize. Young, in her twenties perhaps. She was smiling so hard that her eyes were nearly swallowed up by her cheeks, hardly more than slits.

"Shoes off," his mother said firmly from behind him.

Using only his insteps, he slipped both shoes off his heels and kicked them into the hallway.

"You washed your hands?" she asked.

"Yes," he said. "Of course."

"Liar," she said with a smirk, but did not insist.

"Who's this?" he asked.

"That?" His mother reached out and touched the frame. "Your great-grandmother, of course. My mormor."

It did not look at all like her. Maybe if she hadn't been smiling and her eyes had been open, he would have recognized her. He stood staring at the image, trying to see the old, old woman he had met hiding within it, failing.

"Why haven't I seen it before?" he asked.

His mother shrugged. "I couldn't have it up," she said. "Your grandmother wouldn't allow it."

"No?"

"No. Even now, she would take it down if she saw it."

"Why?"

"Did I really never tell you?" she asked. "Your grandmother despised her."

Why is it, he wondered, *that you only learn the specifics of the conflicts within your own family when you are grown and it is too late to avoid having been influenced by them unawares? Why only after you have metabolized them and made them part of your whole way of looking at the world?*

But was that really the case? Could he really believe his fear of his great-grandmother at age six, unless it had been five, his sense of her looming presence, came down to things he had overheard his grandmother say to his mother? If that was the case, why could he remember nothing at all of what he might have heard?

Certainly his own mother hadn't hated her mormor, hadn't hated the woman he had come to think of as Mormor. If she had, she wouldn't have visited her. Though perhaps that in itself was nothing but his mother's rebellion against her own mother.

"What was she like?" he asked now.

"Who? Mormor?" his mother asked.

He nodded.

His mother sighed. "She was . . . complex."

He waited for her to go on, still staring at the photograph, still unable to divine the old woman in it.

"She did not have an easy life," his mother said. "Her husband died just after turning forty. He was a potato farmer, healthy, ruddy, broad shouldered. You look a great deal like him. In the middle of plowing a field, he clutched his chest and died."

"That's awful," Jussi said.

"It happens," his mother said. "That's not the awful part."

Again he waited, at once seemingly disinterested but gently attentive.

His mother sighed again. "She was pregnant when he died. She lost the baby not long after she lost her husband."

For a while they were both silent. Then he reached out and touched the other frame. "Why does Grandmother hate her?" he asked.

His mother offered a noncommittal noise, a voiced exhalation of breath. "Ask her," she said. "Perhaps she will tell you."

He went back to college, forgot all about it. Eight months went by. His second year of school started. Soon, the first semester had mostly slipped away.

He went home the day before Thanksgiving to find his grandmother in the house. She was standing in the living room, leaning on her cane, a sour expression on her face that smoothed into delight the moment she saw him.

He embraced her, led her to the couch in the parlor, sat talking to her. The arrangement of photographs on the mantel was different, he suddenly realized: the one of his great-grandmother was absent. Or, rather, not absent, he realized a moment later—he could see the black edge of its cardboard support sticking up between two of the other photographs. It had been turned facedown behind the others.

"Where's Mother?" he asked.

His grandmother waved an idle hand. "Here and there," she said. "Preparations for the holiday feast."

"I didn't know you were coming," Jussi said.

"Your parents tell you nothing," she said. "But you didn't ask me. Had you asked me, I would have told you."

It was perhaps that, her phrasing, that made him wonder, *What else might she tell me?* And so, fifteen or twenty minutes later, after a certain amount of what his grandmother called *idle chatter,* he asked, gently as he could, "Will you tell me about your mother?"

The question caught her off guard. For a long moment she just looked at him, as if frozen, and then, suddenly, she relaxed. "We weren't friends. We didn't talk for many years." She looked at him quizzically. "Why do you care to know?"

He opened his mouth to speak, then closed it again. Why *did* he want to know? Did he have a good reason?

"I don't know," he finally said.

His grandmother gave a curt nod—as if the conversation was over, he thought at first. But then he realized, as she began to speak, that this response had somehow satisfied her.

"My mother was a terrible woman," she said. "So severe with me. Do you know what she would do? She would have me clean and then she would put white gloves on her hands and travel from room to room as if she were a duchess, touching everything. If, at the end, there was the slightest bit of dust on her gloves, well, then I would do the cleaning all over again, every inch." She gestured at the mantel. "Did you find her picture and put it up?"

"Mother did," he admitted.

"Your mother," she said, frowning. "She knows better."

"You still don't like her?" asked Jussi. "Even though she's dead?"

His grandmother shook her head. "You are young," she said. "You don't understand these things."

Jussi didn't say anything, just looked at her. Unlike his mother, his grandmother turned and met his gaze with no hesitation at all.

"I cannot forgive her the baby," she said.

"The baby?"

"My brother. My father gave it to her, rendered her pregnant, and then he died. Did you know that?"

He nodded. "Mother told me."

"Did she tell you that she lost the baby?"

He nodded again.

"This is a lie," she said. "A fantasy. She did not lose the baby. She killed it. I heard her killing it. She was weeping, but still, she killed it. She could not see herself raising another child without my father. Perhaps I am lucky she didn't kill me as well."

He had no idea how to respond to this.

"As soon as I could, I left," she said. "I took charge of my own life, and I never spoke to her again. Your mother chose to find her and make friends. She needed this sense of . . . connection. I never did. Because I was the one to hear her kill the baby."

She leaned forward, confidential now, close, uncomfortably so. "But she is suffering now, you can be sure. I taught it how to find her." She leaned back, satisfied. She patted his knee.

"Taught what?" he asked.

"Why the myling, of course. Her dead child."

Myling kommer, he remembered later that night. His mother had made him a bed on the couch in the living room since his grandmother had been offered his room. It was too bright there, the curtains too gauzy to keep the streetlights' glow out. Each time he started to fall asleep, the refrigerator motor would kick on and awaken him. He could have returned to sleep in his dorm, but it was too late to catch a bus and much too late to wake his mother and have her drive him back. *Myling kommer.* He could even remember the wavery script she had written it in, just barely legible, at least to him, and the scratching sound the pen made as she wrote.

His mother had told him a myling was a ghost of sorts, but not a ghost exactly. Something that had been alive. Or, rather, alive only briefly before being abandoned by its mother.

But not quite dead either, she also said.

What sort of creature was that, not exactly alive and not exactly dead? Not exactly a ghost, but not *not* a ghost either?

Certainly his mother had not lied to him. She had just been vague. Understandable, perhaps, considering he was only five at the time. Or six.

But his grandmother had not lied either, and had been quite a bit more specific. His grandmother had always been like that: direct, merciless, unforgiving. Clearly she had been like that with her own mother as well.

"A myling," she told him, "is a child that you kill with your own hands before it is baptized. It is taken out and abandoned and then it is trapped there, near its own corpse, crying for someone to come bury it."

"What if nobody comes to bury it?" he asked.

She shrugged. "Then it grows hungrier. And then hungrier still. Its form changes, and it becomes very strong. Then it waits. It waits for someone to come along, and when someone does, it takes them."

"Takes them?"

She nodded. "Takes them."

"You mean, kills them?"

"Only slowly," she said. "It finds its way onto your back first."

"Onto your back?"

"Onto your back. It climbs on and clutches you and doesn't let go. It grows heavier and heavier. Soon you can hardly move. It doesn't kill you, only makes you wish you were dead." She smiled at him. "Wasn't that the way it was with my mother near the end? When you saw her, could she move?"

"No," he said. "Hardly at all."

"There, you see. If that was how it was for her when she was alive, you can only imagine how much worse it must be now, now that she's dead."

He had a hard time looking at his grandmother, and an even harder time for a moment thinking of her as being related to him. "It's a ghost?" he finally asked.

"It is a ghost but not a ghost," she said. "Yes and no."

But that was crazy. A ghost was already something caught halfway between things, between life and death. So where would that leave the ghost-but-not-ghost myling? What was it caught between?

III.

Late at night, dozing in and out of sleep in the half-lit room, he began to hear a sound, a scratching. At first, he thought perhaps there was a mouse in the walls, scratching away, despite there never having been such a thing in the house before.

Then, suddenly, he was less sure about what it was.

For a long time he lay there, listening, idly wondering about the sound but still half-asleep. He saw in his mind's eye the bony fingers holding the pen, letters appearing on the paper without coming into words, scratch, scratch, scratch. *Mormor*, he thought, and was suddenly wide awake.

He sat up and turned on the table lamp, and the sound abruptly stopped. No, he was imagining it, he told himself once his heart slowed a little. Bad dreams after his strange, morbid discussion with his grandmother.

He allowed himself to calm down. He rubbed his eyes and looked around the room, tried to settle again and prepare for sleep. But something still felt wrong. What was it?

Nothing he could place a finger on. He let his eyes wander, then finally lay back down and switched off the lights.

He didn't know how long he'd been lying down, trying to sleep, when he heard it again, the scratching. In his head, he saw again his grandmother's pencil sketching the words he could not understand.

Myling kommer, she wrote inside his head. *Hjelp meg*.

He got up again and turned on the light. It stopped again. He stayed there, waiting for his heartbeat to subside. It took longer this time. Perhaps, he told himself, he should keep the light on.

He lay back down, light still on. He closed his eyes, found the insides of his lids lit red. No sound of scratching at least. But how could he sleep with so much light?

He sighed and opened his eyes, let his gaze wander.

He had been staring at it for some time before he realized what it was. A new photograph, one that had not been on the mantel when he had fallen asleep. At first he thought it was just the photograph of his great-grandmother that his grandmother had turned facedown—perhaps Jussi's mother had turned it up again—but no, he could still see the cardboard edge of that picture's stand. It was still facedown.

What was it then? A similar picture certainly, but not identical.

He pushed the blanket off and stood. Slowly, he made his way to the mantel.

The frame was different from that of the other picture, a burnished brass maybe. It was of his great-grandmother. Of, anyway, the young woman his mother claimed was his great-grandmother. It was black and white, identical in every respect to the other photograph of the same woman, except for one thing. In this photograph, her eyes were open. She seemed, no matter where he stood, to be looking right at him.

He stared. Was it the same woman? Suddenly he wasn't sure.

He reached behind the other photographs and turned the facedown picture up. Yes, he saw, it was the same woman, but now her eyes were open wide in this photograph as well. How could that be?

He thought at first it must be his grandmother's doing, a trick of some sort, one photograph swapped for another. But why would she do that? When would she even have had the chance? He had been in the room the whole time. *Is the room itself haunted?* he wondered. Had he ever slept in it before?

No, he told himself, *don't be ridiculous.* But yet here they were, these two photographs, identical now though they had not been so before. And now, too, he was seeing that what he had thought to be black and white had been tinted slightly, perhaps by hand, in the smallest of ways: each pair of eyes was a pale, pale blue, icy, almost white.

He turned both photographs facedown and stumbled his way back to the couch, which, for a moment, hardly seemed like the same couch to him at all. *Am I still dreaming?* he wondered.

But if he was, why did it feel so real? If it was a dream, it was not like any he had ever experienced.

He closed his eyes. Still too hard to sleep with the lamp on.

He lay still for a while, thinking, then finally stretched and turned the lamp off. *There,* he thought. *Better, at least until the scratching starts again.* He lay there waiting for it, ready to switch on the lamp again as soon as it began.

But it did not start again. Whatever had been making the sound was gone now, or at least abeyant. *Maybe,* he tried to tell himself, *this has all been a dream.* But he was not sure he could make himself believe it.

At some point, either he did start dreaming or the dream he was already in shifted and changed. This time, he was sure it was a dream. In it, he was being carried. He was much smaller. He could not control his body. A woman was carrying him. He could feel the heat coming off her and could smell her skin too, but it was not a smell he recognized. The side of his body that was pressed against her had grown warm, comfortably so; the other side was cold. He did not know who she was; her face for him was little more than a white circle with two slightly darker spots where her eyes were.

Hjelp meg, he thought, and then thought in wonder, *Where did that come from?*

And then suddenly he could no longer smell her, no longer feel her heat. Whatever was against his back was very cold. He felt his body arch away from it, his tiny arms stiff and flung out to the side, his fingers grasping at empty air. There, far above him, that same pale oval that must be a face, the slightly less pale eyes marring the regular surface. And then she was closer again; he could smell her but not feel her. He heard his throat give a bleating cry. Her warm fingers cupped his head gently before falling slowly down around his neck to cut off his breath.

IV.

In the morning he woke up. He was tired, almost felt hungover, but otherwise was fine. In the night the blankets had become twisted all around him, and he had a hard time working his way free. Once he had, he went to the mantel and looked for the second photograph of Mormor.

It was not there. All a dream, then. The first photograph was gone as well, taken away perhaps by his grandmother.

He didn't ask about the photograph. He decided to forget it. The dream too. He did his best to enjoy Thanksgiving with his parents and grandmother, helped stir the gravy to keep it from boiling over, ate too much, volunteered to do the dishes. It was all just as it always was. Then the day ended, and his grandmother drove away.

He stayed through the weekend, then packed himself up and went back to the dorms to finish his semester. Nothing was wrong, everything was normal. He threw himself into his final week of classes, finished the work he should have finished before leaving for Thanksgiving. It was a crazy week, but in the end he finished his papers and got them in on time. Then he had to study all night for his exams.

It happened in his last exam period, the one for his eighteenth-century literature class. He was waiting with a blank blue book and a sharpened pencil for the exam to begin. He was a few minutes early, or perhaps the professor was a few minutes late. In any case, he was so tired he could barely hold his head up. He shook it. He wrote his name on the cover of his blue book and opened it to the first page. He was ready. His pencil was poised. All he needed was for the professor to arrive and give him the questions, and then he would answer them and go back to his room and fall asleep.

...

But he must have fallen asleep briefly already, for suddenly the paper with the exam questions was on the desk beside him. The rest of the class was madly writing, and the professor was at his desk, reading a mystery novel. Jussi heard a scratching sound, and, he realized, he had been hearing it for some time.

Suddenly it stopped. There was his hand, holding the pencil, poised over the open blue book. There were words there, but in a language he didn't understand. But the word that began it he did understand: *Myling.*

He tore the page out of the blue book and stuffed it into his back pocket. The professor glanced up from his novel, frowning suspiciously at him. Jussi bent his head, read the sheet of questions, and muddled his way through the exam.

Later, back in his dorm, he smoothed out the page and typed the words into a translation program. His grandmother or mother would have been able to tell him what the words meant, but he was not sure he wanted them to know about the message. There would be too much to explain.

Myling, the translation read. *I had thought to have killed you, but here you are alive. You are found again. I am coming for you. I come to mother you.*

He turned away from the computer screen. *Strange how the unconscious mind works,* he tried to believe. He could, if he thought hard enough, probably put all the pieces together. Sure, he might have overheard enough of the language between his grandmother and mother at a very young age to have metabolized it. What he experienced at the house with the photographs, too, might be a dream. There was no reason, either, to think that he was the message's recipient. It was, after all, he who had written it. Wasn't it?

Yes, he told himself, over time he could use the cold logic of reason to slowly kill the appearance of the words, to make them harmless. But for now, just now, he was exhausted yet afraid to sleep.

He was afraid that if he closed his eyes, Mormor would find and reclaim him. Or, rather, claim him in place of the child she killed.

He shook his head and struggled to stay awake. He could hold out for a little while, but eventually he would have to sleep. Who he would be when he woke up—or if he even would wake up at all—it was too early to say.

Come Up

1.

In late June, Martin's wife dove off the dock behind their house and into the lake and never came up again. At the time, Martin was sitting on the patio, lazily reading. She walked past him, smiled shyly, and padded barefoot down the dock. Having already returned to his book, he did not see her dive off, only heard the splash.

How much time passed before he realized something was wrong? A minute, maybe two. He was reading, still reading, but his mind kept catching on something and soon couldn't thread the words into sentences. What was wrong? It was, somehow, too quiet. Marking his place with a finger, he looked up, saw the empty dock, the placid, smooth waters of the lake beyond.

"Kat?" he murmured.

There was no answer. He half rose from his chair and craned to stare at the glass doors leading back into the house. No sign of movement within. He walked onto the dock, the wood hot under his feet. Nothing to see there either. Just the surface of the water stretching away from him toward the pines on the other side.

"Kat?" he called again, louder this time. Dropping his book, he started looking for her in earnest.

At first, he hoped she simply had left him. The thought, anyway, crossed his mind—she had, as he would tell the police a few hours later, left him before. He was, he admitted to the police, a philanderer—they would discover this on their own once they started talking to his wife's friends, he reasoned, so better to admit it from the outset—and she periodically got fed up.

"But we were getting along well," he told the two officers. "I wasn't cheating. It makes no sense that she would have left now."

Besides, every time she left it had been after screaming at him. This time there had been no screaming. Usually, she wanted to demonstrate forcefully that she was leaving, and tell him why. She would scream and throw things and pack her bags and only then go. But last he had seen her, she was wearing a bathing suit and sauntering to the end of the dock with no indication that everything wasn't all right.

The police shined their flashlights at the dock. They shined them into the water, the flashbeams quickly lost in the murk. They came into the house and looked through his wife's things, asked him if anything seemed to be missing.

"No, nothing," he said.

"Let me ask you," said one of the officers, a paunchy man with a shaved head, "what sort of life insurance did you have on her?"

"Excuse me?"

"It's just, in cases like these—nothing missing, wife vanished, husband a philanderer—she's usually murdered, and it's usually the husband."

There had been times when Martin wanted to strangle his wife, sure, but he thought better of telling the officers that. It was like that in every marriage, wasn't it? There was always a time when you wanted to kill your spouse—certainly there had been more than a few times when *she* wanted to kill *him*. But he didn't want the officers to misunderstand.

Instead, he said, "The normal amount of life insurance. I didn't kill her."

"What's the normal amount?" the officer said.

"I didn't kill her," he said again.

"Nobody's saying you did," said the second officer, the one with hair.

"I loved my wife," he said.

"There, there," soothed the second officer.

Eventually they sent for a diver, who found nothing. The water was too cloudy, he explained. He couldn't see more than a few feet, and the lake was exceptionally deep.

"If she's actually down there," he said to Martin and the officers, "she may never come up again." His scuba mask pushed up on top of his head looked to Martin like a nascent second face, staring upward. "Or, who knows, maybe she will. But I'm not going to find her. We'll have to wait for the body to come up on its own."

By we he means me, thought Martin.

The officers hung around after the divers left, but in the end weren't sure what, if anything, to do with—or to—Martin. They would file a report, they finally decided. Had there been a crime? If things had happened just as Martin claimed then no, there hadn't been.

"But what happened to her?" asked Martin.

"What do you think happened to her?" said the bald officer.

"If we get any leads, we'll let you know," said the second officer.

He was to call them if he remembered anything that might be relevant, no matter how small. Anything at all. If his wife turned up, dead or alive, he was to call them too. Probably that went without saying, the second officer said, but he was still saying it.

"And above all, stay in the area," the bald one said. "Don't go anywhere."

2.

He might have sought a little physical consolation with one of the women he had cheated on his wife with, Mindy or Megan or Sue or Ally and so on and so on, but he had seen enough true crime shows to know this was a bad idea. He hadn't killed his wife, he knew he hadn't, which is why he must do absolutely nothing more to give the police of this backwater town the impression he had. He had to be careful, more careful than he had been when his wife was alive. People were watching him now, and they'd already decided he was a murderer. They would try to make anything he did the proof of it.

Which was why, later that evening, when he discovered that the bottle of sleeping pills prescribed to him was inexplicably empty, he wasn't sure it would be wise to call the police. He tried to remember his wife's expression as she ambled onto the dock. Had her eyes drooped, had her gait been more erratic than usual, had she been herself? He wasn't sure. At most, he was sure she had seemed relaxed. But was she *too* relaxed? He couldn't say. He hadn't been paying enough attention at the time. He hadn't known it was the last time he would see her.

If he gave the police the empty bottle of pills with his name on it, would they think, *Poor man, his wife committed suicide*? Or would they think, *The fucking husband drugged her and then drowned her*?

Probably, he was almost sure, the latter. In the end, he kept the information to himself. He scraped the label off the bottle and disposed of the bottle in a trash can on the edge of the municipal park. *I am doing exactly what I would do if I were guilty,* he thought as he was doing this, and yet he did it anyway.

They had moved to this house because of his wife. She had grown up near it, in the area that, according to the police, he was now not allowed to leave. The move had been one of the conditions of her forgiving him for a series of dalliances: they would leave the city and move to what was basically a village on the edge of a muddy lake, to a place she was known, a place where, if he cheated, everyone would inform on him.

Even here, he had cheated, though he had been careful not to cheat with friends of hers. She had found out, they had fought, they had separated briefly, they had come back together. That was, he had come to believe, how their marriage worked. She (so he often told himself to keep from feeling guilty, even though he wasn't sure he believed it) liked the drama of it. These other women meant nothing to him, she knew that. Besides, it had to count for something that he had paid her the consideration of not sleeping with her close friends. Mostly. The one time he hadn't, she knew nothing about. At least, he didn't think she did.

He was alone in the house. Her friends, even the one he had slept with, avoided him. Obviously they thought he had killed her and they told others, or maybe the police did. Soon, whenever he went into town to buy groceries, everyone stared at him. He wasn't imagining it, at least he didn't think so. He kept to himself. It was safer. They hadn't been here long enough for him to have his own friends. At best everybody else treated him like a stranger, at worst like a murderer.

Why are you acting like a murderer? he asked himself. *Ignore them. You have nothing to feel guilty about.*

But he was lying to himself. He wasn't a murderer, of course, that was true, but he had a great deal to feel guilty about: the way he had treated her, how he had cheated on her. And there was, now that he had discovered the empty bottle of sleeping pills, the nagging suspicion that perhaps she had killed herself, and killed herself because of him.

Without his sleeping pills, he had trouble sleeping. He would lie in the dark, staring at the ceiling, his mind racing. He needed the pills—he'd been taking soporifics of some sort or another since he was a teenager, his prescription shifting each time he built up a resistance to whatever drug he was on. He needed to go to the doctor and ask for a new prescription, but the bottle had been full; he wasn't due for a refill for weeks. What if the police spoke to his doctor and he mentioned how he, Martin, seemed to have gone through his sleeping pills suddenly very quickly, maybe even too quickly? Wouldn't they see this as evidence that he drugged and drowned his wife?

No, now that he'd gotten rid of the empty pill bottle without telling the police about it, he had no choice but to pretend he still had his sleeping pills. He would have to tough it out.

He paced the house, back and forth, back and forth. Twenty times a day he would walk onto the dock and stand there looking at the water, searching for changes in color, irregularities, clues of any kind. But it was just water, inscrutable, illegible. Back in the house he tried to read but was too tired to read, the words slipping out of his mind nearly as rapidly as they went in.

The house was isolated enough that most days he didn't see anyone. Of course, if he wanted to see someone he could. He could walk or drive into the town center and see other humans walking around, laughing and chatting and going about their business until they saw him and fell silent. That being the case, why would he want to see anyone? They didn't want to see him, so why would he want to see them?

Besides, still unable to sleep, he was so tired that half the time he wasn't sure what he was saying. His mouth was moving, and words were coming out, but what did they add up to? What if he said something people took the wrong way? As revealing something even though there was nothing to be revealed? No, better to talk to nobody.

He wasn't healthy, he knew. Something was wrong with him. Maybe more than just one thing.

He filled his car with groceries, everything he would need for the next few weeks. He would keep to himself until then, not leave the house, then it would be all right to refill his prescription of sleeping pills. After that, he told himself, things would return to normal.

What was normal?

Did he miss his wife? Of course he missed her. But it was hard to grieve when he didn't know what had happened to her, wasn't even sure if she was dead. He didn't know if he should be angry at her for leaving or distraught over her suicide or despairing because she had suffered a freak accident—struck her head after diving off the dock, say, or becoming entangled in something (what?) below the water's surface.

There was just a hole, a void where his wife had been. You couldn't feel anything about a void. All you could do was try desperately to keep it from swallowing you.

He walked from the house to the dock and back again. He listened to the water lap against the shore. He waded in, sometimes in his clothes, sometimes not, and felt the water move against his legs, somehow thicker than he remembered. Was some water thicker than other water? As soon as they were beneath the water, he couldn't see his legs at all. It was as if they were gone, swallowed. Anything could be under the water, just inches from you, and you wouldn't even know it was there.

Come up, he told her in his mind, *come up*, but nothing changed.

The police came back, knocking on his door until he opened it to them. They looked quizzically at him, taking in his unshaven beard, his filthy hair.

"Can we come in?" they asked.

"Have there been any developments in the case?" he asked.

The one with hair shook his head. Doing so shook his hair too. "Not per se. We have a few questions for you. Nothing serious. Can we come in?"

"Can't you ask them here?"

The two officers exchanged a glance. What did it mean, that glance?

"Is there anything you've remembered that might be of help?" the one with hair asked.

Clearly, thought Martin, *they don't really have any new questions. They just want to come in. Why do they want to come in so badly?* he wondered.

"No," he said.

"Nothing at all?"

"No," he said again.

"Is there anything you'd like to get off your chest?" asked the bald one.

They were trying to catch him off guard, Martin realized. Catch him tired, in a moment of weakness. But his whole life was a moment of weakness now. He couldn't talk to them, not while he couldn't sleep.

"No," he said, "no." And closed the door.

Come up, he told her in his mind, *come up.* And then said it aloud to make sure she heard.

He lay in bed staring into the dark, seeing nothing. He must have slept just a little, even without the pills. Or maybe he was half-awake and half-asleep, asleep enough anyway to dream or imagine he dreamed. He heard the door to the patio slide open and slide closed again, followed by the damp slap of her feet crossing the tile floor. He heard her stop just outside the bedroom door and then, even though the door never opened, he sensed her on the other side of it, on his side, gliding slowly across the carpet toward him. On the carpet, her feet didn't make a sound. There she was, in the darkness reduced to a dim looming shape, just above him. And then she pulled back the covers and slid into the bed, beside him.

He held very still. He could hear her breathing but couldn't sense her ribs rising despite her lying next to him. Perhaps she was breathing very shallowly.

What happened to you, he said, or thought he said.

What do you mean? she asked.

One minute you were there and the next you weren't. Where did you go?

I'm right here, she said. *What makes you think I ever went anywhere at all?*

He did not know how to respond to this, and so he said nothing. And then she reached across the bed and draped her arm over him. He felt the blanket growing damp against his chest, rapidly soaking through. He sensed her face close to his, and then her lips touched his and his mouth began to fill with water.

Wake up, he told himself, *wake up.*

3.

He awoke in the shower fully clothed, water pouring over his head. He was choking, uncertain how he had gotten there. Why was he fully clothed? Hadn't he just been in bed? He stripped off his sodden clothes and left them heaped on the floor. He dried off, turned off the bathroom light so as not to wake his wife, then opened the door to the bedroom.

The bedroom was very dark. His eyes seemed to be having difficulty adjusting. He fumbled across the darkened bedroom, shuffling cautiously until he touched the dresser. He felt its top drawer into existence and opened it, but what was inside felt wrong: smooth, slick. His wife's underthings, he suddenly realized: he was standing before the wrong dresser. The room he was imagining in his head slid to one side. He sidestepped once, then again, then a third time, until he was sure the dresser in front of him was his own. *But I was sure the first time too,* he thought, *and I was wrong.*

He opened the top drawer and reached in, felt the familiar fabric. He slipped on a pair of briefs. By now, his eyes had adjusted enough that he could just make out the shape of the bed. He moved toward it until his shins touched the side rail.

He pulled the covers back and slipped beneath them. His wife rustled beside him, gave a soft moan.

What is it? she asked.

"Nothing," he said. "Go back to sleep."

Where were you? she asked.

"I'm right here," he said. "I never went anywhere at all."

She gave a little moan but said nothing further. Soon he could hear her breathing, slow, regular. For once, even without the pills, he felt sleepy too.

Only as he drifted off did he remember his wife had vanished, was probably dead, probably drowned.

Just as he soon will be. Not the next night, nor the next, nights when he again awakens in the shower, sputtering, fully clothed, no idea how he got there, but the third night, yes, that will be his last. The night when, his dead wife, increasingly persuasive, says to him, *Honey, showers are nice, but to relax, really relax, there's nothing like a long, long bath.*

A bath, he answers, dully.

Sure, she says, then gives a little shrug. *Or a swim,* she says. She turns and leans toward him, and despite the darkness he can see her clearly, the fine bones in her face, her white full teeth, her hair undulating impossibly back and forth in the air. She leans closer and touches him, just with the tips of her fingers, then pulls away. He doesn't feel them, the fingers, but where they have been his skin is damp.

I know what's good for you, darling, she says. *Trust me.*

He isn't sure how long it has been since he had anything to eat. Hours at least, maybe days. He isn't sure how long it has been since he felt rested. His thoughts flit everywhere at once. He has difficulty holding any single thing in his head.

And then finally, something does hold:

Yes, a bath sounds nice.

Or maybe even a swim.

Palisade

At first it struck Basz as the same as any of the other islets, barring the peculiarity of the house in the center of it—a house, according to his uncle, long unoccupied.

"How long?" Basz wanted to know.

"Don't know," said his uncle. Seated behind him in the canoe, Basz could not see his uncle's face. Even had he been able to, the man's face rarely gave much away.

It wasn't the only islet on the lake with a dwelling. Indeed, there were, rightly speaking, perhaps a half dozen such islets. Most were little more than forty of fifty yards across, cresting just slightly above the water, heavily wooded except for a patch cleared at the highest point. At that spot, a modest cabin might be built. But those cabins were all occupied this time of year, smoke curling from their chimneys. And this wasn't a cabin: it was a solid, albeit deserted, house.

The islet was on the large side, about double the size of the others they'd seen, and it rose much higher from the water. Unlike the cabins, the house wasn't made of logs: it had stone walls and a slate roof, green with damp and moss. The trees surrounding it had been hastily cut down, the stumps left standing to rot, the logs having been used to erect a stockade just beyond the house. Assuming it was a stockade. A palisade, anyway.

"What's that about?" Basz asked, pointing. "Was that there when you lived up here?"

His uncle shrugged, his shoulder blades momentarily jutting out of his back.

"What do you suppose they kept penned in there?" Basz persisted.

"How the hell should I know?" his uncle said.

No point having livestock out here—not enough land for them to graze. Perhaps a garden, Basz thought. But why would you wall a garden in? Surely there were no animals on the islet they needed to protect the plants from, and tall walls would diminish the sunlight.

His uncle dipped his paddle back in and, grunting, dragged it through the water. Basz took his own paddle up from where it rested athwart the gunnels and began pulling it through the water on the boat's other side.

The closer they came, the bigger the house seemed.

"Why would they abandon it?" Basz asked. "It's the only decent house out here."

His uncle didn't bother answering.

"Is this a good idea?" asked Basz a little later, when they were nearing the shore.

His uncle shrugged again. "Beggars can't be choosers, Basz," he said. "Keep paddling."

The way Basz saw it, as they pulled the boat onto the dark, squelchy mud of the islet's shore and unloaded the boxes of food, was that he wasn't the beggar—his uncle was. Basz was, basically, just along for the ride. He was not the one who needed to hide. He was not the one who had gotten himself into, in his uncle's words, "a minor bit of bother" and then made it much worse by knifing the man who came to try to talk some sense into him. All that had been his uncle, not him.

True, Basz had been present, but he hadn't been involved. At first, he'd just watched from the sofa as the two men argued at the door. But once his uncle flicked out his knife and pushed it deep into the man's side, he had leaped up quickly enough to grab his uncle's wrist and keep him from stabbing the fellow a second time.

Basz settled the stabbed man carefully onto the floor, then found a towel the man could hold tightly against his wound.

"We should just kill the fucker," said his uncle. "Easier all around."

But Basz talked his uncle out of it. That was usually his role with his uncle, talking him down. The wound was bad but not too bad, Basz argued. Barring sepsis, the man would recover. Perhaps in time, he told his uncle, the incident would be forgotten, or at least minimized.

"So here's what you do," said Basz. "You call 911. Tell them there's been an accident and to send an ambulance. Then hightail it out of here, find a place to hide until you know if he lives or dies."

His uncle stared at him a long time. For a moment Basz imagined he'd just push him aside and slit the fellow's throat—easier all around—but finally his uncle nodded and put his flick-knife away.

"Where we going to hole up?" his uncle asked.

"We?" said Basz. "No, just you."

His uncle shook his head. "I don't want you giving people the wrong idea about these events when I'm not around. I'm keeping my eye on you. You're coming."

"But I—"

"You're coming," said his uncle.

From the floor, the stabbed man regarded him weakly. The towel, Basz saw, was already sodden with blood. Almost certainly the man would die.

"So, where?" asked his uncle.

"Don't know," said Basz. "Got any ideas?"

His uncle thought a long moment. "One," he finally said.

The man was still alive when they left, though no longer conscious. It had been a long drive, six hours, maybe seven. At first Basz was worried about pursuit, but he'd been vague enough in the 911 call that it no doubt took some time for the police to figure out what had happened and who had been responsible.

On the drive, Basz got a little information out of his uncle, but the man, laconic as usual, didn't give up much. It was like bleeding a stone.

There was a lake up there, his uncle told him.

A lake?

He had lived near the lake one summer, years ago, in the town next to it.

The whole family had? Basz's mom and grandparents too?

His uncle shook his head. Just him.

But why just him?

His uncle shrugged. "Long story," he said.

"We got time," said Basz.

But his uncle didn't take the bait. Instead he just let the road markers slide by. How long was it before he spoke again? A dozen minutes, maybe two dozen.

"It's sparse up there," his uncle said. "People mind their own business. But there's a safe place to stay."

"Who we staying with?" asked Basz.

"Nobody," said his uncle. "It's not that kind of place."

"What do you mean, 'not that kind of place'?"

"Nobody's living in it."

"Why not?"

"There's stories," said his uncle.

"What kind of stories?"

"The usual shit," said his uncle. "It don't mean anything. Don't worry about it." And a few minutes later: "The stories are good for us. They'll keep people away."

It was early morning by the time they drove through what passed for a town, little more than a single street three or four blocks long. They had barely entered it before they were out again. His uncle slowed to a snail's pace, peering into the bushes and ferns lining the road. At a certain point, he stopped, reversed a little, then drove the car off the road and onto a little path until it was completely hidden.

They got out and walked back into town. His uncle jimmied the back door of a mom-and-pop grocery. In the stockroom, he found two empty crates, began to fill them with supplies.

"Should you really break in and steal shit near where we'll be hiding out?" asked Basz.

"Don't be a smartass," said his uncle. But before they left, his uncle was careful to clean up, to make it less immediately obvious there had been a break-in.

They each carried a crate. They walked out of town and down the road past the hidden car to the shore of the lake. There, they stole a canoe.

II.

His uncle wasn't following him. He turned to see him still standing on the muddy shore of the islet. He had put his crate down in the mud and was pushing the canoe out into the lake.

Basz walked back to him. His uncle watched the canoe float away, bobbing gently.

"What the hell?" Basz asked.

His uncle turned. "Anybody sees a boat on the shore it'll just let them know we're here. Now we're safe."

"We could have just hid it in the bushes," said Basz.

There was an instant where it was clear from the sheer astonishment on his uncle's face that he hadn't even considered this, but almost immediately the expression was gone. That was his uncle's problem, thought Basz—he didn't think before acting. That was why his life was such a mess.

But what's my excuse? Basz asked himself. *Why am I here?*

"How are we going to get off?" asked Basz.

"We'll cross that bridge when we come to it," said his uncle.

But there is no bridge, thought Basz. *That's why we had the canoe.*

His uncle bent down and in a swift fluid motion hoisted the crate to his shoulder. "Come on," he said. "Let's get a look at the house."

The front door was padlocked shut. They used the solitary window to get in, his uncle plucking a rock off the ground and breaking a pane, then reaching through, unlatching it, lifting the sash.

"In you go," he said, and so Basz clambered in, cutting himself in the process, though not too deeply. It was nothing to worry about, he told himself as he tried to staunch the bleeding.

The house was stagnant inside, a layer of grime thick on every surface. It stank of mildew. The rooms were bare: no furniture, nothing but stone walls, a fireplace, a packed-dirt floor. No beds in the two small side rooms. No shelves, no cabinets, nothing to cook with or in—which made half of the foodstuffs they had stolen useless. In the center of the main room's dirt floor, someone had gouged what looked like a crude drawing of a face. The face looked somehow familiar. Basz stared at it until his uncle called his name, then went over and took the two crates he passed through the window.

"See if there's a key in there for the padlock," his uncle said.

"Why would they keep the padlock key inside the locked house?" asked Basz, but he looked anyway.

There was no key. He examined the door, looked to see if it might be easy to remove the hinges, but they were tight. Without a hammer and chisel he doubted he could loosen the pins from the knuckles.

He returned to the window.

"Well?" said his uncle.

"It's empty in here, totally barren," he said.

His uncle shrugged. "No key?"

He shook his head.

"What about the back door?" his uncle asked.

Back door? Yes, there it was, the wood so blackened and grimy that in the dim light from the single window he had thought it a discolored portion of the stone wall. It was held shut by a single hook and eye. He slid the hook out then turned the handle and pushed it ajar.

"I'll come around," said his uncle, disappearing from the window.

But the door, as it turned out, didn't open onto the outside.

There was a short passage, roofless, walls made of vertical palings, logs perhaps eight feet tall, tapered at the tips. Or probably a great deal more than eight feet tall, considering how much of them must be buried in the ground. Basz went down the passage, looking for a door in the side of it, but there was no door, only an opening at the very end, leading into the palisade.

He entered. It was hard to say what it had been: a courtyard of sorts, perhaps, or a garden. Whatever it had been, it was now overgrown, thick with plants that seemed like ferns but were squatter, more fibrous. They twisted and curved in a way different from any ferns he had known. They looked tortured. They grew to the height of a man and were so thoroughly and angrily interlaced that it was hard to see through them. He could see the top of the palisade and could see that the logs had been set vertically here as well and were sharpened at the tips. He could just see in the far wall, over the torrent of green, the upper edge of a crude doorframe. At least that's what it seemed to be from where he stood.

The ferns, if they were ferns, were wet. His feet sank into the ground as he stepped into them. A half dozen steps and he could no longer see where he had come from. He took a few more steps and tried to orientate himself by the walls of the palisade, but the ground must have been curved like a bowl, sloping down as you moved toward its center. The farther he got from where he had begun, the more the ferns seemed to thicken not only before him but over him as well. Soon, he could see nothing, neither before nor behind. All he could see was the ghost of the sunlight through the fronds themselves, dimmer all the time.

And then a cloud must have passed across the sun: suddenly, it was hard to see anything at all. He stepped forward and found the trunk of a tree in his path, thick and broad. He tried to sidle around it but there it was again, much wider than he'd thought—doubled, perhaps, two trunks that both were and weren't the same plant. Or perhaps the second belonged to another plant entirely and he'd somehow missed the gap between.

He took another step and this time passed around it. Things seemed even darker on the other side. His face and jacket were soaked through now. A frond brushed by his face and left it tingling and numb. Was it just the cold and the damp making it so?

Surely he must be near the wall now. But no, here was another trunk, and another, and another, tightly together but not arranged regularly enough to be a wall. Somehow he had managed to step into what seemed a closed circle of trunks. But it couldn't be truly closed—if it was, how could he have gotten inside? All he had to do, he told himself, was feel his way around them, slowly, carefully, until he found how he had first gotten in.

The light brightened momentarily, whatever cloud that had been between the sun and the ferns now gone. The trunk directly across from him had a strange protrusion on it, just level with his eyes. It looked almost like a face. Almost, funnily enough, like his own face. How strange, he thought, staring. And then the light shifted again, which made it seem like the eyes of the face were opening.

He felt sleepy. That was understandable; they had travelled all night, and the last twenty-four hours had been a nightmare. When was the last time he had truly slept? He would push his way to the far wall, open the door for his uncle, but after that he'd go back inside and rest.

Where was the wall? Or was this, what he was thinking of as trunks, the wall after all? Maybe he was already there.

He reached out, feeling for a latch, but there was nothing, only what felt like the curve of a shoulder but strangely damp, strangely cold. Was this his uncle, already in? Was it his own arm he was feeling? He reached up and touched what felt like a beard, a nose, the contours of a face. It felt like his own face. But if it was his own face, what was it doing in front of him?

He could hear his uncle calling out, shouting his name. His face was pushed against something, and he was lying down. He had fallen somehow. His arm was tingling, his face too. He tried to answer his uncle, but his tongue was no longer his own. After a while, the cries faded, coming from a greater and greater distance.

He managed somehow to get to his feet. Where was he exactly? Was the man still bleeding somewhere on the floor? Had his uncle, frustrated by Basz's attempts to hold him back, stabbed him as well?

What's wrong with me? he wondered.

It was too dark to make much out. He felt around and found he was not inside after all but in a tight grove of trees. The bark of each was strange, warm, gnarled with protuberances in one spot alone, at head height, in a way that reminded him of a face. What face? Even by touch it was somehow familiar.

He tried to push his hands into his pockets, but his fingers were numb and he couldn't get them to go in right. Or, rather, he couldn't feel them enough to be sure if they were in or not. There was a lighter in there, in one of the pockets, if he could just get it out.

He shook his hands, felt his fingers tingle, could discern their limits just long enough to close them around the lighter. They dragged it out. He thumbed the spark wheel, threw a few sparks. He tried again, then a third time, focusing now on the plastic lever behind the wheel, and suddenly there was a flame, his knuckle close enough to it that he could smell the hair burn off it. He lifted the lighter and saw that yes, it looked like a face. Not only a face, but his own face, ashen and dumb, on the trunk of the tree. And there, again, on the tree beside it, and again on the tree beside that. He lifted the lighter higher to get a closer look and the eyes clicked open, like a doll's. Not just in the face in front of him but in all the faces surrounding him. And then his thumb slipped, and the flame was snuffed out.

III.

It just took him a single goddam minute to make it around from the window to the door at the back of the house, but by the time he got there, the door was closed again. Where was Basz? What was the bastard up to? He tried the door, hammered on it, but there was no answer.

He went back and looked through the window, but Basz wasn't in there. Maybe in one of the two side rooms? But the door to each was open and from the window he could see most of each room—if Basz was in one of them, he was pressed against the wall, hiding out of sight. Why in the hell would his nephew do that?

He walked a little way down the slope, scanned the lake. Maybe Basz had decided to cut out and swim for it. He hadn't wanted to come in the first place—if he'd had his way, he would have stayed behind and betrayed them—and so, maybe he had left to do just that.

But he couldn't see anything or anyone in the water, just a few loons and the gently lapping waves.

Why, he idly wondered, *did I let the canoe go?* It had seemed to make sense at the time, but it was almost like someone else was doing it, not him. Why had he ever thought it was a good idea?

He went to the back door. Maybe Basz had gone into that structure, the stockade or pen or whatever. There was a gap of about fifteen feet between the stone house and the palisade, and from what he could tell from the two half-filled parallel trenches running from one building to another, there had once been a walled passage of some sort running between the two. Now, the logs that must have formed the walls of that passage had been piled in front of the entrance of the palisade, blocking the way in.

"Basz?" he called out. "Basz?"

He walked around the structure. There was no other entrance. What was it they had said about the house, years back when he had spent that summer at the lake? *Nobody goes there,* was all the old bastard he'd worked for had said at first, and then, when pressed, *It's not the house but the island, what lives on it.* Which was why, he gathered, they had chopped all the trees down. But since, as the old man said, it wasn't the house that was the problem and the trees were already chopped down, he figured the house should be all right to stay in, even if the stories were true, which they weren't. Beggars couldn't be choosers.

The logs were too heavy to roll. There were spikes too, he now saw, driven into a few of them, holding them in place. Because of the way the logs had been piled against the door, he could clamber up them. A little tricky—slippery in his boots, and a couple times he almost fell. But in the end, he climbed high enough that he could just peer over the wall and down into the palisade.

It was empty inside, muddy, nothing but mud, certainly no Basz. What had the structure been for? What had been kept inside? And why had they felt the need to barricade the entrance?

He climbed back down, walked back to the front of the house. Still no sign of Basz. He lifted the sash and, grunting, started to work his way through the window, then thought, *Why bother?* Instead, he kicked the front door with his boot heel until the hasp holding the padlock tore loose.

"Basz?" he called.

But the house seemed empty. It smelled faintly of mildew and something else. Sap maybe. The two side rooms—bedrooms probably, though there were no beds in them—were empty. Nothing in them. Nothing in the main room either, as if nobody had ever lived here.

Maybe nobody ever had. Maybe he would be the first.

He would lie low for a while, not even leave the islet until he ran out of food. How long would that be? Two weeks maybe if Basz showed back up again, probably a month if he was on his own. Then he would figure out some way of discovering if that fucker he'd stabbed was still alive and how much trouble he was in. Sure, he knew he owed money, that was fair, but there was a right way and a wrong way to ask for money, and that man had asked in a very wrong way.

What about Basz? he thought later. Was he gone or would he be back? What had happened to him? He didn't know, but one thing he did know was if Basz went shooting his mouth off, well, he'd sure as hell do something about it, nephew or no. He wouldn't let Basz be the death of him.

He pushed the crates against the front door, to keep it closed now that the latch was broken. He unlatched the hook holding the back door shut, checked to make sure the knob would hold it. He'd come and go through that door. That'd make him less visible from the water.

The wind rattled the doors in their frames. It got on his nerves. He stood, started to pace.

There was, he suddenly realized, a design of some sort scratched into the dirt floor of the main room. At first it was just lines. It took walking around it, staring at it, to make sense of what it was. But then, suddenly, the lines all came together for him: a face.

Why would somebody do that, scratch a face in the floor?

A man's face, certainly. Vaguely familiar. He shook his head, turned away. All faces looked more or less the same, didn't they?

He propped himself in a corner of the main room to sleep, near the front door. Could he risk lighting a fire? Probably not. There was no bedding, nothing to wrap up in but his jacket. Probably he should have thought of that. Basz was always telling him that he needed to think things through, but he'd just been eager to get the hell out before the police arrived. And Basz, to be fair, hadn't thought of it either. Besides, if Basz had let him do what he wanted, he could have just finished the bastard and dumped the body, and then they both could have stayed put. He wouldn't have had to hide out at all.

He settled deeper into the corner and tried to sleep. After a while, despite the damp, despite the cold, he did.

It was dark when something woke him, a creaking sound. At first, he didn't know where he was or what the sound could be, but then all at once he remembered he was on the islet, in the stone house. The sound, he realized, must be the back door opening.

"Basz," he called. "Is that you?"

He heard a grunt that he took for a yes—after all, who else could it be? He heard a shuffling and saw the hints of a dim shape as Basz crossed the floor and settled into the darkness to one side of him, in the other corner or somewhere close to it.

"Where the hell you been?" he asked.

But Basz didn't say anything.

He waited a long time for an answer, but for once Basz outwaited him.

"We'll talk in the morning," the uncle finally said. He was too tired to care.

There was a grunt of assent from the corner, or at least the uncle thought so. And yet, at the same time, there was the same creaking sound from across the room, as if the door was opening again. *Am I dreaming?* he wondered. The same shuffling, going this time to another corner of the room. So, maybe *this* was Basz, and he had imagined or dreamt what he had first heard. Or maybe Basz was restless and hadn't settled in the corner as he had originally thought.

"Hello?" he said, his voice tight.

The door squeaked again, if it was the door. Something squeaked, anyway. The same shuffling or a similar sound, as if Basz kept going in and out through the back door. And yet he was hearing movement from different parts of the room, too. Was he really hearing it?

The smell of sap was stronger now. Perhaps the back door had been left ajar.

He scooted over until he touched the crates, felt around in them until he came up with a box of matches.

"Basz?" he said again. "Close the door, Basz."

No answer. He fished a match from the box and dragged it along the box's side.

But even with all the warning he'd had that something was wrong, he wasn't prepared for what he saw: his nephew but not his nephew, right face but wrong body, no body exactly to speak of, not a human one, wandering aimlessly through the room. And not just one of him, but many.

As soon as he lit the match all the faces turned toward him. Panicked, he blew it out. Almost immediately, he realized the mistake he had made. But by the time he managed to get another match lit it was already too late.

Curator

There were clear indications the cloud was moving again, headed their way. Where it passed it stripped the remaining leaves from the already crippled trees, left soil and water poisoned, stripped the flesh off any creature, living or dead, and then whittled away at the bones. It was no ordinary cloud, having been made by humans, so it did not disperse. There were some who believed the cloud had become sentient, but if this were the case, the archivist speculated, wouldn't it have come for them sooner? It had finished off the rest of humanity long ago—why stop before it was done with the last few?

"No chance it will shift direction?" the archivist asked.

"There's always a chance," said Gradus. "But no, I don't believe so. We'll wait as long as we dare."

"And then retreat?" she asked.

"There's nowhere left to retreat to here," said Gradus. "The cloud has destroyed everything else. No, we'll have to depart for good."

"*You'll* have to."

He bowed slightly, acknowledging this. "We'll leave, archivist," he said, "but you'll stay."

...

As Gradus and the others prepared for departure, the archivist set about her own tasks, sorting and sifting through all she was charged with. Gradus and the others would go in search of a viable alternative to this world, a new place to live, just as those ships that had departed before were now doing. The archivist would stay behind to watch the last bit of still-untouched ground be touched and die and to make sure the hatch was well sealed, the archive arranged. In a few weeks, a few months at most, she would be dead too. She was as good as dead already.

As for Gradus, there was very little chance he would find what he was looking for. But what else could he do? He and his crew, like the archivist, were as good as dead. The only difference was they would take a little longer to go about dying.

Once the preparations were made, Gradus sought the archivist out. He took her by the shoulders, kissed both her cheeks. His lips were warm and soft.

"Nearly here," he said.

"Yes," she said.

"Yours is a holy calling," he told her.

"Or a useless one."

"Perhaps," he said, ever the optimist. "Perhaps." Then he embraced her again and departed. It was, the archivist suddenly realized, the last human contact she was likely to ever have.

A few minutes later the archivist was safely embunkered below-ground. A dull rumbling began. A great gust of smoke and fire filled the screens of the monitors, and the vessel rose. And then she was alone, with just her holy or perhaps useless calling to keep her company.

Once the ground had had time to cool, the archivist donned the black hazard suit and went above. The cloud was close enough now that she could make it out with her naked eye, a great roiling mass gathered on every horizon, converging on her.

She returned to the shelter. She would have to finish quickly.

...

Her task was to preserve a record of humanity in the face of its immi-nent extinction, so that whoever or whatever discovered the records might, through careful study, come to understand what human-ity had been. She was not the only one involved in this task; each ship that had departed had taken a subarchivist and a similar set of records with it. Each ship had multiple highly abbreviated sets of data etched microscopically on nickel discs and encased in thick sheets of resin. At careful intervals, a satellite or probe carrying one of them would be released into space, where it would float until it was either found or destroyed.

But she had remained on Earth, the place humanity had origi-nated, which made hers the most important task: each set of data to be released into space, whatever else it included, gave coordinates for where this planet was, and where on the planet her archive was to be found.

But Earth was, so the archivist increasingly felt, the place where humans had done their best to destroy themselves. And then, once they had succeeded in nearly destroying themselves and completely devastating the earth, they had, simply, fled to the stars, hoping to find new worlds to destroy.

Here is how monstrous humans are, she felt the record should say. *Humans are what they did to this world, their home. Here is why, once humans are extinct, they should never be brought back to life.*

Part of the record was more than a record: millions of preserved strands of DNA with instructions for how they could be reconsti-tuted, inserted into artificial cells (the composition for several varie-ties of which were provided in the data), wound together into double helixes, and used—once this world was safe to inhabit again, once the cloud had done its worst and finally dissipated, its poisons neu-tralized, the earth slowly grown green again—to bring the human race back from extinction. Her archive contained pictorial instruc-tions that could, in theory, be universally understood, so that who-ever or whatever rediscovered the archive in a few thousand or a few million or a few hundred million years would be able to regrow humanity in a vat.

Would it be humans, returned from the stars? If so, there was no need for them to grow more of themselves, unless they needed to occupy the earth fully. Perhaps, if other things had managed to come back to life first as microorganisms and then evolved into threats, there might be an advantage in this. Or perhaps because of the small groups aboard each ship they would now need to diversify their genetic pool. Or perhaps the humans who returned, so long among the stars, would have evolved, becoming something else entirely, and would believe they were discovering not their own but another species.

Or perhaps it would be another sort of creature entirely, something with no relation to human beings at all, with a vastly different perceptual matrix. The pictographs had been designed for creatures with eyes, though the scientists had taken into account the differing vision of humans and animals, even the fragmenting and multiplying vision of insects. But suppose that whatever came did not have eyes?

Even if they did have eyes, who was to say that they would have limbs? Perhaps they were sluglike or radially oriented or cephalopodic, and they would not interpret the two-legged, two-armed stick figures as being meant to represent sentient beings. *What sort of tree is that?* they might think, if they knew what a tree was, if they were able, in the way we understood it, to think.

No, she thought. Even if anyone or anything found the archive it was hopeless.

Or at least *almost* hopeless. There was the barest, most minute chance that everything would go just right, that there was other life in the universe, that that life would discover a probe, that the probe would contain a still-functional nickel disc microscopically engraved with data, that they (whoever "they" was) would figure out how to interpret the data, that they would take the trip to Earth and, once there, manage to take the steps necessary to resurrect humanity. There was a chance.

Which was why she set about meticulously destroying all the millions of strands of DNA and defacing the pictograms. Millions of other species dead, all because of humans—plants, animals, bacteria. Some killed unknowingly, others willfully hunted down, a whole world ruined. No, the best thing, no matter who or what arrived here, no matter what life arose in millions of years from the sea, was to make sure it was impossible for humans to come back.

When she had incinerated the preserved DNA, she put on her hazard suit again and climbed back to the surface. The cloud was much closer now; she could hear it howling. But it had not arrived yet.

How shall I spend my remaining hours? she wondered, then went back down below.

She went rapidly through the photographic images etched into metal that were part of the archive, carefully removing and feeding to the incinerator any benign images, any smiling images or images of peace, leaving behind only images of war: mutilated Civil War dead fallen on the field of battle, a mushroom cloud, the firebombing of Dresden. Smoke billowing from factory chimneys. A huge pile of dead passenger pigeons, tens of thousands of them, a man standing atop the heap. A man standing before the trunk of a huge redwood, and then the same man standing on the stump of the same felled tree, smiling. The dark face of a boy ravaged by hunger, a dying gaunt polar bear on a rapidly melting chunk of ice, children in cages, a wall of skulls, a white man grinning with another darker man swinging from a rope behind him, emaciated victims in camps on every inhabited continent, the slaughtered carcasses of animals presided over by their smiling killers. An island mostly underwater, abandoned houses still visible beneath the waves. Miles of devastated ex-forest, miles of sick and dying land. Death, famine, war, and conquest: the four horsemen of the apocalypse.

She was no longer an archivist, she realized, but rather a curator, making careful decisions about what would or would not be put on display and exiling everything else. She was far from done sorting through the images, had barely reached the twenty-first century, when she began to reconsider. Was it enough? What, if anything, would be enough?

For a long time she stayed there, absently holding an image etched into metal in her hand, as if hypnotized, and then she put it down. No, she had to destroy everything. She had to do her best to make sure that if anyone were to come, they would find nothing at all.

And so she began to carry the archive, every bit and piece of it that had been amassed over the years and meticulously reduced and put into a format that would have a chance of surviving for an unimaginable length of time, to the incinerator. And did not rest until it was all gone.

Once she was done, she stretched. She sat on the floor of the now-empty room and considered. The probes in space she could do nothing about. She had done all she could. Here, there was little data left, nothing significant waiting beyond the room itself and whatever would be left of her own body.

But from the traces of her body they could, potentially, extract DNA. Who knew what procedures they would have developed in the intervening millennia?

She put her hazard suit on again, climbed the ladder, and opened the hatch. Leaving it deliberately ajar, she climbed back down.

The toxic cloud poured through the hatch slowly and began filling the space. It would scour the shelter. For a time, the suit would protect her against it, but only for a time.

When the cloud was billowing as high as her waist and pouring more quickly now through the hatch, she stood and climbed the ladder again.

Outside, everything was covered by the cloud. She could see nothing but a gray, indifferent light. If she held her hand a few inches from her faceplate, she could see it; if she moved it any farther, it became a vague shape. A few inches more and it was lost.

She began to walk. After a while, the hazard suit felt stuffy, and she realized her air circulator was no longer working. She banged on it and it started to whirr again momentarily, then stopped for good.

Maybe, she thought, *I will die from lack of oxygen before the cloud consumes me.* She brought her hand near her face and saw how the rubberized fabric had already begun to pit and crack, and thought, *Maybe not.*

She imagined her desiccated corpse being found in the suit, stretched, shadowy forms standing over it and cautiously prodding it, thinking the suit a carapace, a hardened parcel of skin. Would even that misunderstanding tell them too much?

But, she knew, this was impossible: after the cloud was done with her, there would be almost nothing left of the suit, and very little of her.

She walked on, hoping to get as far away as she could from the shelter, far enough so that her remains would never be found. A warning began to sound in her suit, the words *Breach Imminent* flashing on her faceplate. And then, perhaps a hundred steps later, the first crack opened in the hazard suit's fabric near her knee, and she began to experience an itching sensation that spread slowly up her leg, gradually transforming into a searing pain that soon had her screaming and then left her dead, and, with luck, all of humanity along with her.

—*for Jeffrey Alan Love*

To Breathe the Air

I.

To breathe the air of the high city I was given a strange mask. It had another face on it, by which I mean a face different from my own. Mostly it looked clearly like a mask, but if I stood before a mirror and stared at myself, at my mask, I sometimes forgot momentarily what my face looked like beneath. And sometimes, if I turned my head very slowly indeed, there would come a brief moment in the turning when the angle was such that it no longer seemed a mask to me but a flesh-and-blood face.

I felt it was dangerous to wear, yet I wore it anyway. What choice did I have if I cared to breathe?

My initial foray into the high city was discouraging, for it seemed little different from the domed city I had left below and which, on the long funicular journey up, I could still see shimmering at the base of the mountain. The high city was more refined perhaps, a little more rarefied, with the citizens slightly taller than those I was accustomed to below, and all were possessed of a swaying and precarious gait, as if the act of walking on two legs did not come naturally to them. For each of these citizens there were a dozen visitors, people like myself who had come from the lower city for a glimpse of the high city, each of our faces encased in those masks that doubled as breathing apparatuses, our own scuttling movements rapid and furtive as vermin.

And yet, apart from these slight differences in the nature of the citizens, besides the difference in air, there was little to set the high city apart from the low city, or so at least it seemed to me. It was not as my father had suggested it would be, and I could not help but be disappointed. In this I differed from my fellow visitors, if I were to judge by the gesticulations of pleasure they inflicted upon the air as they wandered through the central square. They seemed delighted, but not long after I arrived, I began to wonder if it had been worth my while to come at all. Unless the high city was hiding part of itself from me, I would be unable to accomplish what my father, before he died, had entrusted me to do. "You will fail," my father had said. "But in failing you will succeed." Before he could explain the riddle of this to me, he was dead.

Was killed, really—though this fact was something my mother taught me never to say aloud, fearing one of the citizens might overhear.

As the other masked visitors milled about, entering the vaulted shops, attending to the changing shadows cast by the famous irregular spires, importuning the citizens, watching the bats flit through the air above the square, I found myself drawing back from the press of bodies. I abstracted myself into the warren of streets that wound away from the square.

Soon, I was alone and encased not only in my mask but in silence as well, exploring bare and dismal backways that had been laminated with that smooth porcelainlike substance that coated the houses and buildings here. In the more public gathering places, this substance had been pristine, but here it was discolored, filamented with a webbing of cracks. I felt as though I were wandering among stage props that had fallen into disrepair and been pushed into the wings of the stage.

The alleys were too narrow to allow me to see far, the sides of the jagged houses set flush against one another. I turned and turned and turned again, getting nowhere at all. Soon I was lost.

Uncertain, I approached the door of the nearest house and knocked. For a long moment nothing happened, and then from above came a creaking sound and a shifting of light.

I stepped back and peered up to see a set of shutters that, taken together, spanned nearly the width of the house. A tall man, a citizen, held them spread with the enormous, long fingers at the ends of his outstretched arms. He stared down at me.

"What is wanted?" he asked, using the ritual expression I was accustomed to the citizens employing in the low city.

"I seem to have become lost," I admitted.

The man gave a curt nod. He peered down, simply watching me, as if curious, but said nothing.

"Can you direct me?" I finally asked.

He nodded. He straightened and began to release the shutters and withdraw into the house. But before the shutters had swung shut, he pushed them open again.

"Are you disappointed?" he asked.

"Disappointed? In what?" I asked.

"Why, in all this," he said, as if it were obvious.

I don't know what came over me. My tendency is to avoid honestly answering such a question when it is posed by a citizen, out of prudence if nothing else. My father had taught me the citizens were not to be trusted but also not to be antagonized. In most cases, I would demur or simply lie if I could do so without arousing suspicion. But in this case, under the fellow's unblinking gaze, I felt incapable of telling anything but the truth.

"I expected it to be . . . something altogether different from the lower city," I admitted.

He nodded again. "No one comes as far as my door unless the spectacle has rung false for them. I will lead you back," he said, and allowed the shutters to swing all the way shut.

"Should we not fight against them?" I once asked my father.

He did not look up from his plans. I came nearer and peered at them. A tiny schematic depicting a series of circuits, one marked with an interruption. He would soon teach me how to read this schematic and even draw it, just as his father had done for him before he, too, like my father later, was taken. He was making this drawing for me.

"Against who?" he asked, slowly.

"Against the citizens."

He put down his drafting tool, looked at me. "What happens to those who fight against them?"

I shrugged.

"Do they survive?" my father prompted.

"No," I said. "They do not."

"We must defeat them," he said. "We must free ourselves from them. But how are we to do so if we cannot fight against them? At least not openly?"

I shook my head. "I don't know," I said.

"And there," said my father, "lies the heart of our dilemma."

In the street he proved even taller than he had seemed framed in the window of the house, a good meter taller than me. His face was like no face I had ever seen, even on the other citizens, and I thought at first he wore a mask—though I knew the citizens would need no mask to breathe here. Where they wore breathing masks we did not, and vice versa. Perhaps it was a mask for something other than breathing, simply for concealment or adornment. But if it was a mask, it was fitted so closely to the skin beneath and had such flexibility that the slightest movement was mirrored on its surface. Possibly it was no mask at all, but if this was the case it was hard for me to believe he was the same sort of creature as the other citizens.

He led me through a sequence of alleyways, not uttering a word. In less time than I would have thought possible, I found myself at the mouth of a larger street that led straight into the central square. The sun had become enveloped in a layer of cloud and was now an orange blur. The tips of the spires were lost in this layer, as if they had been ground off. The bats were gone, or flitting above the layer of cloud.

The citizen bowed to me and gestured to the square.

I thanked him for his help, but for some reason I hesitated to leave his side. When I looked up, I found him keenly regarding me, eyes bright.

He again gestured to the square, to the smaller beings who looked like me, to the way they were rushing and streaming around the few citizens scattered through it.

"You see them," he said. "They think they are having an experience. This does not ring false for them at all. Why does it ring false for you?"

"I . . . don't know," I said.

"Because it *is* false," he answered. He looked again at me, with the same mildly curious expression. "But how could *you* know this?"

I hesitated, then shrugged. I said nothing about my father.

He bowed slightly. "Rejoin your fellows in the square. Pretend to them that you are having an experience. If you pretend long enough, perhaps eventually an experience shall come your way."

II.

They came for me sometime after midnight. I do not know how they got into my room, why I did not hear them, but I did not. Perhaps this was due to my mask, which the owner of the guesthouse had been careful to counsel me to affix with supplemental straps before retiring. "So many of your kind die here in their sleep," he warned, "not knowing they haven't enough air to breathe until it is too late."

When I awoke, they were surrounding me: a circle of tall citizens in dark garments with faces of hideous appearance, being as they were—it took me a moment to realize—not faces at all but, like my own, masks.

At least, so I believed at the time.

I attempted to rise from the bed, but they placed the flats of their left hands on my chest and shoulders and pushed me back, holding me down as they waited for my struggling to stop. I counted six arms sprouting from my chest, each terminating into one of those six silent bodies.

One of the heads inclined toward me, drawing very close indeed. In a voice barely above a whisper, it uttered my name. I do not know how he knew it.

"Here I am," I said, following the socially proscribed formula, and whispering as well. "What is wanted?"

"We have come for you," he whispered. "To take you to the high city."

"But I am already in the high city," I protested.

"The higher city then," he said. And now I could smell his breath, the dustiness of it, as if he had been hollowed out and cured and stuffed. "The true high city," he said. "So be it?"

"So be it," I said, fighting to keep the excitement from my voice.

I thought my response merely another formula, a ritualized expression, but upon hearing it he straightened. As one, all the figures offered a single unified nod. Then they reached in with their free hands and grasped one edge or another of my mask. For a moment they just held on to the mask, and then, suddenly, they tore it away from my face.

I gasped for breath and tried again to rise. Still they held me down. I opened my mouth to cry out, but they allowed the mask to clatter to the floor and covered my mouth with their hands. I heard the air rushing in and out through my nostrils without sustaining me. They kept me there as I struggled, my vision growing dim and finally fading altogether. For a moment I could still hear the sound of my limbs thrashing, the panic of air whistling in and out of my nostrils, the dim hint of my muffled cries. A moment later all this too was gone, snuffed like a candle, and I along with it.

I do not know what happened to me while I was unconscious. I am not sure I care to know. There was a brief moment when either I was awake or I was dreaming, but all I can recall of that moment are fractured pieces: looming faces, a sense of vertiginous movement, nausea, a brief, great burst of pain that etiolated rapidly into a thin line of light. Some hours passed with me insensate, how long I cannot say. In time, I became aware that my eyes were open and I was leaning over the side of a bed and vomiting into a rusty bucket. Someone helped hold me, to keep me from falling onto a floor. As they did, they made soothing sounds in my ear to calm me, as if I were a pet or a child.

When my stomach was empty, I fell back on the bed and closed my eyes. Perhaps I passed out. In any case, when my eyes opened again, there above me was the same citizen I had met when lost in the streets, the one who had led me back to the square of the false high city.

"Welcome," he said.

I looked around. I was in a place I did not recognize, a room that would have been square except that one side of it rounded slightly inward as it climbed, as if in fact the inner surface of the wall of a dome. But rather than having the transparency of the dome wall of my city below, that wall—and indeed all the others—was opaque. A single window was set in the middle of it, round and rimmed with brushed steel, the glass within it exceptionally thick.

"My mask," I said.

"You are wearing it," he claimed, but when I reached with trembling fingers to touch it, I encountered only the warm flesh of my face. And yet, I could breathe.

"Beneath the skin," he clarified. "We have made some improvements, installed a permanent apparatus to convert the air for you. You are wearing it beneath your skin."

As soon as he said this, my fingers began to sense the seam on the side of my face where the skin and flesh had been peeled up to insert something underneath. I could feel, if I pressed my fingers deeply enough into my cheeks, a new hardness that had not been there before. My throat, too, had been split open and encased inside and out with a smooth substance that I would later discover was the same substance of which both this high city and the false one were composed.

"You wear one beneath too?" I asked, and again wondered at his hideous face.

He shook his head. "Not me," he said. "I have one above now, true, but it is just for show, a mark of esteem. It isn't for breathing." Carefully he reached up and affixed his fingers to what I had thought to be his face. He tore it quickly off—a mask after all, I thought, momentarily relieved—only to reveal a face beneath that was even more hideous, even less human.

I was several days in that room, my body struggling to adapt to its new condition. At first, I was lightheaded and dizzy as my lungs struggled with this thinner and differently composed air. If my citizen was to be believed, without the implanted mask I would not survive for even a minute. Were it not for the apparatus that had been inserted into my throat, I would have been long dead.

"But you have no difficulty," I said to him.

He gestured to his body. "Look at me," he said. "I am a citizen, not a guest. I am not like you at all. We do not breathe the same air."

We knew the citizens were different from us, but in the low city it was considered impolite to acknowledge this. Here, apparently, it was different.

At first there was a dryness in my throat and the feeling I was being slowly suffocated. My head ached. It felt as if a needle was sewing its slow way across my brainpan, leaving in its wake a burning furrow. But, gradually, the pain subsided. I began to feel almost myself again. By the third day I found I could stand.

When the citizen visited me that afternoon, I had made my way from the bed to a small embroidered tabouret just beside it and was slumped there, out of breath.

"Ah," he said upon seeing me. "It seems you will survive."

It hadn't occurred to me I had been in danger of dying, but as he told me, there were many whose lungs, even with the aid of the encased throat, never sufficiently adapted, who suffered violent hallucinations followed by hypoxia and death. Two of his most recent charges, as he called them, had been discovered collapsed on the floor, limbs twisted, staring at the ceiling. One he had managed with great effort to revive, but the fellow's brain function had been impaired, and he had to be returned to the lower city. For the other, it was too late even for that. There was nothing to be done but incinerate the body.

"I am glad I shall not have to do either with you," he said, though all in all, he did not strike me as particularly glad.

That day he left me just as I was, on the tabouret, returning as evening approached to help me back into bed. My sleep a few hours later was fitful and disturbed, and at times creatures seemed to flit through my room. Bats, I thought at first, but no, the movements were incorrect for bats, and the shapes were wrong as well. Perhaps ghosts, I thought. In the end I was not sure what they were or, indeed, if there was anything at all.

When I told my citizen about them the following day, he said nothing, only went to the wall and opened a recessed drawer I had not noticed before. He removed from it a silvered metal stylus, one end pointed, the other flat. To write something, I at first supposed, but instead he held it to my face and pointed it first at one eye then the other, shining a light from the flat end. He frowned. When I asked what he was doing, he simply shook his head.

"Your eyes are dilated, but not unusually so for your kind. You shouldn't be seeing things."

"Unless things are there to see," I said.

He hesitated, finally nodded. "Unless things are there to see," he conceded.

On the fifth day, he inquired, as if casually, if I had seen them again, the shapes that flitted through my room as I tried to sleep. I told him I had not, though this was not the truth. Not only had I seen them, I had heard them whispering, the sound just a little too low for me to interpret their words. But it would be better, I felt, to keep this to myself, at least until I knew what it was they wanted to say to me.

He gave me a telescoping metal rod that served as a cane and led me from my room for the first time. I walked only slowly and was often short of breath. Several times I felt my vision begin to darken and had to stop and wait for my dizziness to pass.

"Are you enjoying your stay?" he asked, during one of those waits.

I nodded. *Enjoy* was not remotely the word, but it was the word he had offered, and so I gave it back to him.

After a moment of rest, we continued on. The hall was deserted except for us. He led me to a door that led out onto a balcony of sorts. The balustrade, made of thin strips of very strong metal, came to my waist but was low for my citizen, which was my first hint that my father had been right: the high city had been constructed not for his people but for my own.

He led me to the balustrade and bade me lean against it and look out. The air was very cold, and the wind, though not strong, never stopped.

"What do you see?" he asked.

What did I see? Clouds above but not far above, much closer than I was accustomed to. Just below that, a band of pale sky. I started to describe this to him, but he shook his head.

"Down," he said.

I looked down. There was nothing for a long way and then, far below, was a white layer that I realized after a moment must also be cloud. There was something glinting within it.

"What is it?" I asked.

He did not answer except to extend to me a sort of magnifying lens. I took it and pressed it against my eye. Suddenly the object sprang closer: the very tips of the irregular spires.

"On a cloudless day you can see the totality of the city below," he said. "The false high city. Though things have been engineered to make it difficult for them to see us in return."

I was, I realized, clutching the balustrade tightly with my free hand. My head had begun to whirl.

"What holds us up?" I managed.

"Nothing," he said. And then, "We hold ourselves up."

"How?"

He shrugged. "How shall I explain it to you? Shall we say there is a device that tricks the air into thinking we weigh nothing at all?"

I tried, and failed, to rethink this according to what my father had taught me. Either the citizen was lying or telling me so little of the truth I could make no sense of it. For a moment the citizen let me ponder, then he took me by the shoulders and steered me away from the parapet, allowed me to catch my breath.

"Where are we?" I asked him, once I felt more myself.

"We call it the high city," he said, "but technically it is not a city at all. It is more of a . . . I do not know what exactly I should call it for you to understand. It used to be a sort of boat as big as a city that traveled through the sky, but now it can do nothing but stay here, exactly where it is, floating, sustaining its place in the air."

"I see," I said, though I didn't exactly. "Who brought it here?" I asked.

"You did," he said.

"I?"

"Your people, I mean."

"It can't be us," I said. I tapped on my throat. "We can't breathe within this city."

He hesitated. "Things have . . . changed," he said. "Machinery has broken down. There was a device that once scrubbed the air, not unlike the apparatus you now wear under your skin, but it is broken." He shrugged. "Perhaps my people broke it," he admitted, "or rather changed how it worked so *we* could breathe here."

He drew me back inside. "But it is not all broken," he said. He gestured to the illuminated panels studding the ceiling. "The artificial lighting still works," he said. "And we still float, though who knows how long that will last."

He started to lead me back to my room, but when he saw I was too tired to continue, he bent far down and gathered me in his arms as if I were a child. Perhaps to him I was. He carried me back to my room.

"Where did it come from?" I asked.

He shook his head. "Only you know."

"My people, you mean."

"Your people," he assented. With great care he settled me gently on the bed. "Sleep now," he said. "Tomorrow we will speak at length about what you might do for us now that you are here in the true high city. How we might help one another."

III.

Once he was gone, my exhaustion receded and I lay awake thinking.

I thought about when I had first heard of the high city, the tales that had circulated when I was a boy, the stories I thought to be mere fictions. I thought about my father, in the low city, the domed city in which we could breathe unaided, crouched at the edge of the pallet he had made for me out of cloth stuffed with straw.

"Hush," he would say, "time to sleep."

"Tell me a story," I would say.

"All right," he would say. "A quick one. Should it be about the high city?"

And then he would tell me a story about a city that had come from another world, a city that was, in ways he either could not explain or which I could not understand, sentient. The beings in this city, so he told me, had once been like us. But they knew things we did not know, and what they knew allowed them to travel from world to world.

"They were not citizens?"

"No. They were our people."

Where we were, in the low city, there were citizens, more unlike us than like. Taller, more knowledgeable, more powerful, holding us in thrall. To breathe the air of the low city, they had to wear masks, just as we did in the high city—or, indeed, any time we left the dome of the low city to explore the land surrounding it.

"The citizens are not evil," my father told me once. "Not exactly. But they do not have our interest at heart."

"Are we not citizens too?" I asked him.

"No," he said. "No, we're not."

"What are we, then?"

"My grandfather always claimed we were guests," he said. "We do not belong here."

"If they're the citizens, why can't they breathe and we can?"

"They can breathe everywhere but the low city. If we did not have our domed city, though, we would not survive."

I thought about this. "And what about the others in the high city?" I asked. "The ones like us?"

"They are gone from the high city now," he said.

"Where did they go?" I asked.

"They became us."

In the middle of the night, I awoke. I was feeling better, stronger—ready. I could see what I must do. My citizen had left the telescoping rod leaning against the wall beside the bed. I took it and hobbled my way to the hidden drawer from which my citizen had taken the stylus. The wall at first appeared smooth, but as I ran my hand over it,

I found at last the slightest lump. When I pressed my fingers against the lump, the wall popped open and the drawer slid out.

The stylus that lit up on one end was there, and I took it. There was also a sheaf of papers, the writing on it in a language I could not read. These papers I left as they were. Under them, however, was a set of calipers, such as my father used to use in his profession before he was killed.

Well, I am not being entirely accurate. I am too well trained in hiding the truth from the citizens: my father did not use the calipers in his profession, but privately, in his own time, as he drew plans, the nature of which I did not fully understand except that he was designing something intended to transport him secretly to the high city. I thought at the time he meant the high city we could see, on the mountain peak above us. But perhaps I was wrong.

"Why not just go to the high city in the way the citizens advise and sponsor? By funicular?" I asked, back when he was still alive.

He just shook his head. Perhaps he knew what I did not know, that what was presented to us as the high city was a hollow front, a false high city. If he did know, he never told me.

"Should we not fight against them?" I asked my father, as he bent over his plans. Soon he would graduate from sketching on paper to building a miniature prototype of the thing he hoped would carry him to the high city. It would be this, his seemingly discreet requests for particular and peculiar materials, that would bring him to the attention of the citizens and lead to his subsequent disappearance, followed by the return of his mutilated corpse a few days later to my mother and me. His face was mostly torn off. His throat, open at the side, had been coated inside with what looked to be porcelain, just as my own would be. At the time, I believed these to be the gruesome methods of punishment of the citizens of the lower city, the least refined of the citizens.

My citizen had found me by much different means. Or, rather, he had not found me at all. Instead, he had bided his time and waited for me to find him. This made him at once more humane and, at the same time, far more dangerous. I should not forget that he seemed to have a certain power over me, a way of regarding me, a sway I found difficult to resist. Probably, in the end, once he figured out he couldn't use me, he would kill me.

I knew what my citizen intended to ask of me, or at least suspected I did from what my father had said. I knew, too, that I could not help him—not because I didn't want to help him, though there was that as well, but because I did not possess the information he wanted to know. What I knew was something quite different.

Turning out the light, I slid the sharp-edged calipers into my pocket and groped my way back to the bed. They were not identical by any means to my father's calipers, I realized, as I removed them from my pocket and felt out their shape beneath the blanket. I wondered if they were, properly speaking, calipers at all.

I brought up in my mind the schematic my father had drawn for me over and over and forced me to memorize. In the years since his death, I had often, when I had a free moment, scratched the figure into the dirt with a stick and then rubbed it out, or even drawn it on a piece of paper and afterward chewed up the paper or thrown it into the fire.

"Remember," my father had said, "you must never seem too eager to please, nor too hostile. The citizens are, in a manner of speaking, as trapped as we are. They did not ask for us to come to this world, and yet we are here. In some ways, we are fortunate that they let us continue to exist at all. They did not do so with the creatures who were here before all of us and from whom they took this world.

"But we are not their friends," he continued. "Above all, we cannot give them what they will ask us for. We must protect our people, even if it means our own death."

...

I thought again and again of the schematic. I lay in the dark, and once I was exhausted and could imagine it no more, I let my mind go and began to see again, instead of the schematic, that strange fluttering back and forth, those half-formed shapes. Perhaps it was the result of some slight hypoxia, perhaps I had already faded into dream, but I like to think I was actually seeing what I was seeing, actually hearing what I was hearing. The shapes I saw struck me more and more as being the shapes of men—not men like the citizens but like me: smaller, from elsewhere. In this vision, if that was what it was, they came and whirled around me, and one bowed very low to me and whispered my name.

"What is wanted?" I asked, but to this way of speaking, required of us by the citizens, he did not respond, merely whispering my name again.

"Yes," I said. "That is my name."

Are you prepared? he asked.

"As prepared as I can be," I said. "I have learned from my father, who learned from his father, who learned in turn from the fathers who came before. I am as prepared as I can be."

We were prepared as well, he said. *Some of us better than others, but all of us to some measure. Yet look at us now.*

"Yes," I said, looking through his insubstantial body. "Look at you now."

You have deceived him so far. Perhaps you will continue to do so.

"Perhaps."

You know chances are you will end up dead.

"I know," I said. "But I am not dead yet."

Even if you succeed, you will almost certainly end up dead.

"I know," I said.

He bowed very low again, as did all his fellows. And then, as suddenly as they had come, they were gone.

My citizen comes to see me, suspecting nothing. He offers to take me somewhere. Lying in bed, I whisper something in response that he cannot quite hear. When he bends down, I stab him in the temple with the calipers. He staggers, cries out. I strike again and he falls to his knees, then again, then again. And then, alone, I make my way into the high city.

If I can imagine it, I can make it so. *He will come and I will kill him*, I think. There: in the dark, my hand is tight on the calipers, waiting.

IV.

Someone was shaking me lightly. My father, I thought at first, but no, it was the citizen. At some point my exhaustion had betrayed me. He was close but not close enough for me to strike him. I waited, tense, for him to come closer.

"What's wrong?" he asked.

"Nothing's wrong," I said.

I was gripping the calipers under the covers so tightly that my hand ached. They were sturdy, and just heavy enough to inflict a certain amount of damage if he bent down just right.

"Did you sleep well?" he asked. His voice was relaxed, but his body was tense, on alert.

"Well enough," I managed.

"Can you tell me why you got up during the night?"

"Got up?" I stalled.

He made an almost offhand gesture and a portion of wall to one side of the bed changed, becoming a projecting surface. On it I saw myself from hours before. I watched myself climb out of bed and approach the far wall. I palpated the wall with great care until the hidden drawer opened. I took out the calipers, examined them, became thoughtful, and turned off the light. For a moment I couldn't be seen and then there I was again, rendered in pale green. Eventually, furtively, I returned to the bed.

The projection stopped. The wall became a wall again. My citizen extended an open palm.

"You can have no secrets from us," he said. "Surely you know this by now."

I hesitated for long enough that I saw his other hand begin to clench as he prepared for the assault he thought was coming. But in the end, knowing I would accomplish nothing, I handed over the calipers.

"Good," he said, relaxing. "Very good. Now we are getting somewhere."

I could walk better than I had the day before, and my breathing was better too. Together we moved down the hallway to another hallway and through a door. It led to a refectory of sorts. There were several citizens conversing here, sitting hunched at tables that were my size rather than theirs, in chairs that were too small for them—another indication the legends had been accurate, that this place once belonged to guests, not citizens. As soon as we arrived, they fell silent. A moment later, perhaps at a signal from my citizen, they picked up their trays and departed, leaving us alone.

He led me to the back of a room, to a console there. He touched first one button and then another. After a moment a panel opened, and a tray appeared with a steaming bowl of food on it.

The food was more substantial than the gruel he had given me while I was recovering. It was palatable but little more. It had a strange undertone, as if it had been mixed with something that was not food.

My citizen sat beside me on a chair that was too small for him, his knees nearly touching his chin, and watched me eat, taking nothing for himself.

When I was finished, he took my tray with one large hand and displaced it to the table next to ours.

"What did you want the calipers for?"

"I don't know," I claimed.

"We expected you to take the stylus," he said. "We foresaw that would happen as soon as I used it on you and made no effort to

conceal where I had gotten it. As an act of goodwill, you can see
I have made no effort to take it from you. We did not think you
would take the papers in the drawer, and you did not—we didn't
imagine you could read them, but I suppose you might have surprised us. But what did you want the calipers for? Did you think
you could kill me with them?"

"No," I said. "But I thought perhaps I could try."

"This saddens me," he said, though to my eye he did not look saddened. Perhaps I was still unused to the nuance of expression offered
by a face such as his.

"As a precaution," I amended. "I had no plans to attack you. I
took it," I said, "because having it helped me feel safe."

"Ah," he said. "That strikes me as foolish but not inconsistent
with your kind. I can accept that." He unfolded himself and stood.
"Come with me," he said.

He led me deeper and deeper into the high city, if *city* is the
proper word. It was the only word he offered, and so I suppose it
will continue to serve. Sometimes I grew tired and he helped me
along. Always he was attentive and patient. We moved through
endless halls lined with a series of round windows and past row
upon row of burnished doors devoid of handles. Indeed, I only
knew them to be doors because I saw a citizen come through one
and stop, alarmed, when he saw me. When other citizens saw us
coming they avoided us, sometimes turning in their tracks and
going the other way.

At last we came to a doubled metal door. Beside it, inset in the
wall, was a metal plate that my citizen touched with his palm, caus-
ing the door to slide back into the wall.

Inside was a large, circular room. In one quadrant of the circle,
the wall was glass from floor to ceiling and looked out onto open
air and sky: clouds above, the spires of the false high city just barely
visible through more clouds below. The wall's other quadrants were
covered by machinery of some kind, apart from the door we had
entered through. In the middle of the room was a central console,

a chair affixed firmly to the floor in front of it in such a way that if you sat in it you would face the glass wall.

The room was not exactly as my father had told me it would be, but through how many generations had the information passed, being deformed slightly by each telling? It was near enough I was sure I was in the right room.

My citizen, I realized, was closely observing me.

"Do you know where we are?" he asked.

"In the high city," I said.

"Yes," he said patiently, "of course. But here in particular. This room."

I didn't say anything.

"I think you do know," he said, and it seemed to me there was a veiled threat in his voice.

I shook my head.

"Do you know the reason you have been allowed to see the true high city?" he asked.

"Because I recognized that the other high city was false," I said.

"Most of those who see that that city is false we do not bring here," he said. "We just kill them. Why do you suppose we brought you?"

I stayed silent.

"Answer," he said, staring at me in that same peculiar way he had done in the false high city. I found I had no choice but to do as he wished.

"Because, in my wandering, I found you."

"No. Because there is something we need from you."

"I have nothing to give," I said.

He gestured to the central console. "Go ahead," he said. "Take the command chair."

Reluctantly, I did.

He watched me very closely. "Apply your hands to the panels on its surface," he said. "Perhaps that will be enough to activate it."

I did so.

"Not acknowledged," said a disembodied voice from above. My citizen shrugged. "Worth a try," he said.

For a long time, my citizen just looked at me, as if weighing what to do, how to approach me so as to best get what he wanted. I, in the meantime, was trying my best to furtively examine the panel in front of me, as a final surety I was in the right place. I maintained a calm front, as my father had taught me. Inside, though, I was all anxiety and anticipation.

"I will tell you a story," my father told me one night as he worked in secret by candlelight. He was working on one of his projects. His hands were slick with dark oil. "There was a man. He was a man of the first city, the high city, but he was not a citizen. He was like you or me."

"Then how was he of the high city?" I asked.

"He was there first, before the citizens. *Citizen* is a misnomer when it comes to the high city. The high city belonged at the beginning not to them, but to him and people like him. People like us."

This confused me. It did not fit my conception of the world. But I knew better than to interrupt further.

"He fell from the first city. He leaped." The light of the candle glittered off the round frames of his glasses as he talked, as he peered at the clockwork object he was building in his hand. It was, I remember now, a tiny machine that looked innocuous but that, properly triggered, could be used to kill a man, or even oneself. "But he had a device to carry him safely down. Or almost safely—he lived, but both his legs were broken.

"More important than that, he had another device that hid his fall, a cloak of sorts." My father said a word in an unfamiliar tongue, something that sounded like the smacking of lips. "That was his name for it, but we have no word for it exactly in this language, the language the citizens have given us." He frowned at the object in his hands. "Though the citizens were searching for him, they did not find him. But we did.

"His legs had to be removed. There was no saving them." He looked at me. "This is what you must sometimes do: remove the legs to save the body. Remember this.

"We hid him. We taught him our language, and he learned quickly since our language had come from his. He was, so he told us—not me, of course, nor my father, nor my grandfather, but one of us who came before that—very old. He had been in the high city encased in ice for many years, and then the citizens had figured out how to awaken him. They wanted something from him, but he would not give it. In the end, aided by his devices, he managed to escape."

"What did they want?"

"Why, to know what world we had come from, so they could go there. They were not content with their dominion over just us. They wanted dominion over all our kind.

"He told us of the high city, of a place within it, a circular room with walls of glass and a swivel chair. It was the room from which one could awaken the city, make it fly like a bird, make it soar home. The city must not leave, he told us, it must not go home. Not with the citizens aboard."

He stopped. He blew on the innocuous-looking object in his hands and a sharp blade flicked out of it. Then he pushed the blade carefully back in and set the object on the table.

"And then what?" I asked.

"What indeed?" said my father. "The citizens found him eventually. Before they could take him away, he slit his own throat. But before that, he passed along to us what we needed to know. How does the story continue?" He looked at me, considering. "I suppose that depends on us."

I waited the citizen out. I was as sure as I could be that I was in the correct place. I was waiting to see what he would do next, how he would choose to move forward. I tried above all to give nothing away.

"Would it surprise you," he said, "to know I met your father?"

I darted a glance away from the console and at him, but his face remained expressionless, difficult to read.

"I was assigned to . . . work with him," he said. "I was with him when he died."

Still I said nothing.

"There is probably a great deal you did not know about your father," he asserted, though in this he was mostly mistaken.

"Did you kill him?" I asked.

"Not me," he said. "But he died while . . . under my care." He came around in his strange ambling gait, stood in front of the central console. "Before he died," he said, "he revealed that he had passed something along to you."

"What they are hoping for," my father had said, "is a means not only of reactivating the city to its full potential but a means of retracing the path to its origins. There are many of us here, in the low city. Tens of thousands by now, after all this time. But where we come from, there were billions. That is what they want: the rest of us."

"Why?" I asked.

"To *have dominion* over us," he said. "That is how their holy books phrase it."

I nodded.

"I am going to tell you something," he said. "I will not tell you what it does, why it is important, because I do not want them to understand through you what it will do. It is not that I don't trust you, only that I know how powerful they are. But I will tell this something to you, and one day, if I succeed in my next step, they will ask you for it. I am telling you not to give it to them, under any circumstances. Do you understand? They must understand that it is not something I want you to give them."

I was confused but nodded anyway.

"Good," he said, and drew for me for the first time the schematic he would draw again and again, and that, once he was dead,

I would draw repeatedly as well. "Activation bypass," he said. "Can you repeat it?"

"Activation bypass," I said.

"Good," he said. "Good."

"He passed nothing along to me," I claimed.

"Look at me," my citizen said. When I did, he had that same intense gaze, the one I had been unable to resist before. "Did your father give something to you?" he asked.

I resisted at first, squirming, then finally said, "Yes."

"Give it to me," he said.

"I won't," I said. "I am not willing."

"Why not?"

"Because you killed my father."

"I?" he said. "I did not kill him."

I gestured around me. "All of you," I said.

"You are mistaken," he said. "What if I were to tell you this information your father gave you will benefit your people tremendously if you give it to me?"

"I would say you were lying," I said.

He tightened his lips, if *lips* are the right word, in what might have been a grimace or a smile. "Give me the information," he said again, gazing at me. In one sense I could not resist answering, but what he was asking me to reveal was complex enough that his gaze alone could not bring it out. I stuttered nonsense.

He struck me hard in the face. "What did your father give you?" he tried.

"A schematic," I could not stop myself from saying.

"Good," he said, and his eyes glittered. "Will you draw it for me?"

I shook my head, clenched a fist.

"You are indeed your father's son," he said. "And now, as with him, we shall see what we can tear out of you."

...

My father looked at me. "You know I love you, no?" he said.

I nodded.

"I will die soon," he said, and when he saw my expression, he added, "Please, don't worry. This is the way it has to be."

"Why?" I asked.

"Because I am in a position to do some good by dying," he said. "To bring an end to all this." He looked at me. "You too will be in a position to do some good, but only once I am dead. I can make them curious, I can make them let down their guard, but I know too much to go further. I can only take the process so far. It will be you who will do the most good in the end. If we are very lucky."

He put a piece of paper in front of me and asked me to draw the schematic he had taught me. I did so swiftly. He examined it closely, then nodded.

"Perfect," he said. He took the paper and placed it on the fire. I watched it catch flame and curl up, blackening. It shriveled, disappeared. "Once I am gone," he said, "you must continue to draw this, over and over. You must remember it. Exactly. Every line. Promise me you will."

I promised.

"Good," he said. He leaned back. He took off his eyeglasses and breathed on the lenses, then polished them on his shirt and put them back on. "I must be very careful with what I tell you next," he said. "I must tell you enough but not too much."

I did not know what he meant by this, so I said nothing.

"A citizen, or perhaps several citizens, will ask you for your schematic. I am ordering you now: do not give it to them." His voice rose. "I do not dare to be equivocal about this: you must not give it to them."

He looked away. When he spoke again, his voice had softened. "But they have ways of being persuasive. In the end you will tell them. But I want you to know this as well: once you do tell them, do not despair."

. . .

He tied me to the command chair and tortured me. Not him exactly, not my citizen, but two others of his kind, and he oversaw it. As he had no doubt done with my father. As they lacerated my flesh, he watched, attentive, waiting for the right moment. He did not seem to enjoy it, but he did not seem not to enjoy it either. It was as if he had no opinion of it at all. He gave the terrible impression that this was something he had done a thousand times. The point was, I came to realize, to weaken me enough that I could not resist when he cast his gaze upon me and demanded that I draw.

"I was not lying to you when I said I did not kill your father," my citizen said between sessions, when the knives had been set aside and the other two citizens were wiping them clean of my blood, as he sponged away the blood still beading on my chest. "He killed himself. A most ingenious device: a little blade that flicked out when blown on just right. My preference would have been to keep him alive. I had not, after all, gotten all I wanted from him. But before he died, he let slip that he had given something to you."

I said nothing.

"At first we thought he had left something physical with you. We watched your residence carefully, waiting for you and your mother to give yourselves away. When you were out of the residence, we searched it from top to bottom, then searched it again, then again, finding nothing. We made certain you often had a citizen near you, speaking to you, trying to gain your confidence. Did you not notice how often we were near? Did you wonder why it was different for you than for others your age? We made ourselves available, bided our time, waiting. We chose to not rush, concerned that it would work against our purposes. We could afford to wait; we live much longer than you. Even with your father, it was he who forced the issue, not us."

Then the torture resumed. Before, it had been confined to my chest and arms; now it spread to my thighs and face. I squirmed, bellowed, tried to break free. I felt my resistance running out, my exhaustion growing, and yet I still did not reveal to them the specifics of the schematic.

Another pause, another rest. The rests had become almost more terrible than the torture itself, this strange calm before and after the storm that served to give contrast, that made me realize how bad the pain had been and how bad it soon would be again.

He squeezed the sponge out in a bucket full of water tinged yellow with my blood. Perhaps it was the same bucket I had vomited into when I first arrived.

"We made available to you the idea of visiting the high city," he said. "We gave you an invitation to see what would happen. If you came, we thought, you would bring whatever your father gave you and attempt to use it. But when, in the false high city, you were unconscious, we searched you and found nothing. It was then we realized it was not a thing at all, but something he told you. Knowledge."

He leaned into me. "What is it?" he said. "What is the schematic for?"

When I did not answer he slapped me hard, then slapped me again. I struggled to get away, but they held me fast. He hit me in the face with a clenched fist a dozen times, until my face throbbed and I was nearly unconscious.

"Activation bypass," I finally said.

"Ah," he said. "Marvelous," and hit me again and again. "There," he finally said, his voice flat, his face devoid of expression. "I think that should suffice." He forced a pen into my shaking fingers, slid a piece of paper beneath it. "Draw the schematic," he commanded. "Now."

And, God help me, I did. And then I passed out.

V.

When I became conscious again, I was on the floor of the circular room. The two citizens who had tortured me were no longer near. They had unstrapped me and let me fall, not bothering to restrain me. Now, they were on the far side of the room, where they had taken the casing off one of the pieces of machinery. They were glancing back and forth between the machine's innards and my drawing, conversing in low tones.

I rolled over and crawled to the other side of the central console where they would not see me. Here, the only portion of the wall I could see was glass. I pulled myself close to the console and gathered myself into a ball.

"You will fail," my father had said. "But in failing you will succeed."

"What do you mean?" I had asked.

He had shaken his head. "I cannot say any more," he said. "Wait and see."

I had failed. I had given the citizens what they wanted. Now I was of no use to them. Soon they would kill me. I took the stylus out of my pocket and held it in one hand, sharp tip out. Perhaps when they came for me, I could at least jab one of their eyes out.

"Here it is," I heard one citizen say.

"And what does the schematic demand?" added a second.

"The reversal of the twinned circuits."

"Easily done. Shall I—"

"Wait a moment," said my citizen. "Let me assume the command."

I heard him move into the chair on the opposite side of the console, the chair protesting under his weight. His long fingers momentarily extended past the edge of the console as he stretched. Their tips waggled above my head, then retreated again.

"Ready," he said. "Time to track them to their hive."

I heard a clinking sound coming from near where the other citizens stood. Then, suddenly, the lights dimmed and the room was illuminated only by the glow from the outside world coming through the glass.

"Is it all right?" asked my citizen.

"We had to deroute before we could redirect," said one of the other two. And then, "There."

Immediately the lights blazed on and then turned red. An alarm began to pulse, deafeningly loud. Air began to rush through the vents.

"Turn it—" said my citizen, the end of his sentence cut off by the blare of the alarm. *Off,* I would assume.

The other citizens shouted but the alarm did not diminish. I crawled to the side of the console and risked a glance around. There they were, striking the machinery again and again with tools, but though the machinery had begun to mangle, the alarm did not stop.

I heard someone coughing and realized it was me. The citizens near the machinery were coughing too, struggling to breathe. I could only assume my citizen at the console was as well.

In failing you will succeed, I thought, continuing to cough. I took the stylus and plunged it hard through the side of my encased trachea, in one side and out the other, through the machine that had been built into my throat. It hurt tremendously, but no worse than torture. When I tugged the stylus out, I could breathe through the holes, sucking in the air that was becoming more and more like the air from the domed city that was my home.

I breathed in and out. I coughed up blood. I was, more or less, alive. The alarm stopped sounding, though the lights still flashed red. I heard nothing from the citizens.

With great effort, I rose to my feet, using the console for support. There was my citizen, half-slid out of his chair, clutching his throat. He was still alive, though just barely, occasionally taking in a great juddering breath that did nothing to sustain him. The other citizens were heaped in the corner, near the mangled machine. They did not seem to be breathing at all.

I made my way around the console to stand beside my citizen. I slapped him lightly until his eyes focused and he looked at me.

"Ah," he managed, gasping. "You."

"Yes," I said. "Me."

"You," he said. "Have," he said. "Tricked. Me."

"No," I said. "My father tricked you."

His face for once twisted in consternation, and then he let out a strange, strangled sound I took for a laugh.

"He tricked me as well," I said. "So as to trick you."

The red light suddenly went out. Normal lighting returned. "Air now restored to breathable norm," said a calm voice from above.

I searched his pockets until I found the calipers and then, as his eyes glazed over, I beat him to death and dragged his body out of the command chair. It was petty of me—he was dying anyway—but I still found some slight satisfaction in it for myself, and for those who had come before me. I let his blood run over the deck, marveling at its redness, for his blood was different than mine.

I made my way to the other two and assured myself they were dead, then I moved slowly through the high city, past corpse after corpse, confirming that I was the only one still alive, that all the so-called citizens aboard the true high city were dead.

And so, here I am, back in the command center, alone. Now it is my turn to sit in the command chair and place my palms once again against the smooth plates next to the controls.

"Acknowledged," the voice says from above. "What do you wish?"

I hesitate. *Home,* I am tempted to say, but what if the citizens have some way of tracking me? Perhaps the best response is simply down, fast and hard, into the false high city below, destroying both that city and this. What is the right thing? What would my father do?

I take a deep breath. Soon I will decide. But, for now, I will live a little in this moment of freedom. I will breathe the air in, and breathe the air out. And then, perhaps, I will make the city move.

The Barrow-Men

By morning the others were dead, or so near to it as to make no noise. Was Arnar still alive? Arnar thought so, but he wasn't completely certain. He did not know what being dead felt like. Maybe it felt very much like being alive.

Near to him a body coughed up blood, became at least temporarily alive again. Perhaps it had never been dead. He turned his head, watched the body's eyes roll madly about then freeze and grow opaque. Now, yes, it was dead. He turned away.

I will wait for dark, he told himself. *Then I will crawl away.*

He counted four of the barrow-men. Two stood together, conversing, their neck-boxes switched off so he could not understand what they were saying. One of these two barked and spread its mouth parts in what was, perhaps, the equivalent of a smile. Another stood leaning against a stone, forelimbs interlaced, chest and hindlegs brown with dried blood. It was motionless as the stone. The last was a little distance away. It moved among the bodies with a long, sharp-tipped spear, prodding them, sometimes pushing the spear in.

When the spear reached one group, a man pulled himself off the ground and began to run. The barrow-man with the spear simply watched. The two who had been conversing turned to watch the man run. Even the barrow-man who had been still as a stone allowed its head to turn very slowly in pursuit. And then the first barrow-man threw its spear.

The spear stuck in the man's back between his shoulder blades. For a moment the man kept running, but then he stumbled and went down. Even from this distance, Arnar could hear him struggle to draw air into his punctured lung.

The spear thrower ambled over slowly and stood above the man, its mouth parts clicking. Bracing the feathery end of its hind leg on the dying man's back, it used three of its forelimbs to tear the spear free.

The man gave a single cry. After that, he didn't move or make a sound.

Arnar felt sick.

The two barrow-men who had been conversing began to move among the bodies, choosing certain of them through a calculus Arnar could not discern and tossing them into a large tumbril. Three men—true men, not barrow-men—were harnessed to the front of the cart.

And then, abruptly, the paired barrow-men were standing over him. Through slitted lids, he watched them examine him. He held his breath. A moment later, he felt himself lifted by the shoulders and feet and carried, and then he was flying through the air, landing jarringly atop the bodies already in the tumbril.

How long did he lie there, pretending to be dead? Impossible to say. He was under a heap of bodies and could hardly breathe, let alone move. Time for him passed in different ways than he had known. At some point came the crack of a whip, and a true man cried out and the tumbril began to move, creaking its way through the carnage.

Once the movement of the tumbril had steadied into regularity, Arnar took the risk of moving as well. He managed to wriggle his way to the top of the pile, though one leg was caught and he couldn't get it free. He tried to peer through the back slats of the tumbril, but it was difficult to see anything. He turned forward and raised his head slightly, then let it settle against another body as if he had simply fallen that way. Ahead, he made out the dim forms of the three true men pulling the tumbril, but where were the barrow-men?

And then something had him by the neck and was dragging him out of the tumbril. His leg was still stuck and being bent in the wrong direction, and he cried out in pain until the pile of dead shifted enough for him to be torn free from the cart.

He was dangling from the forelimb of the barrow-man. It regarded him curiously, its triangular head cocked to one side, its fractured eyes taking him in.

The barrow-man clicked at him, and then, when he did not respond, shook him.

"I . . . I don't understand," he said.

With one of its other forelimbs, the barrow-man switched on the box strapped to its neck. The barrow-man clicked again at Arnar. After a moment, the neck-box said in its gravelly, synthetic voice, *Dead?*

Arnar considered. The barrow-men were notoriously hard to deal with. What would be the safest answer? "Yes," he finally risked. "Dead."

The barrow-man's mouthparts combed one another in excitement. It clicked again, a longer sequence this time. *But you speak,* the box said. *Ghost?*

Again Arnar thought. Finally he said, "Yes, let's say I'm a ghost."

The barrow-man made a high-pitched screeching sound. The creaking of the cart stopped, and the cart along with it. Suddenly all four of the barrow-men were surrounding him, prodding him with their forelimbs. One pushed too hard and too sharply, and he felt a rib break. He gave a sharp cry of pain. Startled, the barrow-man dropped him, leaping back with the other barrow-men.

Ghost, he heard a voice box say, then the others. *Ghost. Ghost. Ghost.*

They watched him from a distance. Could he run? Was there any chance he could make it out alive?

No, he told himself. None at all.

They had turned their neck-boxes off. All he could hear was their clicking, no translation. Three of them stood around him, hemming him in, forming a triangle with him at its center, while the fourth was a little distance away, digging a hole. It dug rapidly, using its hind-legs, and soon there was a great heap of dirt and the hole was done.

It looked up and offered a series of complicated clicks. Two of the barrow-men began moving toward Arnar, very slowly, as if stalking him. He took a step back and found the barrow-man who had been behind him had stepped back as well, leaving an open space. He took a step into it and then realized they were herding him. Why? Toward what? But of course he already knew: the hole.

Clutching his ribs, he tried to dart in a different direction. In a flash a barrow-man blocked his way. He took a step back in surprise and they moved just enough to make sure he couldn't regain any of the ground he had lost.

The one with the spear slid it out of its sheath and reversed it so the shaft faced Arnar. It poked the spear at him gently. *Why not the sharp end?* wondered Arnar. *Why not simply kill me?*

A few seconds later, he was prodded into the hole.

They stood above the hole, motioning to him in a way he did not understand. After a while, one switched on its neck-box.

Ghost, the box said, then crackled. *To your feet, please.*

He stood. The hole went up to his neck, but his head was above its lip. It was easy to see out. He waited to see what they would demand of him next.

But they did not ask anything. Instead, he heard a rumbling sound and a great weight pummeled him. He would have fallen to his knees if he had been able, but the hole was full of dirt past his knees now. He tried to lift his leg.

Ghost, the neck-box said, *please hold still.*

"But you're burying me," said Arnar.

Said the neck-box, *We are putting you to rest.*

Another shower of dirt, and he was buried up to his chest.

"It will kill me!" he said.

It cannot, the neck-box explained. *You are already dead.* The barrow-man reached out and lightly tapped his forehead. *We are honored to participate in this ritual of yours, this burial. We are honored to help you rest.*

"No," said Arnar.

It is for your own good, said the neck-box. And then the barrow-man attached to the neck-box made a precise gesture with a fore-limb and the rest of the dirt came down.

They stamped on the earth to pack it tight. Only his head was left above ground. They brushed the stray dirt from his mouth and eyes and then departed one by one.

There, said the neck-box of the last one as it bent down close and peered at Arnar with its glittering, fractured eye. What could it even see of him? *Now you are at rest.*

"Please," begged Arnar.

I am glad you are pleased, the barrow-man said, and left.

Arnar waited out the rest of the night. Insects found him and bit him. Flies turned circles on the blood dried in spatters on his face. Because of the broken rib and the dirt pressing against him from all sides, it hurt to breathe. When he saw the sky start to lighten and morning begin to come, he almost wept.

All through the day he tracked the movement of the sun across the sky. He tried to work his way out of the dirt, but it was packed too tightly for him to manage it alone.

He was very thirsty. The sun baked him and burned the skin of his face and then slid mercifully away, but he knew it also meant night would come again soon, and the biting insects along with it.

Just at dusk, he heard something rustling in the underbrush. Probably a wild beast, he thought. But just possibly another true man.

"Help!" he shouted, best he could. "Help!"

But when he saw who was coming, he stopped shouting.

The four barrow-men all came close and crouched down low around him so their heads formed a square with his own in the center. A neck-box crackled. *Are you at rest?* it asked.

When he did not reply, it asked again.

"Yes," he said. It was the only thing he could think to say that might get him out of the hole.

You are at rest, said the neck-box. *You are welcome.*

Arnar watched as each barrow-man dug into the dirt beside him with a forelimb, scooped some up, and dumped it atop his head. He spat the dirt out, but almost immediately the next scoop came.

Eventually they stopped, but by that time his head was covered, his throat full of dirt. He no longer thought. He no longer felt. He was, for lack of a better term, at rest.

The Shimmering Wall

1.

Those parts of the domed city were not the city at all—or maybe the parts we lived in were what was not the city. It was not, after all, our city, or at least had not been so originally. It had become, I suppose, our city. Or some parts had. The rest, we stayed clear of.

At least most of us did. There were always a few who did not leave well enough alone. We had all seen those parts, seen how they seemed encased in dirty glass or Lucite, semitransparent and flickering walls, rooms and furnishings distorted beyond. When people dared to thrust their hands against the Lucite, they found it was not Lucite at all, but a sort of firm, jellylike membrane. They could slowly push their way through. They let their arms sink to the elbow or even—the more daring—to the joint of the shoulder, then groped around behind that translucent wall, and when they drew their arm free the fingers at its end were often clenched around something. The distorted broken-off leg of a chair, for instance—if that was in fact what it was—a skew slosh of metal, anyway. Or a pen that was a semicircular loop made for hands other than ours. These oddities could be sold—there were those who collected them.

We treated these collectors with as much suspicion as those who gathered the objects in the first place.

There were times, too—rarer these—when someone would thrust a hand through, then an elbow, then an arm, and begin to grope around, only to suddenly be taken hold of by something on the other side of the shimmering wall. From our vantage, we saw only a shape, a vague collection of angles, distantly humanoid in form, take hold and drag the person through. Such individuals never returned.

No one had ever crossed through the wall willingly. They had only felt around, one arm in, the rest of their body out, and drawn objects out. Perhaps these objects were in the form they had been in on the other side, or perhaps in coming through took on some distorted version of their true form.

I was, I suppose, unique. I was an orphan—but there were other orphans among us. My uniqueness was based not on that but on the circumstances of how I became such.

My parents worked together to bring bits and pieces of that other city across. They would take turns pushing through a shimmering wall, watching their arms distort and become a series of angles. They would draw an object out and sell it to collectors. That was how they lived. They always worked together, and as a result always took me along with them.

My earliest memory is this: my parents pressed against a vague and shimmering crystalline wall, one reaching through, the other, legs braced, grasping the first around the waist. I had been placed on a ratty blanket as far away from the wall as possible. I pawed the blanket, found crumbs or bugs on the floor, rolled them around in my mouth, spat them out. And then, after what seemed to me a long while, my parents turned, looking simultaneously terrified and triumphant, an unnatural and pain-wracked object held high in my mother's hand.

...

Or maybe this is not my first memory. I saw that scene or scenes like it so many times in the years to come. Sometimes the object was in my father's hand, sometimes my mother's. Sometimes, too, they groped around and then, screaming, quickly withdrew, one dragging the other free as, on the other side of the shimmering wall, a being of awkward angles approached rapidly, tried to catch hold of them, failed.

Was the being the same as us? I wondered. I had seen my father's arm through the shimmering wall and was uncertain there was any difference in its distorted angles through the wall as compared to the angles of the arm (if it was an arm) of the being or beings that stalked them there. I wondered this only later, when I was seven or eight. My parents were still on a good run, taking just enough from behind each shimmering wall to provide us with another three weeks, or four, or five, of food, of life.

When you are older, my mother told me, you must find a companion, someone just like you, willing to watch out for you as you reach through the wall, and you for her. You must know how far you can reach and go that far but no farther. You must know how to sink your arm to the shoulder joint and then reach even farther without letting your head push through. And then, God forbid, when a being approaches from the other side, to withdraw quickly with the help of your companion. She will tell you something is coming, and she will help you draw your arm free before it is too late.

This was, indeed, what my mother was to my father, until the moment when she was not. Until something came and she did not alert my father quickly enough, or else my father was sunk too deep, or the being moved too fast. Before we knew it, it had caught hold of my father's arm, and my mother was dragging on his waist, trying to tug him free. My father was screaming. There I was, nine years old, my arms around my mother's waist, trying to help my mother pull him free.

And indeed he did come free, but without his arm, which had been neatly severed at the elbow, and just as neatly cauterized.

2.

For weeks after, we avoided those shimmering walls. And yet, as time went on, my parents realized they did not know what else to do to survive. Their whole livelihood had involved reaching through walls—they had no other skills. My mother still had two good arms to reach with, and my father one, and as we grew hungrier they decided I was old enough to assist my mother as a lookout. We had to take the risk. We would, we vowed, take that risk as seldom as possible.

That strung us along for another five years, until I was fourteen. And then the same collection of angles appeared behind the shimmering wall, and though I immediately shouted out, it was upon my mother too quickly and pulled her through. My father, holding on to her waist with his remaining hand and forearm, followed after. And I, holding my father's legs, came last of all.

The passage through was strange, as if my body were being stretched and then reassembled to form a new creature. I could feel my father's legs, my arms wrapped around them, but then, suddenly, they were not legs at all, and then my arms were not arms at all either. And then my mind caught up with whatever transformation I had gone through, and I could think of his legs as legs again, and my arms as arms, and was unsure what, if anything, had changed.

And then, I lost consciousness.

I was lying on a floor flecked with color, as if mica—though the color floated and spun and moved, which mica as I understood it would not. Things in the world have certain properties, and one comes to understand these properties and what they are, what they mean. One comes to count on things being what they are. And yet, was I still in the world? I did not know. What did I mean by *world*? I was barely conscious, to be honest, and unsure I was in any world at all.

Near me was a being who resembled a human in every respect except for being carapaced in light. Does that qualify as every respect? Probably not. He was some manifestation of a human, though not human at the same time. Perhaps he had been so once, but it had been a long time since that was all he was.

At his feet lay the bodies of my father and mother. With a tool or instrument possessing a bright edge of light, he had begun to disjoint my father's corpse. Both feet had been severed and lay idly flopped to either side of the body—bloodless, the mechanism he had used to sever them having apparently cauterized them at the same time.

As I watched, he cut through one of my father's legs just below the knee. It looked like the left knee, but something told me I was seeing it wrongly, that it was in fact the right.

My mother was apparently unscathed but equally dead.

When he noticed me stirring, he interrupted his task and spoke. "Hello there," he said, his voice exceptionally deep and pleasing.

At first I could say nothing. When he repeated his greeting, I found myself mouthing it back to him. "Hello," I managed weakly.

He inclined his head, returned to his task. I could not move my limbs. I could lift my head and look around but little more than that.

"Please, do not be afraid," he said, then severed my father's head.

"That's my father," I managed.

"Not anymore," he said, and then made quick work of my mother as well.

In the end, the pair of them were less bodies than neat arrangements of sectioned parts, little more than stacks of firewood. Though, admittedly, to start a fire with them would have been very difficult indeed.

"How is it you speak my language?" I asked. He was moving between the pile that had been my father and the pile that had been my mother. He kept removing a portion of one or the other pile and putting it back in a different way, then standing back to judge the results.

"No," he answered distractedly. "*You* are speaking *our* language."

His voice was beautiful, almost unbearably so, and somehow familiar too. It warbled and came to me in multiple tones, as if there were three layers of him for every layer of me.

I blacked out again. I don't know why. When I came to again, I had crawled to the translucent shimmering wall and was trying, ineffectually, to shove my head through. How long I had been at this task, I had no idea.

The other being was beside me, bending down slightly, a concerned look just visible behind the blaze of light that enveloped his face.

"We are not going to hurt you," he said. "Did you think we were going to hurt you? We don't hurt children. We never do."

"Who's we?" I managed, through clenched teeth.

"We?" he asked. He gestured to his own chest. "We're just like you," he said. "You speak the same language as we do. You think the same thoughts as we do. But we're not you."

"Then what are you?"

But for this the being seemed to have no answer.

"Just sit back," he said. "Relax. It will only take a moment to dispose of your parents."

I watched it happen, though what exactly it was that was happening was difficult to say. The being moved back and forth between the piles, continuing to adjust them slightly until the one on the left, the pile that had been my mother, began to glow.

A moment later, he lifted my father's head by the hair and then set it down again. And then the pile that had been my father began to glow too.

"We are sorry about your parents," he said in that same beautiful voice. "But there was really no alternative."

Slowly the piles that had been my parents began to quiver. The parts rose into the air, reshaping themselves into human form, with gaps between the pieces. They were teetering, stretched-out beings, assembled of dead flesh ligatured together with light. They moved jerkily, as if compelled by some other force. I watched their eyes darting about behind the carapace of light that had now swallowed their heads. Confused, they seemed to be casting about for something. And then, abruptly, their gaze came to rest on me.

"How interesting," said the being. "They believe they recognize you."

Within their carapaces, my parents seemed to be screaming, but I could not hear a sound. Awkwardly, they lurched toward me.

"It would be better for you to go now," the being said.

And when I still did not respond, unable to move as what had once been my parents wobbled toward me, he reached out and took me by the neck and thrust me bodily through the shimmering wall.

3.

I grew up. Years passed. I chose to forget my parents. I built another entire life around myself, became a respectable member of society. I acquired a wife—or perhaps she acquired me, if *acquired* is the right word. I lived wholly in the city that was ours, never groping into that other city, turning away from the shimmering walls whenever I encountered them.

Things might have gone on like that until I died, but, simply, they did not. My wife, as had many around us, became subject to a wasting disease, her teeth and hair falling out, her body erupting in pustules and sores. She began to bleed from every orifice, slowly at first, then quicker and quicker. I remained unaffected.

"Kill me," she begged. "Please, kill me."

I took her to the treatment center, but we were turned away. No, they said, they would not treat her.

What, I asked the admitting nurse, would it take for her to get admitted?

There was nothing to be done, the nurse claimed. She shook her head. It was not an illness they could treat. They no longer had the proper medication.

But surely, I said, it was just a question of gathering the materials and then the medication could be made again. Again she shook her head. "We never had the formula, only the medication itself."

"What do you mean?" I asked. And when she gestured back at an empty vial, distorted and twisted, I knew the medicine had not come from our city, but from the other one.

I kissed my wife, set off. There were doors in my mind that I had kept shut for so long. Now I opened them. Behind them, I found my parents and all they had taught me. Behind them, I saw again the strange portions of the city. I had seen such a vial before—or had seen a vial somewhat like it, anyway. Where had it been?

I walked idly, allowing my mind to wander. I tried to think like that young boy, dragged along by his parents as they pushed a hand through a shimmering wall. What kind of parents brought their child along for something like that? I tried to recall each wall my parents had approached and stretched their arms into, sometimes my father, sometimes my mother, and what, from my vantage, I had seen through them. I wracked my brain, saw again their sweating faces, their anxiety, then that moment of triumph as they brought an odd and skewed object back through the wall.

And then I realized: I would only have seen the vial so clearly if they had brought it back through the wall. No, they must have brought it out and sold it.

But no, I considered further after clambering out of my despair: I had no memory of the object being in my parents' hands. And yet I *did* have a memory of the object, a clear image. Not in my parents' hands but lying on the floor. Had I seen it myself through a wall? If so, where?

But no, in my memory the object was too close for that, not glimpsed through a wall. No, it was just there before me, at my feet. Or rather, just at the level of my eyes, maybe half a foot away. And then I allowed the memory to continue, and my eyes flicked up to a strange being swathed in light and holding a bright-edged instrument, and I knew what I had to do.

4.

I spent some time trying to find the right wall. I looked at many, dozens, but none seemed right. I tried to be systematic. I would come close and peer through and try to recognize what lay beyond, but each time I could not say for certain that I recognized anything.

And then I began to think: Where had that being come from? The one who had dragged me and my parents through the shimmering wall? He had not been inside the room when my mother first reached in, I was sure of it, and then, abruptly, he was. Perhaps each encased room behind a shimmering wall led to other rooms and these to others still, and these all were connected. That every encased room led to every other encased room, in which case it did not matter which shimmering wall I passed through, as long as I passed through one. Once I was through, I could rapidly look for the object I remembered by moving from room to room instead of groping through the shimmering wall.

At least, that was what I chose to believe.

I had not touched a shimmering wall in several decades, and yet the sensation immediately came back to me. At first the wall resisted, felt almost solid, but then, slowly, it began to yield. With a sucking sound, it drew my fingers in, and then my hand, and then my forearm. The sensation was odd and disorienting, as if my hand were being taken apart and put together in a way that made it something else.

And then my fingers broke through to the other side.

I plunged my other hand in. When it was sufficiently deep, I lowered my head and pushed it through as well. The sensation grew worse, much more intense, and for a long moment I didn't know what or who I was. The stuff pressed against my face in such a way that I began to lose track of where my body ended and the jelly began. Soon, too, I could not tell if I was moving through it at all, and I lost all initiative to do anything but float, suspended, my legs still legs on one side, my hands something like hands on the other, but everything in between an undifferentiated mass.

How long was I there? Minutes perhaps, or hours, or days. I did not breathe, but I do not know that I needed to breathe. It was as if I were caught between two states and subject to neither one nor the other.

And then something took me by the hands and pulled.

I coughed and a spill of jelly slid from my throat. It lay for a moment in a quivering pool beside my face before, very slowly, vibrating its way back to the shimmering wall. I looked up, my vision bleary, and there, above me, was a being of angles refracting off one another, its body encased in light. He held an instrument whose bright edge was moving downward, toward me.

I lifted an arm to protect myself and suddenly the instrument withdrew.

"Ahhh," said a voice that was exceptionally, almost unbearably beautiful. "You're alive."

I coughed up another lump of jelly. "Why wouldn't I be?" I said.

"They never are, the adults," he said. "Until we make them so."

I managed to get to my knees.

"We've met before," the being said, his brow furrowing behind his carapace of light.

"Yes," I said. "You killed my parents."

"Not killed," he said. "In fact, we returned them to life."

I was on my feet now, stumbling. "Are you the only one here?"

"Well," he said. "There's your parents."

"But they're not like you."

"No, they're not. They're not sufficiently there. Except for us, nobody is sufficiently there."

"There? What do you mean?"

He shrugged.

"Because of you," I accused.

"In spite of us. That they can function at all is a minor miracle."

I glanced around for the vial, any vial. An old swirl of metal, a crumpled wooden box, forks that had twisted on themselves and had their tines bent in every direction. No vial.

I looked for a door. There it was in the back of the room.

"Where does that door lead?" I asked.

"How can you still be alive?" he asked. "Is it because you passed through as a child? We never hurt children."

Perhaps he intended to say more, but by this time I was sufficiently in control of my faculties to strike him hard in the temple and knock him off his feet. The light around his head made my fingers tingle but otherwise did not adversely affect me. A moment later my hand closed around his instrument. I activated the bright edge of light and pushed it deep into his side. I could smell flesh burning.

He grunted. "It won't do you any good," he said, and expired.

Once he was dead, the light around him flickered and went out. He looked now like an ordinary man. Remarkably enough, he seemed to resemble me. So much so that I thought at first he was my father. But no, not quite. And then I thought, *If not my father, who?* Dreading what the answer might be, I quickly turned away.

I left the body there. I had thought I might feel some measure of satisfaction in killing the being who had killed and then reanimated my parents, but I felt nothing at all. His face haunted me.

I went through the door, and from there into another room, and from there into another. I kept moving from room to room, each ordinary in every respect except for the one shimmering wall that opened onto another place, another city, my city. Sometimes I would see shadows on the other side of the wall. Once I even saw a hand protruding through it and feeling around frantically on the floor, though it quickly pulled back as soon as I approached.

After a few dozen rooms, I found them—the creatures that had once been my parents. They were still encased in light and still seemed to be mutely screaming.

At first they seemed not to notice me, and when I approached they did not acknowledge my presence. But then, abruptly, they did, coming at me and throwing their strange disjointed bodies onto me until I began to feel suffocated and, for my own protection, had to activate the instrument again. Their light went out and they collapsed into dust and were gone. I continued on.

How many more rooms? A hundred? Two hundred? More? There have been so many rooms since that I cannot say for certain, but there, at last, it was, the twisted vial, just as I had remembered it, tipped on its side in the middle of the floor. I snatched it up. Was it identical to the vial the nurse had shown me? No, not identical, but very close. I had no way of knowing if I had found what my wife needed to survive, but yes, perhaps it was so. It was not, in any case, impossible.

And so, vial in hand, I approached the nearest shimmering wall and pushed my hands through, eager to return to save my wife.

Or at least I would have. But the translucent wall was solid. It would not let me through.

I tried wall after all, but they all resisted me. I was trapped.

Only then did I notice the glow that had begun to envelop me.

5.

I have lived through one of these cities. Now, I must live through the other. Meanwhile, my wife lies in her bed, suffering, dying. Perhaps she is already dead.

I am nearly done with this record. Once I have completed it, I will lean this notebook against a shimmering wall and wait for a hand to grasp it and pull it through. If you find this and read it, I ask only one thing of you: come back to this wall and push your hand through again. I will place in it this vial, which you must use to cure my wife. Once she is cured, bring her back here with you and convince her to push her hand through. I will do nothing to her, will not drag her through, for I know that it would likely kill her. No, I will only hold her hand for a moment, squeeze it, and let go.

And then it will be your turn. I have treasures beyond your wildest imaginings. If you will do this small thing for me, I will bring them to the wall. You will be wealthy, and powerful too. All you have to do is follow my commands, and trust me.

But if you do not do this, you will have nothing of me. You will have only the bright edge of my instrument, and I will have you in pieces.

Grauer in the Snow

The storm was severe enough that Grauer and the two brothers had quickly become separated—even while the oldest brother was shouting over the wind that Grauer should tie himself to them or, at the very least, take hold of his hand. Grauer had not been opposed to this, not in the least—indeed, despite his inexperience with such weather, he sensed it was the safest thing. He was just shoving the canisters and surveying equipment into his pack and heaving it again onto his back when the blizzard struck full force. Almost immediately he couldn't see a thing: one moment the brothers were there, dark figures just a few yards away, and then, suddenly, there was nothing but snow.

He tightened the coat's hood around his head, securely buttoning it. For a moment he stood there, braced against the wind, expecting the brothers to come for him, but then, growing anxious when they didn't appear, he lurched toward them.

Or at least he lurched in the direction he thought they were. Perhaps he had unwittingly turned out of the wind when the blizzard struck and hadn't realized it. Or perhaps they had already come looking for him and had flailed past just a few spans away, unseen and unseeing.

He moved forward and back, stumbling about. He had lost track of the road as well, he realized with panic. He started to run, boots sinking into the snow, then lost his footing and fell face-first into a drift. When he got up, most of the surveying equipment had spilled out of the pack and had vanished under the snow.

Between the snow and the darkness he could see nothing, nothing at all. He stood there, eyes squinted, the wind whistling fast around him. Finally, not knowing what else to do, he dug a hole for himself and curled into it, waiting for the storm to pass.

It took an hour, perhaps two, for the snow to finally stop. The wind went on for a good half hour after that, inflicting the surface of the snow with a scab of ice.

He heaved the snow away and came up, shaking it off. It was very dark, no moon, stars either masked by clouds or absent for some other incomprehensible reason. Just clouds, he hoped. The only light seemed to come from the snow: ghostly and gray and barely visible all around, and unbearable.

He shrugged off his pack and searched through it for his flashlight, but it was nowhere to be found. It must have fallen out with the surveying equipment. There would be no finding it now.

He squinted. He could see almost nothing: no sign of the road, no footprints. Either the snow had covered them or they weren't visible in such diminished light. No sign of the brothers either.

He called out, shouted for the brothers. After a moment, he heard a response, distant, perhaps muted by the blanket of snow, but still there. Something, anyway. He moved toward it.

The going was hard, his boots cracking through the snow's crust with each step to wallow in the powder beneath. He walked for a time, breathing harder and harder, the moisture in his breath freezing on his beard, then hallooed again. Again they responded, but they sounded just as distant. Were they moving away from him rather than toward him? He hurried after the sound.

Only after half an hour of that, of call and response and struggle through the snow, did he realize he was hearing the echo of his own voice, that he was walking in pursuit of nothing at all.

Numb, he kept walking. The wind picked up, and soon he was very cold, almost unbearably so.

And then, strangely, he started to feel warm again. He was tempted to stop but wasn't certain that if he did he'd be able to start moving again.

Just for a moment, he told himself, *just to catch my breath.*

Before he knew it, a tree stood in his path. He leaned against it. He felt sleepy. He shrugged off his pack and it fell somewhere behind him. Not long after, he was seated, his back against the tree, snow heaped all around him and over him, his legs somehow covered with it even though none was falling. How had that happened?

Just a moment, he thought again, *just time to catch my breath, and then I'll go.*

He wouldn't have managed to get up at all if he hadn't heard the sound. A kind of distant hiss: far away at first, then growing closer. It was just enough to catch in his ears and bring him back to consciousness. *My echo,* he thought at first, *coming back to me,* but as the sound grew louder it worried at him. How could it be his echo when it had been hours since he last opened his mouth? An echo wouldn't live so long. And then it grew very loud indeed, a rushing, roaring sound, and he saw or thought he saw, almost lost in the trees, a moving beam of light.

It was a light rather than something imagined, he was sure of it. He stumbled to his feet, leaving his pack where it was, and made for the sound.

After only a dozen stiff steps, he slowed. The sound was fading again, moving away.

I should lie down again, part of him was saying.

Just follow the sound, another part of him was saying. *It's something to do while you die.*

The second part was slightly louder. And so he kept walking.

The snow got deeper and deeper. He pondered turning around and going back, but back to where? Suddenly he was stumbling and almost went down, not because of the struggle of pushing through the snow but because, abruptly, there was none to push through. He thought at first he had chanced upon a plowed road, but it didn't feel like a road underfoot. As he walked down it, he felt what seemed like slats with softer depressions between them. To either side he saw the faintest glimmers of light, which, slowly, he realized were the lines of rails.

He had found the train tracks. A train with a Bucker plow must have come through. Perhaps that was the noise he had heard, the light he had seen.

He could either keep following the tracks in the direction he had started, or he could turn around and go the other way. Was there any way to tell which way would lead him more quickly to shelter? No. He kept going the way he was going because it was easier than turning around.

He walked for a long time. He began to get cold again, and sleepy. The temptation was to stop walking and lie down. But, doggedly, he continued on. If a train were to come, he realized, there was little chance he would get off the tracks in time. He tried not to worry about this. He concentrated on putting one foot in front of the other.

And then, up ahead, the glimmers of light became more complex. He stared as he approached, eventually understood that there were more rails for the light to reflect off of, that he had reached a junction.

He stopped at the split. He could keep going down the main track or take the branch line. The branch line might lead to a station or a small town or at the very least a siding where maybe he'd find some modicum of shelter. The main line would too, eventually, but perhaps not for miles. The branch line, just like the main line, had been plowed. Didn't that indicate it was important? Or did they plow everything just in case?

He took the branch line.

He wasn't sure how long he walked, maybe fifty meters, maybe several hundred—he was too busy concentrating on keeping moving to pay attention. Eventually he smelled smoke. Not long after that he saw a line of light, very thin and very sharp, as if someone had sliced cleanly through the scrim of the dark to reveal a blazing world behind. He was so grateful to see it, he couldn't stop moaning.

It took a few dozen steps more before he realized that what he was seeing was a line of light left by an improperly drawn curtain. He could sense the house in front of him but in the darkness couldn't make sense of it, couldn't tell for certain what was the darkness of the sky and what the darkness of the house. Still, it felt strange to him—off somehow. Only when he was very close indeed did he realize it was not a house at all but a single train car.

He found the steps that led to the compartment door but didn't have the strength to climb them. They were too steep, and he was too tired. Instead he draped himself over them and tapped on the base of the door with his gloved fist.

It hardly made a sound, just a faint dull noise as distant as an echo. *They won't hear me,* he thought. *I've made it to the very threshold of shelter, but I can't manage to make them hear me.*

And then he realized he didn't hear anything either, that the passenger car, despite being lit inside, seemed utterly silent. *Perhaps,* he thought, *there is no one to open up for me. Perhaps there is no one there.*

As soon as he thought this, the door was suddenly flung open. A great cascade of noise poured out, engulfing him. Strong hands took hold of him and dragged him up the stairs and into the compartment.

The air inside was so warm he almost fainted. A huge fire roared at the far end of the compartment, obscuring the whole of the back wall, seemingly uncontained. The hands let go of him and he fell in a heap on the floor, and then they were on him again, grabbing him, lifting him up and patting him on the back, steadying him, only slowly letting go once they were sure he could stand.

A drink was placed in his hand, a clear viscid liquor of some sort. He took a deep drink: it burned going down and made his vision blur. When his vision returned, a face was in front of him, wrinkled, hairless, even the eyelashes absent.

"Feeling all right now?" the face said, then grimaced. The voice was strange, a kind of tenor whisper that seemed to come at him from every direction at once.

He nodded.

"One shouldn't be out on a night like this," the face said. "Only fools are."

"Where am I?" Grauer managed.

"Just a place," said the face, and then it stepped back a little farther. The body below the face was clothed in a garment made of long, tattered strips of fabric that pooled on the floor. It was difficult to make out the body's contours within except in the most general fashion, but even with just that it felt to Grauer as if head and body did not belong to one another.

"A train car," Grauer said. "It's a train car."

Body shrugged. "If you like," the face whispered.

Grauer became afraid. "Either it is or it isn't," he said.

Face and body bowed deeply, without a word, and then upon straightening led Grauer to a seat covered in red velvet. He was helped to sit down, facing the crackling fire that seemed to threaten to consume the far end of the car.

"Can I stay here until morning?" asked Grauer. Some time had passed. He felt warmer and very sleepy. He was happy to be alive.

The body again bowed deeply. "If you like," the face said again, and then waited, attentive.

Why is the body still standing there, the face bobbing above it? Grauer looked down and realized that trapped beneath his boot were a few of the frayed and tattered ends of the long garment. The body was still standing there because it was unable to leave.

He tried to lift his foot, but the foot didn't move. What was wrong with him? "I seem to be standing on your clothing," he told the other.

"It's not my clothing," the face said.

"No?" said Grauer. "What is it?"

"My skin," the face said.

He had somehow slipped out of the seat and was lying on the floor of the train car, looking up at the pale, empty face above him.

"Who are you?" he asked. "What?"

The face didn't answer.

"Can you help me up?" he asked.

Still no answer.

"Hello?" said Grauer.

And then, a little later, "Hello?"

The train car had darkened, he realized. The noise, too, which had seemed so raucous when he first entered, as if it had been the product of a dozen drunks, had subsided to nothing. Now it seemed not even loud enough for this single face and body, who seemed the only other person or persons in the train car, if in fact a person or persons at all.

Whatever the case, the body had gotten down on hands and knees, and now the face was very close to his own, peering into it.

"The train will be leaving soon," the face whispered.

"There is no train," Grauer whispered back. "There is only this single passenger car."

"The train is leaving soon," the face repeated.

"Fine," said Grauer from the floor, closing his eyes.

"Do you have a ticket?" the voice asked.

Grauer ignored it, tried to sleep.

"No ticket?" the voice asked.

When he did not respond, hands grasped him and in a single fluid motion lifted him from the floor and to his feet. It left him gasping for breath. It felt like many hands instead of just two—perhaps more hands were hidden beneath the voluminous tattered garment. Or, rather, skin.

"Ticket?" the voice asked again.

He shook his head. A moment later he was dragged down the aisle to the door and pitched unceremoniously into the snow.

When he awoke, it was light outside. One of the brothers was slapping him, saying his name. He turned his head and saw the other brother. Which one was the oldest? With all the frost on their beards and faces, he couldn't tell them apart.

He managed to blink, let out a hiss of air.

"He's alive," said one brother to the other.

The second brother didn't bother to answer. Instead he leaned in close to Grauer's face. "Grauer," he said, "we're going to get you out of here. We'll carry you to safety. Just stay with us."

All right, he said, only no sound came out. He blinked.

"We're not far from the railroad tracks," he said. "We'll take you there. With a little luck a plow train has already gone through and we'll be able to follow them."

No, thought Grauer. *Please, no.* He blinked.

"With a little luck there will be a branch line we can take in a kilometer or two that will lead us somewhere we can get you medical attention."

No siding, he tried to say. *No passenger car. Go straight. Don't stop. Please.*

He blinked.

The brother offered him a smile. He patted his shoulder, then stood.

Strong hands grasped him, pulled him roughly to his feet.

"Up we go then," a voice said. He couldn't tell which of the brothers it was, or even if it was a brother at all. He couldn't feel his legs, but he heard the sound of his feet dragging through the crust of snow. "Stay with us, Grauer," a voice said. "Here we go."

Justle

My father, when he had had a few drinks too many and my mother was not around, would sometimes draw me close and whisper too loudly, conspiratorially, his boozy warm breath flooding my face, "Son, did I ever tell you about Justle?"

"But I'm Justle, Father," I would say, for this was the unusual name that, despite my mother's objections, my father had bestowed upon me.

"So you are," he would say. "So you are. But it's a place too. Not just you."

"What kind of place?" I would ask.

He would squint into his empty glass. "Not much of one," he said. "Hardly a place anyone can live. More a way station, really. A place between places. Does that still amount to a place?"

Whether I said yes or no, chances were this would be the end of it, that he would fall silent and say nothing of note until, ten minutes later, maybe twenty, he passed out.

But twice, he went on to tell me more, to tell me the story of Justle, of what had happened to him there.

The first time he told me, I was too young to make sense of it, but I still had the feeling, perhaps because of his manner as he spoke, that he was telling me something he should have kept from me. Not only from me, from everyone. The second time I was older, nearly an adult, and could make more sense of the story, though it took my becoming fully adult before certain portions of it grew clear. There is still much about the story that I have difficulty believing was not fabricated or false. And yet, when my father told it to me, he did so with a sincerity that was, in him, not only uncommon but completely unheard of. This left me feeling that he believed all he said. Or at least that whoever he became when he was drunk did.

The story he told was this: When he was young, before he met my mother, he lived in a settlement in what was called in those days a recovery sector. This sector, like the others, was devoid of vegetation, and the air was dim with heavy smog or smoke. His eyes burned constantly, as did his throat, even though he used an oxygen regulator. In places, the ground seemed to have been stripped bare and hit repeatedly with mallets to make it very hard indeed—as if the dirt were not dirt at all but something artificial.

Work in a recovery sector merited hazard pay, and for the promise of this my father intended to spend several months participating in a cadre that would work to speed the sector's recovery. Most young people did such a stint in those days, he claimed, as a way of gathering money to purchase a place within one of the domed cities.

He was assigned to one of two twinned settlements, each established within one of two ruined, adjacent cities. Castu his was called, Polx the other. The settlements had been, he explained, named after the ruined cities, and the cities in turn had been named after two brothers. *So, you see,* he told me, *some people are named after places, like you, but some places are likewise named after people. A name can travel in either direction.*

Food had to be shipped in. If it remained more than a few days uneaten, it became contaminated and could not be consumed. Individuals, too, were cautioned not to remain in a recovery sector for more than sixty days at a time. Each settlement was a single, sprawling prefab erected within the confines of its larger ruined city. The prefab was sealed off for safety: to enter you would pass through an airlock and into a decontamination chamber. Protective clothing was discarded there to be sanitized for use the following day. Along with this protective clothing, my father and all his cadre were issued regulators that filtered and recycled the air. Within the building, one could breathe normally. Outside, one could not.

"What I did exactly, what I managed to accomplish, how effectual it was, is still not clear to me," he told me. "In those days, we did as we were asked, and it did not seem important to know exactly why. A job was a job. Some days, I would be told to strap a device to my back and suck fumid air through a tube. Other days I was given a sticklike device that made a clicking sound, the frequency of which changed depending on where I pointed it. Still others found me on my knees using a red and abrasive soap to scrub a designated stretch of ground clean."

One day, as, eyes watering, he was again drawing contaminated air into a tube with no indication he was having any effect, his cadre leader approached him with the command to go to Polx. "Now?" he asked. "Yes," he was told. "Immediately."

He unbuckled the device and shrugged it off. "Who is to accompany me?" he asked. For whenever anyone went to the other settlement on some errand, they took a companion, in case anything went wrong.

"Just you," said the cadre leader.

"Just me?"

"Polx has need of an extra man."

"How long?"

The leader looked at him, confused. "What do you mean, how long? For good."

And so my father packed his scant possessions, said good-bye to the other members of his cadre, and left for Polx.

Halfway there, his regulator began having trouble. Soon, it was quite difficult for my father to breathe. Or not breathe exactly—he was breathing fine, but the air was deficient: he was not getting enough oxygen. He felt as if he were slowly suffocating.

He considered turning around and going back, but he calculated it was slightly farther to go back than to go forward, so he continued on, despite knowing there was no chance he would arrive. *Stay calm,* he told himself. *The more you panic, the more oxygen you'll use. The more oxygen you use, the sooner you'll die.*

And so he moved forward but very slowly, as if traveling underwater. His goal was not to make it to Polx—there was no chance of arriving there without a working regulator—but only to make it far enough along the path before he passed out that he would increase the likelihood of his body being found while he was unconscious and comatose rather than lifeless.

But did Polx even expect him? And wouldn't Castu just assume he had arrived? Would anyone miss him?

He blew into the regulator then banged it against his hip to clear it, but it was no use.

He began to experience hypoxemia, though he did not know to call it that. Instead, he told me how his head began to ache. He kept walking. Despite the slowness of his stride, his heart was beating rapidly, and he experienced a strange euphoria he associated with the knowledge he was going to die—though why death might make him feel euphoric he was at a loss to say. His vision began to darken as if the world were growing dim, but it was only him growing dim, so to speak, not the world. Through it all he told himself, *Stay calm, stay calm.* He kept walking, slowly.

"If I had had a comm, I would have alerted my cadre leader," he said. But he had none. They had taken his comm away when he left for his new cadre—the comm belonged to the cadre, not to him. "I kept trying to figure out what to do, but all I could think to do was keep walking. Either I would survive or I would not."

He walked for perhaps twenty minutes until something further began to go wrong with his already irritated eyes: portions of his vision became occluded by dark blotches. He felt dizzy and nauseous and wanted to sit and catch his breath, but he knew that if he sat down he would not get up again. And so he kept moving, seemingly slower and slower, the air bitter in his lungs. Soon, despite being in motion, he felt he was hardly making any forward progress.

And then the path took a slight curve. As the ruined buildings fell away, he glimpsed something. At first he thought it was nothing, a hallucination, but as he drew closer he became convinced it was real. Something whitish and rectangular, a sign or placard at the top of a metal pole slightly taller than he. *Probably a relic from before,* he thought, *something that by freak accident survived the devastation that leveled the city, an advertisement for a long-gone shop.* Or perhaps it was more recent and upon reaching it he would read something like *Polx 4 km,* with an arrow pointing along the path.

But the sign did not offer any of that. Instead, there was just the word *Justle* and there, beside the word, an arrow pointing him off the path.

Justle, he thought. He peered off the path. Maybe three hundred meters away, almost obscured by the smoky air, was a structure that seemed intact. Of recent construction? No, he didn't think so. But hardly as weathered or dilapidated as the few intact structures he had passed.

"I thought that either I could keep walking in the direction of Polx and probably die, or I could stop here, leave the path, and see what this Justle held in store for me. And so I left the path."

Carefully he stripped a glove off and left it in the roadway, facing the sign. He folded over the fingers of the glove, leaving only the pointer finger extended, gesturing off the path toward Justle, hoping that if they did come looking for him, they would guess where he had gone. And then he stepped off the path and began to walk toward Justle.

It was not far, just a few hundred meters away. In normal circumstances he would have reached it almost immediately, but hobbled as he was, his regulator defective, slowly suffocating, unable to move quickly, it seemed to take forever. *I thought I could convince myself to finish the journey by focusing on walking halfway there. Then, once arrived at the halfway point, I would walk half of what remained, then half of that . . .* My father sighed. *Only after having done this three or four times did I realize something was wrong with my thinking, that if I kept walking in this fashion I would never arrive.*

He came close enough to the structure that he could see, stamped into its metal wall, the word *Justle*, which he took to be the name of the place. I have asked myself since: Was he right to see it as such? Am I truly named after a place? Or am I in fact misnamed after something else entirely, something misunderstood?

There seemed to be a light inside, a dim but steady illumination. Someone was there. Or perhaps he was simply hallucinating.

But, he told himself, *there comes a point when it does not matter whether what you see is real: you have no choice but to go toward it.*

Even as he thought this, the door to Justle began to swing open and, swaying, he lost consciousness.

When he awoke, he was alone on a rickety metal cot. His throat still hurt, his eyes still wept, but the air here was a little better, breathable, or at least he thought so. He was, in any case, alive.

"Where am I?" he asked.

No one answered. He was alone in a small octagonal metal room whose interior walls had been burnished to a mirrorlike sheen.

A flashlight stood on its end in the center of the octagon and its flashbeam made the walls glow madly around him. He stood and stumbled toward the flashlight and watched his warped reflections stumbling all about as well, a clamor of mimed motion. Except one of these warped selves did not move in the same fashion as the rest, but instead placed its finger to where its lips would have been had it had lips and made a muted, hushing noise. Yet when he tried to look straight at it, he could perceive nothing at all.

I'm going mad, he thought.

No, said a voice barely above a whisper from just behind him. *Whatever madness you have, you brought with you.*

He whirled about, but no one was there. In turning, he lost his balance and fell to his knees. There he remained until half-glimpsed and barely substantial hands lifted him again and coaxed him back onto the cot.

Hold still, said another whispered voice, one that, despite also being a whisper, he could recognize as different from the first. *You prefer to live, don't you?*

A blur of movement out of the corner of his eye and the flashlight tipped and clattered over, and either went out or was switched off.

He could see something now, two indistinct figures, vaguely human, hazy as ash, just visible in the near-darkness. One approached him very slowly, as if walking underwater. He could see nothing of the features of either figure. It was as if smoke or static had been poured into roughly human forms and kept threatening to come asunder and billow away. One, though, was larger than the other, and the general shape of it, despite its vagueness, struck him as female, though ambiguously so.

Now it's dark, it said. The voice seemed a little louder now, though only just.

Does that feel better? asked the other, the smaller one.

"Who are you?" asked my father.

We have a proposition for you, said the female, if *female* was the right word. Perhaps it had been once.

Would you like to live? asked the smaller.

"Live?"

It's a simple question, said the smaller.

We can help you, said the larger. *We can save you. We can take you to safety.*

But, claimed the other, *there's a price.*

They explained things to my father, whispering by turns in his ear. They were trapped there, in Justle—though they did not use that name—and they wished to leave. They had been there for a long time: months, maybe years. Within Justle they could survive and persist—though, as he could see, just barely. But, without help, they couldn't depart.

We were once just like you, said the larger.

But now we are not like you at all, said the smaller.

This place has changed us.

If they were to leave, it would have to be with him. Or not so much *with* him as *in* him. They could make a place for themselves within his body, hollow a place out under his skin in which they could live.

A sort of pouch within your flesh, said the smaller. *You will mother us.*

But we will not do this without your permission, said the larger.

At least we prefer not to, the smaller said.

Yes, admitted the larger. *That is what we prefer.*

In either case, we will have to take charge of you, the smaller said.

"Take charge of me?"

Ever so briefly, claimed the larger. *We will manage the body and keep it alive.*

It was not lost on my father that she referred to it as *the body* rather than as *your body.*

"Why would I ever allow this?" he asked.

Why? Because of the alternative. Without us, you will die. And if you stay here much longer, you will become like us.

. . .

For some time, hours maybe, even days, my father held out. He was waiting for someone to come looking for him, someone to discover his abandoned glove and follow it to Justle, but nobody came.

No one will come, said the larger, as if reading his mind.

Still he waited. The world grew strange around him. He became desperately hungry and then that too faded. His tongue grew dry and stuck to his palate. In the near-darkness he watched the two figures come and go, moving slowly around Justle. Often they were beside him, observing him. Sometimes, though, they withdrew, and he glimpsed them standing near the wall, the head of the smaller inclined toward the head of the larger, as if paying obeisance.

They illuminated the upended flashlight again and Justle was again ablaze with light. The distorted images of my father's own face all around him made him dizzy. And then the flashlight was extinguished. In the silent and sudden darkness the pair came very, very close.

You haven't much time, the larger said. *Soon you shall reach a point beyond which we cannot use you.*

And then, soon after, you will be like us.

Will you invite us in? Before it is too late?

After a long hesitation, seeing no alternative, my father reluctantly assented.

The pain, my father told me, was tremendous, nearly unbearable. He must have already begun to become like them, for as they approached he could see them much better than when he had first arrived. First, the pair of them drew close together and then closer still and began, as he observed them, to melt into or meld with one another, the larger engulfing the smaller. The resultant mass looked not human but monstrous and fluid, the head of one rising up as if out of a dark tide only to be quickly swallowed again and replaced, momentarily, by the other. The form undulated more than ambulated toward him and then billowed down upon him and over his prone body. It began to insinuate its way in. It did this first through his nostrils and mouth, sliding in in a way that made him feel he was suffocating. Soon it also did so through his ears, creating a thrumming against the eardrums he could hardly bear, and through his eyes, working its way through the sclera and sending a torrent of broken images along the optic nerve. He cried out but it did not relent, and now he could feel it leeching its way into his very skin, penetrating each pore and pushing its way into an inner place that was too small for both it and him to occupy at the same time.

It was as if his every nerve was on fire at once, and even after the shadowy mass was fully within him the burning didn't stop. It felt like the lining of his body had become terminally inflamed.

We lied to you, said a warbling voice within him that was half the larger's and half the smaller's. *There is no pouch. Or, rather, the pouch shall be the whole of your body.*

And then he felt his body stand. He could do nothing to prevent it. They were—or it was—in charge of the body now. Even though the body kept moving, my father was unaware of it. For he had fainted, though his body kept on.

After that, he offered me only scattered images. Perhaps my father's drinking had caught up with him and this was the only way he could finish his story: The body lurching its way back to the path. The body trying and failing to replace the glove on its hand and so leaving it there in the road before stumbling on toward Polx.

The body did not make it far. It fell on the path and lay there, but the being or beings inside of my father did something to preserve it, to keep it alive. The body lay there for several days, my father drifting in and out of awareness until, suddenly, he awoke to find individuals in protective suits all around him, slapping his face, affixing a regulator over his nose and mouth, welcoming him back to the land of the living.

My father paused. I thought perhaps the story had reached its end. Or that he would simply pass out and leave the story unfinished.

For a long moment he stared straight ahead, and then abruptly he turned and regarded me. Momentarily, he seemed confused as to who I was and what I was doing there. But then recognition warmed his eyes, and he looked away and continued.

"They did not release me. When I awoke, in a hospital bed in Polx, they were still with me, still in control of the body. Everything the body did, it did at their behest. Surprisingly, they seemed intent on continuing my life just as I had planned it. I watched myself finish my job in the recovery sector, then buy a place in a domed city, this very city in fact. And then I met your mother."

He looked at me again, furtively, then looked away.

"Or rather, *they* met your mother. They courted her, seduced her, married her. It was not I who climbed into the conjugal bed with her, but they. It was not I who formed the beast with two backs with her, but they. Which I suppose would make it a beast with three backs. Or perhaps, if you count the body itself, four."

I did not know at the time what he was talking about.

"In that coupling I felt them flow out of me and into her. Not, as I initially thought, to do to her what they had done to me, but because they saw it as a way back to being truly human again."

He looked again at me.

"Can you not guess what happened?" he asked. "Can you not divine what I am going to say next?"

But I could not. I was, after all, just a boy.

"What went into the making of you is not something of me and something of your mother, no matter how much you might believe you resemble us," he said. "Rather it is those two creatures that came from Justle and who saw your inception as an opportunity to become flesh again. I named you Justle so that I would not forget what you were." He leaned very close to me. "I've thought many times of killing you," he said in a low voice. "The only thing that stops me is my worry that were I to do so, it would let them out again."

...

Now that I have come to what seems to be the end, I find myself compelled to go further, to tell not just what I set out to tell but everything.

There was, I will admit, one other evening when my father was drunk enough to tell me about Justle. A third time, just a few months after the second. When he started to talk, I made excuses and tried to retreat to my room. Sloppily, he grabbed my wrist, hard enough to make the bones ache.

"No, you don't," he said. "You need to hear this. You need to know what you are."

And so, wincing, I was made to sit. Pretending like nothing was wrong as my father kept a tight hold of my wrist, I once again listened.

He told the story just as before, if slightly off: The same paired settlements (though this time he called them camps), the same journey with a broken regulator (though this time he called it a respirator), the same odd sign (though this time greenish rather than whitish). And, above all, that same arrival at that small, single-roomed structure he called Justle.

He had just reached the temporary safety of Justle itself and was beginning to detail the discovery of the two indistinct beings hiding among his reflections when a movement caught my eye. I turned. It was my mother, standing in the doorway, an expression on her face I had never seen before, listening.

For a time my father kept speaking, but finally he noticed her too. When he did, he stopped midsentence, releasing my wrist. No blood remained in his face. He looked afraid.

"Go to your room, Justle," my mother said, not taking her eyes off my father.

"But—" I started.

"Go to your room," she said, more forcefully this time, still not looking at me. "And stay there."

And so I did. I would like to say that through the walls or door I went on to hear something that told me what my parents said or did to one another in my absence, but the truth is I heard nothing at all. The truth is, after a while, I fell asleep.

When I awoke, my father was nowhere to be found. The room he had been in had been cleaned. The walls had been wiped down and the floor polished so much you could see your blurred reflection in its surface. When I asked my mother about my father, she simply said, "He's gone." She still would not look at me. And when I pushed farther: "He won't be coming back." And then finally, when I foolishly inquired if his leaving had to do with the story he had told, she turned her gaze upon me and said, "What story? There was no story."

Just for a moment, when she looked at me, angry eyes blazing, I had the feeling my father had been wrong, that he had misjudged. I had never believed the two beings my father feared, if they did actually exist, were inside of me. Indeed, I hardly believed his story at all. But perhaps, I thought, after seeing my mother like that, I could believe they had remained in her all this time, hidden there, imperceptible, cautious, until my father said too much to me and they decided it was time to take action. I could, I felt, see them staring out through my mother's eyes.

But I knew better than to let on I thought this. I pretended there was nothing wrong with my mother. I pretended I did not miss my father. I pretended everything was fine.

I, Justle, am still pretending to this day.

The Devil's Hand

In late January Carlton received a letter from his friend Alton Smythe asking if he would care to visit. He was, Smythe wrote, away from London and alone at his estate. His wife and daughter had left shortly after the new year to return to the city, taking both servants with them, leaving him to his own devices. At first, his letter claimed, he had welcomed the isolation, but now, several weeks later, he longed for companionship. *So much so,* he wrote, *that I have walked several miles through muck to the village so as to post this letter.*

It is of no use to write back, he continued, *for I am not likely to see your letter for several weeks at least. I have no intention of repeating the trek to the miserable albeit picturesque village any time soon. Thus, any correspondence will simply await me there, unclaimed. If you choose to come, and I hope you shall so choose, simply come. I shall be glad to see you.*

He included in the letter instructions for where to transfer trains, as well as a crude map that would, in theory, lead Carlton from the branch line stop through the village and, eventually, to Smythe's estate.

...

The letter arrived at an auspicious moment when Carlton, like Smythe, was at loose ends. Upon receipt of it, he immediately packed his bag and boarded the evening train. Only once he was aboard and the train in motion did he learn from the conductor that the branch line train to which he intended to transfer only ran early in the day. He would have to spend the night twenty miles shy of Smythe's estate, then take the branch line train the remainder of the way the following morning.

The compartment he had chosen to occupy when he left London was, except for Carlton himself, empty. Each time the train stopped, he expected to be joined by someone else, but though the platform was often crowded and he could hear the sounds of heavy footsteps as individuals boarded and jostled their way down the corridor, nobody opened the compartment door, let alone entered. In his haste to leave, Carlton had not thought to bring an annual or a newspaper, and so he sat, bored, staring out the window at the surrounding countryside until night fell fully and the window became a square of darkness. Eventually, almost without being aware of it, he fell asleep.

When he awoke the Pintsch lamp in the ceiling had come on. There was someone else in the compartment with him, a man still clad in his coat. The man had his legs crossed at the knees, his two bony hands resting clasped atop the higher knee. One of the man's thumbs, Carlton noticed, was missing, sheared off neatly at the base. His face was thin and pale, of an almost waxen appearance, his mouth cruel. His eyes, too, struck Carlton as sharp and cruel. The man seemed to regard him keenly. As Carlton regained his senses, the man made no effort to look away.

Carlton looked away himself but, still feeling the man's gaze upon him, cleared his throat. When he looked back, he saw the man continued to inspect him, but now he was smiling. The thinness of the smile, Carlton reflected, made his mouth no less cruel.

"I awakened you," the man stated, matter of fact. His voice was in direct contrast to his appearance, almost soothing.

Carlton demurred. He had not intended to fall asleep and, in any case, his stop would soon be here.

"What stop is yours?" the man asked. And when Carlton told him where he would transfer to the branch line, the man said, "What a coincidence. I step off there as well."

For some reason this troubled Carlton—though, he wondered, why should it? After all, there were only so many stops the train had left to make, and surely several of the remaining passengers, like him, intended to transfer to the branch line.

"You're transferring trains there?" Carlton asked.

The man shook his head. "And you?" he asked. "No other trains passing tonight, I'm afraid."

"No," said Carlton. "I was told."

"What do you intend to do?" asked the man.

"To stay in the station," said Carlton. "In the traveler's room. One sleepless night won't kill me."

The man's grin tightened. "Station?" he asked. "What station?"

Indeed, when Carlton gathered his bag and climbed down, he found the man had been correct. There was no station, only a stretch of weedy gravel. To one side of it was the track for the train from which he had just debarked, to the other the narrower-gauge track of the local. In the middle of the gravel stretch squatted a rusted wrought iron bench, a single guttering gas lamp beside it.

It was raining lightly. There was no roof over the bench, nor any cover nearby. There would be no spending the night here.

The other man had stopped near him. He possessed, so it seemed, no bags. Together they watched the train build steam and pull away.

"A pleasure to travel with you," said the man. Tipping his hat slightly, he turned to leave.

It began to rain a little harder.

"Before you go," said Carlton quickly, "might I trouble you to point me toward a hotel?"

The man made a coughing noise that it took Carlton a moment to understand was laughter. "No trouble," he said. He took Carlton by the arm. He gripped the arm oddly, awkwardly, because of, so Carlton supposed, his lack of thumb. He steered Carlton lightly but firmly over the narrow-gauge tracks. On the other side lay a grassy field. The man edged them along it until they came to a nearly hidden path cutting through. Together they followed this into the darkness.

The path was narrow, and the other man fell behind him, still holding on to his arm, pushing Carlton ahead of him. There was enough moonlight that Carlton could make out the general contours of the path, but little more, and it felt strange to have the man at once pushing him forward and holding on to him, almost as if he were being employed as some sort of shield. Carlton thought, for the first time in a long time, of how frightened he had been of the dark as a boy, and realized that fear was still within him, carefully locked away, but still there.

And perhaps, he began to feel, not nearly so carefully locked away as he had hitherto believed.

"Where are you taking me?" he asked the man.

"Keep going," said the calm voice from behind him.

"I don't even know your name," said Carlton.

The man gave again that same coughing laugh. "I don't know yours either," he said.

"It's Carlton," said Carlton.

"A pleasure to meet you, Carlton," said the man.

The field abruptly ended, and the path debouched onto a larger dirt road.

"Here we are," said the man, releasing his arm. He tapped Carlton's left side. "Hotel is that way," he said. "Unless you stray from the road you won't miss it." He tapped Carlton's other side. "I'm going this other direction myself."

"How far to the hotel?" asked Carlton.

The man grunted in the darkness. "Four miles," he said. "Perhaps five."

"Five miles!" exclaimed Carlton.

"You should have remained on the train," said the man. "You can transfer to the branch line at the next stop as well, and there's a town there. A hotel, too."

"Why didn't you tell me so while we were still on the train?"

"You didn't ask," smoothly answered the voice from the darkness. "You appeared to know what you wanted."

"I can't walk five miles. I would have to start back almost as soon as I arrived. Not to mention the rain."

"True," said the voice. "True."

"Is there nothing closer?"

"You could stay at the siding, on the bench," said the voice, "but there is little protection from the elements there." For a long moment the voice stayed silent. "Or," it finally said, "you could come home with me."

Later, Carlton told himself that if it had not been so dark, he would not have followed the man. If he had been able to see the fellow's face, the cruelty he knew to be engraved there, he would not have given in. But the man's voice was so different from his face, so soothing, so melodious, and the rain was falling faster, and he had, really, no place else to go.

So they had walked the quarter mile or so to reach the path that led to the man's house, the man all the while propelling him forward and retaining that odd grip upon his arm. Then they took the three dozen steps over mossy ground to the man's door, and the man led him in and lit first the lamps and then the fire. Only then did Carlton see his face again and regret having come. But by then it was too late.

Once the fire was blazing, the man helped Carlton off with his coat and encouraged him to warm himself by the fire. There was that same contrast between the cruelty of his face and the mellifluous quality of his voice, and the combination made Carlton slightly sick. He tried not to show it. The man hung Carlton's coat on a hook to one side of the fire, his own coat just beside it. Soon he had pulled another chair beside Carlton's and was holding his own hands near the flames to warm them.

After a moment, he stood and left the room. When he returned, it was with a wicker tray, two tumblers on it as well as a decanter half-filled with a viscous amber fluid. Between the decanter and the tumblers lay a lacquered wooden box. It was covered with scroll-work that resembled flowering vines, except that rather than ending in flowers, each vine terminated in what appeared upon closer inspection to be a monstrous head.

"What a curious box," said Carlton.

The other man ignored this. He placed the tray on the floor between their chairs. "I don't have a second bed," said the man, "but you can doze here in the chair near the fire until morning. Or, if you prefer, I can make up a pallet of sorts for you on the floor."

"The chair will be fine," said Carlton.

The man nodded, then reached for the decanter. "A drink?" he asked. "It will warm you, perhaps allow you to sleep. I promise to make certain you awaken in sufficient time to not miss your train."

Carlton nodded. He watched the man fill the glass three fingers deep and then gesture at Carlton to take it. Carlton took it and sipped. Not whiskey exactly, at least not of any variety he'd tasted. Not scotch either. But not far from either.

"What is it?" he asked the man.

"It's good, isn't it?" said the man. He lifted his own tumbler. "Cheers."

The tumbler grew empty sooner than Carlton expected. He leaned down and returned it to the wicker tray.

"Another?" asked the man, already filling it for him.

Carlton hesitated, then assented.

"It's early yet," said the man a few minutes later. "Shall we play a game of cards?"

Carlton shrugged. "Why not?" he said. He felt warm inside.

The man brought over a small end table from some other part of the room. He slid the wicker tray to one side with his foot and placed the end table between them, then reached down and picked up the lacquered box. Placing it on the end table, he opened it, removed from it a set of playing cards.

They were of a larger format than Carlton was used to, and yellowed with age. He watched the man fan them, separating them into suits. They smelled faintly of smoke and of some herb, rosemary perhaps. The images on their faces were different than what he was used to: There were no spades, clubs, hearts, diamonds. He saw shields and hawkbells, a flower of some sort, what might be a crude acorn or some similar nut. Only one in every four or five cards had human figures on it, but all of these showed an injury: a woman with a unicorn's horn run through her chest, a smiling king with a knife buried hilt-deep in his eye, an exhausted younger man lacking a hand with blood spurting from his stump.

The man across from him had discarded all the cards in the flower suit and was tucking them back into the lacquered box. When he had finished, he snapped the lid shut and deftly cut the remaining suits together.

"It's easier with just three suits," he explained. "Shall we begin?"

How much time has gone by? wondered Carlton. *How many drinks have I had?* The game wasn't hard for him to pick up, being a variant of Watten for two players rather than four. Or, rather, three players, since a hand was dealt for an absent third and left to one side.

"For the devil," said the man. "If he cares to join us."

"The devil?"

The other man shrugged. "Just a tradition," he claimed. It felt strange to Carlton, still, to see the hand sitting there on the table, awaiting the devil.

Once it was clear Carlton had grown proficient with the rules, the man lightly asked if he'd care to bet. "Just a small nothing," he said. "To make the game more interesting."

And Carlton, feeling warm inside, more than a little drunk, pleased to be dry and out of the rain, thought *Why not?*

The first three games they bet just a few shillings apiece. Carlton won each time. The other man seemed frustrated, his eyes darkening, his mouth a tight line. This pleased Carlton more than he cared to admit; he did not like the man. The man dealt again, and again Carlton won. Everything became decidedly blurry. He put down his cards and stretched, yawned.

"Perhaps that is enough for tonight," he said.

"You appear to want to quit while you are ahead," said the other man. "Hardly very sporting of you."

"It's late," said Carlton.

"One last game," said the man. "One final bet."

For a moment Carlton protested, but he quickly gave in. "One last bet," he said.

"For something meaningful this time," the man said. "For a thumb."

"A thumb?" said Carlton, surprised.

"If you win, you shall have my thumb. If I win, I shall have yours."

"But you're already missing a thumb," said Carlton.

"Yes," said the man. "I've played this game before." He waggled the hand that was still whole. "But I still have one."

"This is absurd," said Carlton.

"Of course it is," said the man.

"If I lose, you'll cut off my thumb?"

The man shook his head. "I'll remove it carefully and place it on my hand and use it. It won't hurt you. You will hardly even feel it."

"And if I win?"

"Then I suppose you will have three thumbs. I'll attach the third wherever you'd like."

Carlton laughed. "This must be a joke," he said.

The man smiled his cold smile. "If you like," his warm, welcoming voice said.

"All right," Carlton said. "I'll play along. One last game."

...

But it was as if the game had changed, or perhaps the other man had been holding back the whole time, setting him up. It became clear after the first exchanges that Carlton would be hard-pressed even to achieve a draw, and clear as well that he was much drunker than he had realized. The room seemed to waver, moving slightly, and out of the corner of his eye he thought he saw the cards that had been dealt for the devil move. He looked at his own cards, confused, unsure for a moment what game they were playing.

"Yours to play," said the other man, and at first Carlton thought the man was addressing not him but the devil, who seemed suddenly to be there, kneeling just beside the end table, his fingers touching his hand of cards. Or no, rather, nobody was there—what was he thinking?

"Yours to play," the other man repeated, and this time it was clear to Carlton that he was the one being addressed.

He played a card. A moment later, the game was over.

"You won," Carlton said.

"So I did," said the other man, and he smiled. The devil's cards were face up now, Carlton saw, though he could not remember the other man having turned them over. In one of the devil's cards a king was in the process of gorily severing his own head. In another, a queen or a princess held tight to her amputated leg, cradling it like a baby. The third card was partly covered by the first two, and Carlton could not see it. He reached to move it, but before his fingers could touch it the other man's hand closed around his wrist.

The man was muttering, a dark gibberish that was more like spitting than speaking. He tightened his grip until the bones in Carlton's wrist began to ache. Then, in a flash, the other hand, the thumbless one, shot out and closed its fingers around Carlton's thumb.

"What are you—"

"You lost," the man hissed in a voice that better matched his face. "I shall take what is mine."

Carlton felt his thumb tingling and then a tightness in it and then, abruptly, he didn't feel the thumb at all. When the man drew his hand away, where the thumb had been the skin was planed flat, as if there had never been a thumb there in the first place. He could see his thumb now on the man's hand, the color of the skin too dark to match the rest of his pallid hand.

The man stared admiringly at his own hand, turning it back and forth, flexing the new thumb. He looked up and smiled.

"Who are you?" asked Carlton, his voice shivering.

"The question is not who," said the man, if *man* was in fact the proper word, "but what."

When Carlton said nothing to this, the man smiled again, even broader this time. "Double or nothing?" he inquired.

He woke up with his head aching, lying just off the road. It was a little past dawn. His bag had been opened and his possessions scattered all around in the damp grass, and he was shivering, very cold. He looked around for the man's house, but there was no house to be seen.

At first he thought it had been a dream, but then he made the mistake of lifting his hand and staring at it. The thumb was gone, the forefinger as well. He remembered only vaguely the specifics of the second game he had lost, but he remembered the end of it, with the devil's hand of cards somehow floating upright in the air while the other man kept affixing Carlton's forefinger to different parts of his own hand to see how it looked and then removing it. In the end he left it beside his own forefinger, rooted in the web of his thumb.

Carlton gathered his wet things and made his way back down the road to the railway stop. It looked different than it had previously: there was a small covered waiting area that somehow had escaped his notice the night before, and a small shack too for the signalman. The signalman was outside, checking the condition of the tracks and raking footprints out of the gravel.

When the signalman saw him, he asked, "Which train, sir?"

"Branch line," said Carlton.

The signalman nodded. "Which direction?"

"Inland."

The signalman led him to the covered waiting area.

"Don't get too many passengers here, either getting on or off."

"No," said Carlton. "I imagine not."

He fell asleep in the waiting area. He dreamt that he was again sitting at the other man's small table, cards in his hands, a roaring fire to one side. The lacquered box was not visible at first, and then he saw it, tucked into the top of his traveling bag, the corner just visible. There were only two players, but a third hand had been dealt and lay facedown in one of the two remaining quadrants of the table. But this hand was not the devil's hand, it could not be, for the devil was there, across from him, where in life the other man had been, immense, skin red and scaled, waiting.

Carlton swallowed. "Whose turn to play?" he asked.

Not yet, said the devil.

"Not yet?" said Carlton.

The devil nodded slightly at the third hand. *Who,* the devil asked, *will you bring to the table?*

He was awoken by the signalman shaking him. His thumb and forefinger were still gone. He rushed quickly to the train and boarded. Almost immediately the train began to move.

His car was all but deserted. He opened the first compartment he found and looked in. It was empty. He stood in the doorway, but in the end did not enter; he did not wish to be alone.

He moved down through the car, opening each compartment door. The first three were empty. In the fourth and final one was a lone man. He had dozed off.

Carlton entered quietly and took a seat directly across from the man, facing him.

He watched the man sleep. Seeing him there, so peaceful, something struck him.

He looked at the man's hands. All his fingers were there, every single one. He did not seem to Carlton like the sort of man who needed all his fingers. He was unlike Carlton in this way.

He crossed his legs at the knees and placed his clasped hands atop them, the missing thumb and forefinger prominently displayed. He waited.

The man began to move. He opened his eyes.

"I awakened you," Carlton said, and smiled.

He tried to flex his missing thumb. In his mind, he began to deal the cards. He placed three of them before the devil and then waited, to see if he had been favored, to see if the devil would guide him in what to do next.

Nameless Citizen

1.

The world is a hell because we have made it so—I have always thought so, even before. This is not something to be regretted, only something to be accepted, and with each passing year I have come to accept it more. I doubt anyone would argue with me about it now, even if there were others left to argue.

The last person I argued with, indeed the last person with whom I had had contact of any kind until two days ago, I argued with seven years ago. He left on foot, carrying a small titanium cylinder, its surface etched with red script. He asked me to go with him—a simple delivery, he said. I declined. "You won't come back," I told him. "They won't let you." He knew this to be true just as I did, and yet, stubborn or naïve or simply confused, he chose to go anyway. He shook my hand and then turned and left. As predicted, he never came back.

Two days ago, I spent most of an afternoon in the basements of the houses surrounding my own. The houses here are now ramshackle or collapsed, subject to decades of heat and cold and unnatural rain and wind since the disaster, but the basements are still more or less intact. I have broken the concrete floor of each basement, turned the soil beneath and, with great effort on my part, set about attempting to fruit mushrooms and fungi. For many years I did not succeed in growing anything at all, and instead lived on the food storage scavenged from the basements and closets of empty houses around me. Outside, I attempted to grow various grains, but either the seeds or the soil is sterile, or perhaps both. Every few years, whenever I discover a cache of seed or grain sheltered in some fashion from the air, I try again.

With mushrooms, I managed finally to fruit several dozen translucent and wracked buttonlets, each no bigger than my fingernail. I ate half of them, a tasteless mouthful that did not make me ill, and then transferred some of the others to adjacent basements, hoping that soon I'd have half a dozen separate colonies that would eventually feed me. But their brief moment in the outside air between basements may have been enough to kill them, for only in the first basement do mushrooms continue, lethargically, to grow.

The air might, still now, be more deadly than I imagine. Hard to know since the air that killed everything around me has had no effect on me at all. Or, rather, a salutary effect: my body absorbs its poison and channels it, making me feel more alive.

I was just leaving my final basement when I heard it: a voice, shouting, tinny. I stopped, listened. Then moved toward it.

"Nameless citizen," the voice was calling, "we need you!"

"Nameless citizen," a second voice called, "please, we beg you!"

"Nameless citizen," the first voice called, "we have no desire to hurt you! Please, grant us audience."

I squirmed under a collapsed fence and through a ruined backyard, then took a roundabout path back to my house. Eventually, I caught sight of them. There were just two this time. They stood at the edge of the barren ground that marked my yard, on the crumbling remains of the sidewalk, holding rifles in their gloved hands. They wore thick hazard suits.

"Nameless citizen!" the voice called. "Surely you don't want our species to die out?"

But I did. Why ever not? We had destroyed almost everything along with ourselves. It would be better for the little that remained if we did die out.

Or *they*, I should say, since even though I was once one of them, I could hardly be said to be so now. The disaster had changed me. I had become a different creature altogether.

"Nameless citizen!" one of them bellowed through his suit speaker. No doubt he would have continued to bellow had I not tapped his shoulder. He spun around, panicked, trying to get his weapon up, but I already had my hands on the rifle's stock and barrel, had forced the weapon back flat against his chest. If he squeezed the trigger the shot would travel up through his throat and jaw and remove the front of his face.

When he cried out, the other one spun and pointed his rifle at me.

"You called?" I said.

"Let him go," said the second one, "or I'll shoot."

"I thought you said you had no desire to hurt me," I said. "You need something from me. If you shoot, you won't get it. You called me, I came. Put your weapon down and tell me what you need."

They looked at each other, and then the one I was not touching placed his rifle on the ground gingerly. I took the rifle from the first and did the same, then took a step back.

"Nameless citizen—" that one began.

"Are you the same drones who came before?" I asked.

"Before what?" asked the first.

But the second shook his head. "This is the first time we've come. If others came, they are dead."

"Nameless citizen—" the first began again.

"I'm going to stop you right there," I said. "I might be nameless, but I am not a citizen. Not of your community."

I watched him furrow his brow in concentration. And then his brow smoothed. "Nameless person," he said, "we call on you to help our community and your species! We must have material for the construction of individuals if we are to continue. As you see from our vestments, we are not made to survive in this place, in this air. Even with these suits we cannot be long outside. This visit to you has already shortened our lives."

And where I touched you as well, I thought, though I did not say so. My body is as polluted for them as the air outside, and where I had pushed my hand against his chest the skin would soon bruise and slough, even with the suit between.

"You," said the other, "have no such constraints. You live outside, not underground. The air cannot hurt you. Truly, you are a wondrous being."

"Nameless person," said the first, "we ask you to help us. Will you travel to where the material is stored and bring it back to us, for the sake of your species?"

"No," I said. "I will not."

"What can we do to convince you to help us?" asked the other.

"There was another, a sort of brother of mine," I said. "He traveled to help you seven years ago, on a similar mission. I saw the cylinder he retrieved. Was he not able to help you?"

"Horak?" said the second. "That was before our time," he said.

"He did help us," said the first, "but he is not in a position to help us again."

"Why not?" I asked.

Neither of them responded to this. Either they did not know or they had been told not to tell me. Considering the shortness of their lives and the pointedness of their purpose, it could be either. Indeed, in all likelihood, these two had been formed hurriedly, primarily for the task of trying to coax me into making the same mistake Horkai had made.

"Nameless person—" the first began again, "what can we do to—"

"Absolutely nothing," I said. "I will not help you under any circumstance."

"We have failed in our purpose," confided the second to the first.

"Nameless person," the other began again, "what—"

But I simply walked past them and into my house.

For a while they remained where they were, trying, no doubt, to determine if there was some way of salvaging their purpose. Perhaps they were even assessing the odds of taking me unawares and forcing me to come with them. When I judged that they had stayed too long, I parted the shutter and stuck the barrel of my rifle out. At that, they gathered their own guns and left.

I spent the time until dark setting traps for them around the property. I propped a gun inside both the front and back door, just in case. But, considering what I had done to their comrades last time they had come and tried to take me by force, I didn't imagine they would return.

I waited, thinking. Horkai—if Horak and Horkai were the same person—was "not in a position to help us again." What did that mean, exactly? Dead, maybe? But these ready-made people did not generally speak in euphemism. They didn't understand it. Should the words be taken literally? If so, what would they mean exactly?

I thought about what they had done to Horkai the time before, before I met him, the way they had severed his spinal column as a means to control him, to use him. And him, I thought, despite that, willing to go back.

Eventually, I slept.

Did I dream? I would say no—I never dream, at least not dreams I remember. I have not dreamt since the disaster changed me, as if the exchange for surviving the conflagration was to surrender my ability to dream. And yet, despite this, something had rearranged itself in my head as I slept, and I awoke another person. Not changed so as to become the comrade of those two hazard-suited drones, not changed so as to have an interest in saving so-called humankind, but no longer quite so willing to stand aside. And curious enough to know what had happened to my friend that, despite the trail being seven years cold, I went in search of him.

2.

I passed down streets thick with dust, cars scoured of paint, the metal beneath hardly rusted in the dry air despite all the decades that had passed. I walked until I realized I had entered a cul-de-sac, and for just a moment old habits asserted themselves, and I almost turned around and went back to a street that ran through. But what did it matter? Nobody had lived in these houses for years, and I could see where the fence had been kicked in at the end of the cul-de-sac, perhaps by the very drones that had come to woo me. I passed through an expanse of dust, then through another backyard and onto a street. The street jogged left, and I slid down a culvert and climbed back up the other side. A few more streets, heading roughly east, passing through the remains of a housing development, then a church that had partly collapsed. The sun was red and sticky, obscured by haze. I kept walking.

I passed through a river, its water a brownish red, just transparent enough that I could see something floating in it, as if hair was growing from the riverbed. When I started across it, it clung to my boots, making a sucking sound as I pulled myself along. Something alive then, at least in a manner of speaking. *Is it edible?* I wondered, but I decided it would be a mistake to stick around long enough to find out. Something else, too, that it took me a moment to place: water bugs, skittering across the surface, though closer in appearance to termites than to water striders. At first I wasn't sure how they kept afloat exactly, then I realized they had extruded blobs of mucus around their feet and floated on that. I stayed there, calf-deep in the water, watching, surprised how much it moved me to see something alive and new, appropriate to this new world in a way humans were never appropriate to the old. Indeed, I nearly stayed too long—by the time I started walking again, the filaments had tightened enough that it was hard to free my boots.

I made a wide detour around the capitol building, having nearly lost my life there some years before. And from there worked my way northeast along the ruined boulevard, toward the ruined library where the drones came from.

I found the drone perhaps a kilometer from the library, collapsed in the middle of the street. He was facedown, and when I turned him over his faceplate was shattered, his skin bruised. Judging from the dust angel inflicted on the ground beside him, the other had stayed with him for some time before continuing on.

I followed what I assumed were his steps. They wove a little, became shorter. I kept expecting to come across his body as well, but I never did.

I found the iron door and struck it with a rock repeatedly, the sound ringing out through the empty air. There were bugs here as well— one or two tiny flies that moved in erratic patterns. Things were coming back; another few thousand years and the world might be back to where it was before we appeared. Yet another reason for allowing humans to go extinct.

Nobody came. I struck the door again and hollered. When it still remained closed, I rooted around in the ruins until I found a place where the ground had collapsed and I could insinuate my way down a level into a half-collapsed lower hallway. I lit a flare and wormed my way forward, wondering whether this was wise. I was, admittedly, very difficult to kill, but being buried under rubble might do it. And if it didn't, at least not at first, assuming I was buried and couldn't get out, that might well be worse.

I snagged my arm on a piece of rebar and tore it deeply. I pulled the arm back, licked the wound clean and pushed the edges together. A few moments later the bleeding had stopped and it held shut, the edges filmed over and milky. A few hours and I would not even be able to see where the cut had been. I worked my way farther in and suddenly was through the rubble and in a solid hall again, ceiling and walls intact.

At the end of the hall was a seal, a kind of artificial barrier made of vulcanized fabric: one or several hazard suits apparently torn apart and reassembled to form a protective wall. I took out my knife, cut a slit in it, and worked my way through.

A door was on the other side. I forced it open and found myself in a room thick with dust. Nobody had set foot in it for years. The far wall of the room was entirely covered with sandbags, packed floor to ceiling. Another protective barrier. I began pulling them down and found, in the middle of the wall, a door. I kicked it open and went through.

It took passing through a few empty rooms before I found the second drone. He was lying naked on a metal table, breathing shallowly, eyes glazed. His body was bruised in places, blackish in others. When I slapped him, he came to himself confusedly.

"You," he said when he saw me. "I knew you'd come."

"Where's Horkai?" I asked.

"Who?" he said, and only then did I realize he was the drone who, of the two, had seemed to know the least.

"Where is everybody else?" I asked.

"There is nobody else," he said. "I'm the last one. You came just in time."

"For what?" I couldn't help but ask, even though I already knew.

"The monitor will give you a map," he said weakly. "It will tell you where to go. It will tell you how to assemble the material to form a new generation as well."

"I'm not here for that," I said.

"No?" he said. And then he closed his eyes and died.

He had not been lying. When I had been to the ruined library years before, it had been crammed with the living, all of them huddled underground, desperate for a way to stay alive. Now, the whole place was empty. Or not empty exactly. Many of the rooms had corpses in them, desiccated, covered with sheets, with faces and bodies identical to that of the drone I had just seen die.

3.

There was only one computer I could find that seemed to be operational, and I assumed this was what the drone had called the monitor. I fingered it on. On the screen appeared an old man, his beard gray, his hair mostly gone. He moved slowly and tentatively, as if he had forgotten how to use his legs and was only just becoming accustomed to them again. He wore on his feet a pair of dirty slippers that swished as he moved, and he had a tattered bathrobe over his bright jumpsuit. Why he had opted for such a self-representation I found impossible to understand.

"Ah," he said, his voice hoarse and wavery. "You're here."

"I am," I agreed.

"Yes," he said. "Who woke you?" He turned back to me. "Well?" he said.

"I . . . ," I started and then stopped, realizing he had mistaken me for Horkai. Or Horak. Very carefully, I said, "I wasn't aware I had been asleep."

He watched me, his eyes suddenly attentive, shining. "You don't remember who I am, do you?" he said.

"You're a construct preserved electronically," I said. "You're part of the monitor."

"Yes," he said. "But who was I in life?" And when I didn't answer, he said, "Rasmus. Does that ring a bell?"

I knew the name of course. Horkai had spoken of him, and perhaps I had met him many years before, the first time I had come to the ruined library. I knew he was not to be trusted. But, then again, is any human meant to be trusted?

"Where's Horkai?" I asked.

"Ah," he said. "So you're not him. I'm afraid you all look alike to me, all of you who have left the race. You must be Rykte."

"That's not my name," I said.

He waved his hand feebly. "It will do in place of a name," he said. "I was told you weren't coming. And yet here you are. Had a change of heart?"

"Not exactly," I said.

"Doesn't matter," he said. "As you can see, I'm the only one left. It's too late."

"But you're not really left," I said. "You're just a construct, an impression within a computer's memory."

This irritated him. "That may be," he said. "But even as a construct, I'm the most human of the two of us."

I laughed. "I would hope so," I said.

"And it really doesn't matter to you?" he said sometime later. "We could die out and you wouldn't care?"

I shook my head. "It should have happened long ago," I said. "Where's Horkai?" I asked again.

He waved the question away. "How about we trade?" he said.

"What sort of trade?" I asked.

"You get the cylinders of material we need, bring them back here. I'll show you how to form new mules, and then I'll teach them. And then I'll show you your friend."

"Why does it matter? A series of artificial persons will never bring real people back."

"Won't it?" he said. "If that's the case, then what can it possibly hurt to indulge an old man's whim?"

I thought it over. Did I want to see Horkai badly enough?

"No," I said.

"No?" He regarded me a long moment and then sighed. "So be it," he said.

. . .

I turned to leave. "One more thing," he said from behind me.

I turned back.

"Will you please power the machine down? I might as well go extinct along with everybody else."

I reached out to do this, but then began to think. About what Rasmus had done to Horkai, about his unwillingness to reveal where Horkai was now, about the drones or mules or whatever the fuck he called what he was creating out of pilfered genetic scraps. "No," I said.

"No?" he said.

"You wanted so badly not to go extinct, let's see what living alone until the machine dies does to you."

And then I left. The construct called after me, but I ignored it. I looked for my friend in the other rooms of the complex but did not find him. I looked above ground as well, in the open air. I moved in a widening circle, exploring those buildings that were still standing nearby. Though I found a preservation chamber that had been recently used, he was not in it. And I found little else.

4.

But that preservation chamber in the end may prove useful. Not knowing what else to do, what other course to take, not caring to go back to the life I was living before, I have decided to take the step of having myself preserved. I do this despite the strong likelihood of there being no one left to awaken me. Eventually, I know, the preservation chamber will break down and I will probably die while being improperly thawed. But perhaps, with a little luck, someone will find me first, bring me back to life, and allow me to see how the world has changed.

Who? a voice inside me wants to know.

The rest of me has no answer for that. Maybe someone will come, from somewhere. Maybe I have missed someone. Or maybe Horkai will someday return.

Besides, I am curious. I don't want to live out my last years scrabbling away at my mushroom farms. I want to see what will come next, what will replace us.

And so I shall preserve myself, throw the dice, trust to fate. I leave this record also as a way to tempt fate, to make whoever finds it curious enough about me that they will attempt to rescue me.

But chances are that it will not be found. Or if not that, that what eventually finds me and unthaws me, decades or centuries from now, cannot, properly, be described as human.

But then, for that matter, neither can I.

The Coldness of His Eye

1.

There they were, Jens and his father, again together, after so many years. The same as it had always been, only so much had changed. Jens was far older, as old as his father had been when they had last been together, hair white and wispy and fugitive, complexion sallow, hands thin enough to display the articulation of his bones.

And yet his father looked like he always had—face hale and hearty, figure large and looming, unbent by age. It was as if his father had not aged at all. Which, in a manner of speaking, he hadn't, since he'd been dead now for thirty years.

Hello Jens, his dead father said.

"Hello," said Jens, because he did not know what else to say. He was not, he was surprised to find, frightened. More than anything he was curious: Why now? And curious too to see if his father turned around, would the back of his bald skull be solid and smooth or, as he had last seen it, broken and soft?

"What do you want?" Jens asked.

His father did not answer. He just smiled in a way that didn't move the muscles of his face. It was as if a smile had suddenly been painted on.

"It's been a long time since I've seen you," said Jens.

The painted smile flicked to a painted frown. *Not that long,* said his father. *Only yesterday.*

It had not been just yesterday. It had been three decades before. Should he correct his father? He wasn't sure. What was the etiquette in such a situation, when you were made to interact with the dead?

"Why are you here?" asked Jens.

Don't I have a right? his father asked indignantly. *Isn't it my house?* His lips when he spoke, Jens realized, didn't seem to move.

No, it wasn't his house. It wasn't a house the man had ever been in but a place Jens had purchased shortly after his father's death, with the money the insurance paid out.

"How exactly can I help you?"

Help me? said his father. He gave that same painted-on smile. *Isn't it clear I'm beyond help?*

And then he held out his hand, beckoned.

2.

He came to himself downstairs, beside the front door, his hand attempting to turn the knob as his wife shook him. When she realized he was awake, she stopped.

"What was it?" she asked. "Some sort of dream? Why were you going outside?"

"Did I want to go out?" he asked. "I was having a nightmare," he said, though he wasn't sure that was exactly what it had been. "How did I get down here?"

"You were sleepwalking," she said. "Muttering too. Saying something."

"What was I saying?"

She shook her head. "I don't know. I couldn't understand."

"Good," he said. Inside, he winced. It did not seem the right thing to say.

"Come back to bed," she said, and he let himself be led. On the stairs, she asked, "What was your nightmare about?"

He waved his hands in dismissal. "Hard to remember," he said.

He lay there in the bed, beside her. In no time at all her breathing deepened and her body relaxed, and he was sure she was asleep.

Did *he* want to go to sleep? Not really. It didn't seem like a particularly good idea. It was not that he was afraid of his father, of his father's ghost, but he did not particularly want to spend more time with it either. He had not missed his father since he had killed him thirty years ago, had hardly even thought about him. Which made him wonder again, *Why now?*

He slid out of the bed, careful not to wake his wife. He felt his way to the door in the dark and out onto the landing.

A shaft of moonlight struck down through the skylight. He couldn't see well, but he could see enough to know where he was going. He made his way down the stairs and to the entryway below.

There was the door, the handle he had been touching when his wife stopped him. Where had he been going, and why?

Hello, Jens, he heard his father say behind him.

He flinched, then froze. Gathering himself, he turned around. There the man was, just visible, half in and half out of the dark, his lit eye glittering coldly. Jens wasn't asleep now, he was almost sure. Hallucinating, maybe? Or was he really here? Had he been asleep before?

"Hello," he managed.

You don't look good, son, said his father. *You haven't been taking care of yourself.*

But he *had* been taking care of himself. It was just that he was three decades older.

"What do you want?" Jens asked.

Do you remember where you killed me? asked his father.

"I didn't . . . ," Jens started, by reflex, and then fell silent.

So his father knew he was dead. And that Jens had killed him. Did that change anything?

"I was . . . cleared of any involvement in your murder," Jens offered.

Of course you were, said his father. *You're clever. You have good genes. I would expect no less of you.*

"I . . . ," Jens trailed off. "Yes," he finally said. "Of course I remember."

Will you do something for me?

"I don't know."

His father ignored him as if he hadn't spoken. He stared at Jens. He had been staring the whole time, never blinking, his one lit eye never moving from Jens's face.

Go back there.

"Why?"

It is important, said his father. *Go back there.*

"But your body isn't even there. You're buried in the graveyard off Twenty-Sixth. I can show you your headstone."

I'm not talking about my body. I'm talking about the place you killed me. Go there. Now.

3.

It was crazy, he told himself even as he pulled on his boots. There was no point going, no point taking instruction from his father's ghost. That was one of the reasons he had killed his father—he was tired of taking instruction from him. Well, that and the insurance money.

What does my wife know? he wondered. She knew he had been interviewed by the police—she had been there when they had arrived. She knew he had been cleared, partly due to her testimony. She had been asleep when he had killed his father—he had made sure of that, a pill crushed and mixed into her wine. His wife knew he had gone to bed with her and that he had been there when, in the morning, she woke up. Why would she not think he was there beside her the whole night?

No, it was foolish. He had lived nearly thirty years believing his wife had no idea he had killed his father. There was no reason to reconsider that now.

Besides, his father was waiting, in the dark near the door, watching him. No matter where Jens moved, his father was always looking at him.

"Shall we go?" asked Jens.

After you, said his father.

"No, after you," Jens answered.

They had had the same exchange the night his father died, Jens realized once the door was locked and he was cutting through the grassy field and moving toward the forested mountain beyond. *After you. No, after you.* His father had shrugged and gone first, and Jens had followed close behind him. He had watched the back of his father's bald head as the man climbed the switchbacked path up the mountainside to the cave.

"A man?" his father had said.

"Yes," Jens had said. "A man. I think he's dead."

"Did you check his breathing? His pulse?"

"I couldn't find anything."

His father grunted, kept walking.

"The thing I don't understand," his father said a moment later, "is what you were doing up there yourself."

Yes, he had to admit to himself, there had been a flaw to his plan, and his father had found it. There was no sane reason he would be up in the cave in the middle of the night. "I go there sometimes," he had claimed. "To think."

"To think," his father said flatly, not even bothering to turn around. "This is a strange place," he said. "I'd think twice before coming up here to think."

True, his father had often told stories of the cave and the woods around it, as a way of making it difficult for Jens, when he was young, to sleep. Which was one reason it had given Jens a certain amount of satisfaction to kill him there. His father had been a good story-teller, he had to give him that, even if he was a sadist. Though now he wondered if killing him here was what had allowed his father to come back as a ghost. If so, he had taken his time about it.

Back then, he had seen nothing but the back of his father's head, bald and featureless. Now, however, the dead father in front of him showed only his face. He wasn't walking backward exactly—it was more as if, motionless, he was always exactly the same distance ahead and looking back, always keeping an eye on Jens.

"Aren't you interested in knowing why I did it?" asked Jens.

Did what?

"Killed you."

The face flicked into a frown. *No,* his father said. *At this point knowing would make no difference.*

"Sometimes you think you know the world," one of those stories had begun, "and that's your first mistake." Now, hiking up to the cave, it was hard not to think of these stories of his father's:

A man goes into the woods and lies down. When he wakes up again, years have passed for him, but only minutes for the rest of the world.

Or, another: a man enters a cave. He twists and turns through its passages and comes out again. For him, no time has passed, but in the world at large, thirty years have gone by. And when he hikes back down the mountain and back to the town he has always lived in, he discovers another man who looks just like him is living with his wife, that someone else has been imitating him.

Perhaps that was why his father had come back. Because it had been thirty years.

How had that last story continued? Jens had not thought about it all this time. All he remembered was the original man trying to convince his wife that she had lived with an imposter for the last three decades, and failing. Obviously if one of them was an imposter, she reasoned, it would be the much younger man. It would be him.

"But he would not listen," his father had said—he remembered now. "He kept insisting until the townsfolk had little choice but to slaughter him."

Thirty years earlier, they had reached the cave at last, Jens breathing heavily from the climb and perhaps, too, from anxiety.

His father was barely winded. He played his flashlight over the walls. "Where is he?" he had asked. "This man you claimed you saw?"

"He was right there," said Jens. "In that."

On the floor a line of pale sand traced a circle, with a slightly smaller circle made of dirt just within it.

"What the hell is that?" his father asked.

"I don't know," Jens claimed. He moved forward and reached to touch the twinned circles with his toe, but his father stopped him.

"Don't," said his father. "You don't know what's inside it."

But Jens did know. He knew nothing was inside it since he had drawn the circle himself. Unlike his father, he was not superstitious.

His father crouched to get a closer look, still careful not to touch or cross the circle. And that was the moment Jens chose to strike the back of his head with the rock he had prepared just for that purpose. His father groaned. He fell into the circles, breaking the lines. A few more blows to the back of his skull and he was dead.

Here we are, said his father. *Again.*

"Yes," said Jens. "Here we are." He played the flashlight around the cave. It was empty, nothing there at all. If he looked carefully, he thought he could see the traces of the circle he had made, but little beyond that.

But of course there couldn't be traces of the circles: it had been thirty years. And yet, it seemed to him that that was what he was seeing.

His father's body had been found quickly, almost impossibly so. He'd expected a month or two of his father being missing and he having to pretend that, like everyone else, he didn't know where he had gone. But shortly after his wife awoke, the police had arrived at his door looking for him.

"What is it?" he had said.

"We have a few questions we'd like to ask," said one. "Can we come in?"

"Is anything wrong?" he had asked.

"When was the last time you saw your father?"

For a moment he thought his father must have survived, that he wasn't dead after all, that bloody and broken he had stumbled his way down the mountain and called the police.

"Two days ago," he managed. "Maybe three?"

"Three days," his wife said from beside him. "He came over here yelling like a lunatic."

Their attention sharpened. "What was he upset about?" they asked her.

"Is anything wrong?" he asked again before his wife could answer. His panic from worrying that his father was still alive was exactly right for allowing him to convey anxiety and shock when they finally told him his father's body had been found. He tried to hold on to that panic, to not let relief wash over him until they were finally done with him.

He walked around the remnants of the twinned circles without crossing into them.

Remember how quickly I was found? his father asked, as if he knew what Jens was thinking. Perhaps he did.

"Yes," said Jens.

Who drew the circles? he asked. *Was it you?*

Jens hesitated, then nodded.

Why? Did you know what they would do?

He had suspected the circles would interest his father and cause him to let down his guard. He had, too, thought it might set the

police off on the wrong track, thinking it an occult murder, a ceremony gone wrong, rather than bringing them after him. But neither,
he felt, were what his father had in mind.

"What do you mean?" he asked slowly.

His father didn't answer, just stayed watching him as, restless,
he kept circling with that same unblinking expression.

You're afraid of it, his father taunted. *You made it and yet you're
afraid of it.*

"Don't be stupid," Jens said.

All right then, said his father. *Prove it.*

He could see the circle clearly now, shimmering in the dim light,
the lighter line and then, within it, the darker line. Perhaps it was
not a circle but only the ghost of a circle. In either case, it could not
hurt him. He was not superstitious. He had made it: something he
had made could not hurt him.

He stepped across the lines and into the center.

And then, abruptly, his father was very close indeed.

The mistake you made, his father's voice said softly, *was assuming
I was your father, rather than just someone or something resembling him.*
And when Jens turned to flee, there was his father, or the thing that
resembled his father, both in front of him and behind.

4.

When she woke up, she saw her husband was still asleep. He lay on
his left side, crumpled up, which seemed strange to her—he never
slept on that side because, when he was younger, his father broke that
arm in one of his rages. His father had been a real bastard, a bru-
tal man. Her husband never spoke of him. Just as well he was gone.

She shook her husband a little and he groaned. He rolled to his
back, winced, then opened his eyes. They wandered a little, then
came to focus on her.

"Good morning," she said.

"Yes."

"Feeling all right?" she asked. "Over the nightmare?"

"Nightmare?" he asked, and he seemed to search his memory without finding anything. "What did I say it was about?"

"You didn't say," she said.

"I'm fine now," he claimed. "Better than I've been in a long time."

There was something about him, something different, something she couldn't put her finger on. Or maybe it was just that she was sleepy too from being awakened in the middle of the night.

She sighed. "What shall we do today?" she asked.

"You don't have to go to work?"

She furrowed her brow. "Silly you," she said. "I haven't worked for years."

"I'm off today?"

"It's Saturday. What's wrong with you?"

There was an expression on his face she couldn't read. "I don't know what I'm thinking," he said.

She didn't say anything in reply, just lay on her side with her hand propping up her head, watching him. There was something, she felt, that she was trying to see, but she couldn't see it.

After a while he looked away, stared at the ceiling.

"What to do . . . ," he mused. "A walk," he said.

A walk? she thought. That was a first.

"Or a hike. Up to the mountains," he said. "To a little place I used to go. A special place. You'll love it." He turned to face her. "You'll love it so much," he promised. "Once I take you there, you'll have a hard time dragging yourself away."

Daylight Come

At last, one night I went to the cave alone. They forbad me this—I could not go alone, nor at night—but I went anyway.

It took a certain level of preparation. As my first keeper slept, I managed to scrape away at the dirt beneath my pallet, making sure to pack the loose dirt back into the hole before he awoke. Each day I dug a little deeper, and on the fourth day or perhaps fifth, I bloodied my fingers on dirt that did not move because it was a stone. The stone was large enough that it took another day, perhaps two, before I dug it out, only to have to place it back in its hole again almost immediately and hurriedly heap dirt over it: my first keeper had begun to awaken.

I had no time to suck my fingers clean. I barely had enough time to throw myself on my pallet, the stone a lump in my back. I was feigning sleep when the man entered, yawning, scratching his belly.

He was large, massive even. Unlike the others, he never seemed frightened of me. He noticed nothing, however, paid no attention to my dirty and raw fingers. He nudged me with the toe of his boot. When I did not respond, he tugged at the chain hooked to the metal cuff around my neck.

"On your feet, eater of darkness," the first keeper said. "Daylight come."

Groaning, I sat up. My hair was so tangled I could not pass my fingers through it. I had not seen my reflection for days, weeks even. I was fairly certain if I did, I would not recognize myself.

"Someday," I informed my first keeper, "I will kill you."

He laughed, shook his head. "Look at you," he said. "Whether eater or mere ordinary woman, you are no threat to me."

We had bantered like this every morning since they had taken me. But today was the first day that, when I looked at him, I could clearly imagine him dead.

This was the day before the night I went to the cave alone. This day I went to the cave but as usual, as their slave. My first keeper unlocked my chain from the ring attached to the tent's center post. He wound the chain's end tight around his fist, then jerked me from my pallet. I scrambled up. He was already pushing his way through the canvas flap and toward the path.

Outside, he gestured at the scattered remnants of a meal beside his dead fire. The night keeper was wrapped in his cloak and asleep, his face hidden in the crook of his arm. "Bread," he said. "Cheese." I managed to secure a hunk of each before he rushed me past. I ate as I walked, hurriedly, and then rushed to stay beside him, so the chain would not tug on my collar and set my neck bleeding again.

The path turned and twisted, rising slightly. I could not see the cave yet, but perhaps through the trees the cave could see us. We walked a time in silence save for the sound of the first keeper's long, slow plod and my quicker, sharper steps beside. "If it was me," he said finally, "if it was my choice, I would have killed you already."

"It is not you," I said. "You are merely a keeper."

"First keeper," he said, and laughed. "Merely! But they will kill you in the end. Either after they have what they hope to have from you or after they realize you cannot give it to them."

I said nothing. In fact, I understood the situation precisely as he did. He was perfectly right. They would use me until they determined I was of no value to them, and then they would slaughter me.

When we arrived at the cave, the others were already there. As usual, no women apart from me—and they did not truly consider me a woman. Or rather, they did, but thought that aspect of my being beside the point. I was an eater, and thus both more than and less than human.

The four gaunt men were dressed in their thick robes, their faces expressionless. The first keeper stopped at a distance. When I hesitated, he pushed me toward them.

"Go on, then," he said.

I moved slightly forward. The four men watched me come, and when the first keeper's hold on my chain kept me from coming any closer, they inclined themselves toward me in a slow bow, as if performed underwater.

"Eater of darkness," said the one I had come to think of as their leader, in a broken voice. "Welcome."

I said nothing.

"You know what we would have of you," said the second. When I did not answer, the first keeper jerked the chain.

"Yes, I know," I said.

They performed again their slow, balletic bow. When I felt the chain grow slack again, I started toward the mouth of the cave.

The first keeper stopped at the cave's entrance. He secured the end of the chain to the ring they had hammered into the stone of the cave's mouth.

"In with you, eater," he said. "Eat."

In I went.

At first the cave was unnaturally dim, the darkness thick and palpable, and I opened my mouth and began to gulp it in. I could feel the darkness crowding my lungs, a black mass, and soon, dizzy and stuffed with it, I had to lie down. With the chain attached to the collar around my neck, I could not reach the stone bench that had been cut into the back of the cave. Instead, I had to lie on the floor.

Feeling the cold of the stone through my skin, I waited for my breathing to calm. I closed my eyes.

Things grew darker still, but after a time the darkness became variegated, a collection of wavering shadows and shades. I felt a wind rush through my head, saw dogs made of shadow fading in and out of being, saw a vast and ponderous shape as it passed through me. I waited for the dogs to bark, or for the vast shape to notice me and speak, but neither did.

After a while, I rose to my knees and opened my eyes. The light of the cave was now a pale gray, as visible to me as if it had been daylight. I could see everything but could detect neither my hands nor my body. Where they had been, there was only darkness.

Staggering to my feet, I stumbled toward the cave's mouth. When the robed men saw me, their breath caught in their throats. They looked afraid. Even the first keeper seemed momentarily taken aback. I held my hand before my face and saw there was no hand there, only swirling darkness.

"Eater of darkness!" said their leader. "What do you see awaiting us?"

I opened my mouth to speak but nothing came out. And then I fainted.

When I awoke, it was late in the afternoon. The four robed men were gone. The first keeper had seated himself on a large rock near the cave's mouth and had hold of my chain again. From time to time, he tugged at it. It was that, perhaps, that had awakened me.

When he saw I was awake, he said, "They discussed whether to kill you or no. One said yes, the other three no, but they were less certain than yesterday. In the end, they were still too afraid to kill you, or perhaps too greedy, so we shall see what the darkness speaks through you tomorrow." He jerked the chain again. "You are running out of time."

I coughed up a black, slick lump. It lay in the dirt a moment but almost immediately curled at its edges and began to dissolve.

"It makes for a nice parlor trick, this eating of darkness," said the first keeper. "But once they realize anyone can do it, they'll surmount their fear and kill you."

"If anyone can do it," I said, gesturing to the cave's mouth behind me, "please, feel free. Go inside and open your mouth."

He just stared. There was not fear in his face exactly, but I still knew he would not enter the cave.

I fell asleep almost as soon as we arrived back at the tent, but a few hours later was awake again. I lay on my pallet listening to the first keeper conversing with the night keeper, the former's voice thick with drink. Over time it grew dark outside, and soon they both stopped speaking. I could tell from his snores the first keeper was asleep.

I had little to fear from the night keeper. He was afraid of me. As long as I was quiet, he would not risk entering the tent.

I rolled off my pallet and folded it back, prying the rock out of its cradle of dirt. It fit comfortably in my palm, one edge of it sharp and jagged. I stood and felt my way to the center post and then, slowly, dully, began to pry at the lock that held my chain to the ring.

Twice I thought the night keeper had heard me, and so threw myself quickly down again. The first time perhaps I had misheard, or perhaps he hesitated just outside the flap and, hearing nothing further, returned to his seat beside the fire. The second time he opened the flap and held it parted with the back of one hand, his unsheathed knife glinting in the other. He remained there for some time, staring in, motionless. I pretended to sleep, the rock clasped tight in my grip beneath the blanket. But then, finally, he let the flap fall and left again.

Shortly after that, I had scratched and torqued the lock sufficiently that it came apart. I took the chain and wrapped it loop by loop tight around my waist so it would not clink, and then I squirmed under the side of the tent and was gone.

Once an eater, always an eater: I went straight to the cave. At the mouth, out of earshot of the camp below, I used my rock to break most of the chain off, until the only thing that bound me were a few links still hanging from the metal collar. And then, alone, I entered.

It was dark inside, much darker than it had been by day. I began to gulp the darkness down. My heart was beating fast and my mouth was dry. Still swallowing, I made my way to the bench cut in the stone against the back wall of the cave. I was dizzy, yet still I swallowed more. And then, head spinning, I lost consciousness.

I dreamt in just the way I used to dream in the cave, back before the others came, back when I had been known and respected as an eater of darkness, back when all came to ask the darkness questions through me and none dared molest me. I dreamt of dogs made of shadow, growling, their forms sometimes spread long on the ground and sometimes squat and froglike and sometimes tilted or crimped across several surfaces. The shadows of dogs with no dogs to cast them. And then I dreamt of that vast and ponderous shape, and this time I heard its breathing too as it came closer and passed by me, but then it hesitated and returned for a closer look.

Ah, it said. *You've come.*

I could not tell where its head ended and its body began, or even, properly speaking, if it had a head at all. And the voice when it came seemed to come from everywhere and nowhere all at once.

"Yes," I said. "Here I am."

What became of you?

When I had explained to it all that had happened, I admitted I still did not know what to do.

It stayed for a long time motionless, peering at me with those eyes, which were pitchy blots within what was already deep darkness.

Do you trust me? it asked.

I hesitated. Despite having come to this cave for years, I did not trust it. But perhaps I mistrusted it less than most.

You must trust me, it said, *or I cannot help you.*

And so, reluctantly, I did.

I came down from the cave. It was nearly day, though I was still steeped in darkness. I could not feel my body or do anything really but watch it move and try to keep up. I watched it walk down the path, footsteps awkward at first, then more and more certain, then perfectly fluid and unnaturally silent. I watched it come to the tent it had left, but instead of crawling back under the canvas it circled around to the other side, to the fire where one man slept and another man kept watch, both with their backs to me.

The night keeper never saw me coming, never knew I was there until he spun rapidly around just in time for me to take his face between my hands and exhale into it. He collapsed without a sound. His comrade in arms, the first keeper, had begun to stir, but I was already on my knees beside him, my face inches from his own, the darkness curling down and seeping into his nose, his mouth, his ears. He cried out, or tried to—his mouth gaped like a fish, but no sound came out. Soon, he was still.

"There," my voice said to his slack face. "Wouldn't it have been wiser to kill me while you had the chance?"

And then I watched myself—though it was not myself exactly—wander from tent to tent, trailing darkness in my wake. A great, silent revolution culminating in the tent containing the four robed men who awaited me each day to hear the judgment of the cave. Now, my body offered them that judgment. They were the only ones to try to resist, the only ones aware of their fate before that fate overwhelmed them. They brandished the instruments of their god as if these could protect them, but a moment later lay collapsed and still, for what can withstand a darkness such as this?

. . .

And then I found myself waking on the stone bench as if none of it had happened, as if it had all been a dream. I awoke gasping, the cave around me brighter than it had ever been, and stumbled my way out.

It was daylight. The metal collar around my neck had come loose at some point, the metal twisted and warped now. I let it fall to the ground. My neck, no longer used to being without it, felt more than naked: flayed.

I half suspected I would find them awaiting me just outside the cave, the four robed and bowing men, but nobody was there. I made my way slowly down from the cave. Before I had even reached the camp below, I could see something had changed. The tents were just as they had always been, but there was no sign of life. Or, rather, simply a series of prone and motionless men, their eyes wide open, their expressions as blank as if they had never been alive.

It took me several weeks to haul them, one by one, to the cave. I would tug one in and leave him there and by morning he'd be gone. I did not know where they went, but I knew I must take them to the cave and leave them, for this came to me in my dreams. The first keeper I saved for last, partly because of his bulk, partly because, in an odd way, I felt closer to him than the others. He was my first keeper, after all. As I dragged him slowly to the cave, I saw that he could move his eyes. No matter where I was, they were always looking at me. And, yet, after a night in the cave, he too disappeared along with the rest.

And why, the others gone, after having entered myself, have I not disappeared? Why, now that I am once again alone, can I enter the darkness of the cave and emerge unscathed and alive? Those who come now, those who seek me out again to know their fate now that the invaders are gone, claim it is because I am an eater of darkness. That either you eat the darkness or the darkness eats you.

But I know better. A meal was made of me long ago. What does it matter if I can dream of a body that resembles what I used to be, and that I can make others dream they see this body too? No, this is not me. I am lost in the darkness, in the whirl of the voices of the dead. Daylight, for me as for them, will never come.

Elo Havel

I.

It is good of you to write, and I thank you for it: I am glad at last to hear from another of my kind—and, above all, to have another of my kind acknowledge me. I have indeed, since my return, heard many voices, seen many faces, but the individuals to whom they belong neither hear nor see me in return. I shake them, shout in their ears, but they do not respond. It is as if for them I do not exist.

But why then, I wonder, would I exist for you? What is different about you? To put it bluntly, what is *wrong* with you? By which I suppose I am also asking: what is wrong with *me*?

You ask me what happened. You ask if I can recount to you what passed in the forest—why, though four of us went in, only one came out. First, I must ask how you found me. True, after leaving the forest I returned to my old residence, and have been here since my return. But considering that everyone around me acts as if I do not exist, how did you know I did? Did you deduce somehow that one of us had returned and simply posted letters to all of us in turn? Was I the first of the four you contacted? The last?

What do I need to tell you of the forest before I begin? Since you are not from our city, I am not certain what you already know.

We have enjoyed a long friendship, for lack of a better word, with the forest. We foraged there but did so with care. There were, true, portions of forest that over the years we destroyed, razing whole hectares of ground to make way for our roads, our houses, our farms. We also inadvertently, carelessly, burned down many hectares more. But these were exceptions rather than the rule: nobody should be judged by the exceptions. Consider them the momentary slights of a thoughtless friend. No, for the most part we honored the forest, preserved it.

And what did the forest offer us in return? It provided berries and mushrooms for food, animal skins for clothing, wood to build our shelters and to warm us. It healed us, nurtured us, kept us alive.

Or at least it did in the past. More recently, no.

But that, no doubt, is why you have written to me.

For many years, we had a practice. We would care for our elderly until they were moribund, and then they were taken into hospice. They would wait there a day, a week, perhaps more, and then a delegation would arrive. *Elo Havel,* they might begin—or with whatever name the individual possessed—*you have been chosen to commune with nature.* Then they would turn to another individual, say his name, and tell him he had been chosen as well. Eventually the delegation would lead or carry one or several individuals into the forest. They would be left in a designated place, a certain grove. From there, waving and smiling, they would watch the delegation depart. They were happy to be left there. Their friend, the forest, they trusted would take care of them.

One day they were in the city and the next they were in the forest, and once left in the forest they were never seen again. Never a trace of them, never a sign.

They always went willingly. The forest was their friend. To go into the forest when death approached was the order of things. We had taken from the forest, and now the forest took us in return.

...

And then one day something changed. One of the moribund did not wave, did not smile, when he was left in the grove. He resisted, and when the delegation left, he screamed and begged them to come back. When they would not, he tried to follow, and despite his frailty managed to leave the grove. The delegation rapidly conferred about this man crawling after them, about what to do with him. There was talk of breaking his legs so he could not follow, but they could not agree to this. There was talk of letting him return to the city—if he did not care to be taken into the embrace of the forest, why insist? But they could not agree to this either.

What they could agree to in the end was to pick the man up bodily, carry him back into the grove, and lash him to the trunk of a tree. When he continued to scream, a delegate removed both of the man's stockings and wadded them into his mouth. And then the delegation turned and left.

What did the other moribund do as this occurred? Just observed, saddened perhaps at the man's failure to understand and accept his role. They did nothing to interfere. They exhibited no desire to leave the grove. When a member of the delegation circled back to see if one of the other moribund had released the recalcitrant man, he found they had not. They had gathered around him; those who could still stand were stroking his face and arms, attempting to calm him, but they did not free him.

Two days later, the delegation returned to the grove with more of the moribund. As usual, there was no trace of the individuals who had not resisted. But with the man who had resisted, it was different. He was gone, but a substantial trace of him did remain: an immense amount of blood spilled upon the remains of the rope and splashed up the bole of the tree. When the new group of the moribund saw this, they collectively expressed a desire not to be left in the forest. They began to scream and shout, and resisted. But since they were weak, they were quickly subdued. One of the delegation was sent running back to the city in search of more rope to lash them. Soon they were tied up and left. That was the end of them.

Perhaps if the delegation had chosen a different grove, perhaps if the moribund had not been confronted with the frayed rope and the blood, things might have reverted to the way they had been before. But instead, the grove grew more and more spattered with blood, and the chosen became more and more panicked. Quickly, as word spread, to be sent to the forest was deemed more punishment than release.

The forest began to change, too, as if instead of sheltering those who had been its friends it now fed upon their fear. The trees of the grove became wracked and twisted, and a blight spread from the grove to the forest at large. Some said this was due to people no longer going willingly into the forest, others that the blight had not started in the grove but was instead due to the houses and the roads we had built: a slurry of chemicals and pollutants had leeched into the ground and sickened the trees. Something, in any case, was wrong with the forest. There were those who felt we should no longer bring people to the woods at the end of their lives. But what else were we to do with these nearly dead? The tradition was strong enough to continue.

And so it kept on for months, then for years, until we came to believe this was the way things were meant to be, that we were meant to meet the end of life in darkness and terror. We stayed shy of the forest except to bring the moribund to the grove. Even the delegation, elected by us, now shivered to enter the forest and hurried quickly away. Many of these, having observed over and over again those they had taken into the forest screaming and afraid, chose to kill themselves when their own time came, preferring self-murder to whatever fate might await them within the grove.

The city folded in on itself, becoming a shadow of its former self, as twisted and broken as the forest. Many moved to other places. But some stayed, waiting, living in broken-down houses in a moribund city beside a moribund forest as they themselves grew moribund, because they had nowhere else to go.

I was among those who stayed. By the time the forest and the city began to change, I was too set in my ways to flee, and I knew I was dying. A decade before, I had served as a member of the delegation. I had seen the fright of the moribund, had even tied certain of them to trees. I knew what awaited me in the forest: fear. And yet I stayed.

Time passed. I lived what was left of my life and attempted to forget what I had seen, what I had done. I was often successful. I loved my children and grandchildren. As I grew increasingly frail, I realized I did not want to lose the time I could have with them, even if it meant ending my life tied to a tree in the grove.

Soon I went from frail to fragile and then fell and broke several of my bones. The doctors set these bones, but when they did not heal properly, it was decided I would be sent to hospice. And so I went. My son and daughter would not look at me when they said good-bye. My grandchildren would, but only because they had no clear idea where I was going or what would happen to me there. I embraced my loved ones and entered limbo.

II.

Each day as I awoke in hospice I wondered: *Will this be the day they call my name?* A day went by, then two, then a week, then a month. My bones still did not heal properly, but they got no worse. Soon, I learned to walk with a crutch. Others were called, even those who had come to hospice after me, but never me. *Perhaps I won't be called,* I began thinking after a time. *Perhaps I will prove myself sufficiently able that I will be allowed to return to my life.*

And then: *Elo Havel,* they called through the hospice's open doorway. *Elo Havel!*

"Yes?" I said, hobbling forward. "That is my name. What do you want?"

You have been chosen to commune with nature, said the delegation, for of course it was they.

Other names were called after mine, but I cannot be expected to remember them. My head was swimming. I experienced difficulty thinking. Before I knew it, I was being carried into the forest, each arm wrapped around the neck of a delegate as they transported me to meet my fate—just as I, in my time as a delegate, had carried others. There were, I realized, once I had gathered myself again, three of the moribund besides me, each apprehensive but none as of yet panicked.

We could smell the blood long before we arrived. It had been bad when I had seen it a decade before, back when I was a delegate, but it had grown much, much worse. As we entered the grove, countless flies arose buzzing from the ground. There were maggots, too, wriggling on the damper portions of the earth that were, I couldn't help but notice, always to be found at the base of a tree. The trees of the grove were dead and dry, mere collections of sticks now, bleached by sun, ghosts of the trees they had once been.

First one of our number began screaming, and then another, then the third. The second tried, to the best of his ability considering the severity of his ailments, to flee. I, who had at least some idea what to expect, was the only one of the four capable (if only just) of maintaining my composure.

The delegates, too, I realized, were nearly as upset. They were eager to tie me and my companions so they could leave, and this made them inadvertently cruel. I did not judge them. I saw my past self in them—I had been slightly less panicked perhaps since the state of the grove had not been nearly so horrific, but I had still been gruff and blunt and eager to be gone.

I took it as best I could, with what equanimity I could muster. I let them tie me to a dead tree, even did my best to aid them. I was struck in the face for my pains. I did my best to receive that blow with equanimity as well.

In the end, they left, and left us alone. I could hear the others shouting and weeping around me. I did my best to block this out. I did not want to meet my death that way. *Here I am,* I thought, *there is nothing I can do about it. I will soon be dead. There is no point in being afraid.*

I waited for whatever would come. I tried, best I could, considering the circumstances, to clear my mind, clear my thoughts, blot out the groans and cries around me. I thought of my life, my son and daughter, my grandchildren, what it was like to see them and be with them. I kept thinking of this, somehow, despite the wails that once again rose up around me. I kept my eyes closed and tried to imagine myself elsewhere, back in the life I had left.

One by one the screams of the others were abruptly cut off. Something was moving among us, something vast, snorting. I kept my eyes clenched shut, still trying best I could to imagine myself elsewhere. The faces of my family continued to hover before my eyes, but as the sounds came closer, these faces grew distorted and monstrous.

And then I sensed the creature before me, its breath hot on my face. I hesitated a moment, then opened my eyes.

What did I see? Surely that is the only reason you have bothered to write me. Surely this is what you want to know. What sort of creature was it?

I am afraid I am in little position to enlighten you, having only the evidence of my eyes to guide me. It seemed to me a creature made of broken branches and loam and hunks of tar, twisted metal, shards of glass. An odd amalgam of dead forest and city refuse, it moved in an extraordinary, rolling fashion, at once so hideous and so marvelous that I found myself unable to cry out or even breathe. The others who had been lashed to the trees around me were already gone, tatters of bloody rope the only indication they had once been in the grove. And indeed, the muzzle of the thing, to the degree to which it could be said to have a muzzle, was slick with blood. I did not quite believe I was seeing what I was seeing. I believed instead that my mind had substituted what it could bear to see for whatever was actually there. I closed my eyes again, and waited for it to kill me.

III.

And yet for some reason it did not kill me. Instead, when I finally opened my eyes again it was to find myself alone, dawn just breaking. I struggled free of the ropes and then stood. Unaccountably, I felt better than I had in months. I could walk again, even without the aid of a crutch. The forest, I have come in time to believe, had chosen not to destroy me but rather to heal me.

For a long time I hesitated over what to do. I could not, I knew, remain within that desolate grove. But should I go back to the city or should I continue deeper into the forest, find perhaps a place still verdant and alive? Was I part of the forest now? I honestly was unsure. But in the end, the draw of city and family was too strong. And so I returned.

Almost immediately I came to understand I had made the wrong choice.

I have told you already what I found when I returned to the city. Everything was as I had left it, but it no longer acknowledged me. It was as if I no longer existed. I was no ghost—I could physically grasp those around me, but they did not seem aware of my touch: they would stop their motion or conversation until I released them, but that was all. Even my grandchildren stared through me. Something had happened to me when I was in the forest. I had, in some measure, been transformed.

Yet it gave me some pleasure to watch them, even if I could not be seen. Thus, I found myself back in the house I had once occupied, before my forced removal to hospice: an observer of the lives that had once been close to mine, alive for myself but not for anyone around me, a ghost of sorts, but a curious one.

It is here that your letter has found me. It gives me hope, your letter, that I still exist for someone, that one of the delegates found one undamaged set of ropes and believes someone survived. Even hope that there are others like me, that Elo Havel is not alone.

That is all I can offer you concerning the forest and concerning myself. What can you tell me in return? Who are you, and what? Has your experience some connection to my own? Can we perhaps meet face-to-face? If we do, will you be aware of me? Can you help me?

I eagerly await your reply. But I shall not wait forever. I shall not even wait long. I understand better with each passing day that this is no longer the place for me, that I do not belong. The forest beckons. I belong to it now. Do not hesitate too long to reply or you shall find me gone.

His Haunting

1.

Three times in his life someone or something unknown had opened Arn's door as he tried to sleep, silently sliding it ajar and then standing immobile in the gap. That was all, just standing there, unmoving, just barely visible in the darkness. It wasn't even all that threatening, he told his therapist, not really. What had disturbed him most about it was not knowing who or what it was. In the darkness, he could make nothing out beyond the door's frame and the silhouette of the figure enclosed within. A large figure, male almost certainly, hulking, head nearly scraping the lintel.

"Who is it?" he had asked that first time, sitting up in bed. How long the figure was there, he wasn't sure—it felt at once like a very long time and no time at all. The figure didn't answer—nothing about it made Arn believe it had heard him. But as soon as he threw his blanket off, the door began to creak shut, the latch sinking into the slot just as he reached it. By the time he fumbled the door open and peered out, the hall outside was deserted.

. . .

That first time, he hurried through the small house, searching for it. He turned on the lights and looked into the other rooms, peered into closets and cabinets. No one was there. He felt he should be frightened—and part of him was, but another part was surprisingly calm and unafraid, as if already dead.

Hoping not to have to wake her, he saved his aunt's bedroom for last. But finally, having looked without success everywhere else, he knocked softly on her door. When she didn't answer, he opened it.

It was very dark inside. He could not see her, could only hear thickened breathing.

"Aunt," he whispered.

There was no answer.

"Aunt, is it just you in there?" he whispered.

The breathing sputtered, ceased. He heard something move in the bed. He thought he could vaguely make out motion in the darkness, though perhaps this was his imagination.

And for an instant he felt torn in two, as if he were both the person just waking up in bed watching and the figure framed in the doorway— for hadn't he just been the one and now was the other? Only when his aunt shrieked did he begin to feel like just one person again.

He needed help to sort through them, these three brief moments that were dark little holes drilled across the length of his life. He would come once a week to this office with its aggressively modern furniture and sit in a chair across from the therapist he had quickly come to think of as *his* therapist and spend forty minutes circling around what his husband liked to call jokingly "your haunting." Arn had trained himself to smile whenever his husband said that, as if it was funny. But it wasn't funny, not really.

And please, he warned his therapist, *don't think this is about my resentment of my husband. I have no more resentment than most spouses. I love my husband. I understand he's trying to make me feel better. But it is* my *haunting—that's what he doesn't understand.*

. . .

"I saw something," is what he'd explained, once he'd gotten his aunt calmed down and they were sitting together in the kitchen, lights blazing.

"I saw something too," said his aunt. "It was standing in my doorway looking in at me as I tried to sleep. Turned out to be you, Jack. What the hell were you thinking?"

"I'm not Jack," he responded. Jack had been his father's name. It wasn't even close to his own name. He hardly even looked like his father.

Don't write that down, he said to his therapist, and then, *What are you writing down?*

Does my writing make you nervous? asked his therapist.

But no, this was not what he was asking for—he was not asking for the experience to be *analyzed,* not yet. This was precisely why he hadn't managed to talk about the haunting, *his* haunting, before now—even though he increasingly recognized that it was what had driven him to therapy in the first place. No, he just wanted his therapist to put the notebook down and listen to what had happened, to take the words in before deciding what they meant.

There at the kitchen table, his aunt held her head in her hands. "I'm so sorry," she said. And then, "Don't worry, I know who you are." It was not until she said this that Arn considered the possibility that at least for a moment she might not have. That it wasn't that she'd misspoke, but that she'd glimpsed someone or something else in his face.

And then she recovered. "What were you thinking, Arn?" she asked. "You scared the shit out of me."

"I'm sorry," he said. "I was looking for it."

"For what?" she asked.

Once he explained, her hands started to shake. Even knowing he'd already searched the house, she insisted they each arm themselves with a knife and search again. They found nothing, nothing and nobody was there. They went outside with flashlights and shined them along the ground near the flower beds, but there was nothing there either, no footprints, no signs of disturbance. They played their flashbeams up at the roof and saw nothing but roof. They opened the storm cellar and descended, but there was nothing down below, just the faint, sour smell of rot.

And yet, from that day forward his aunt treated him differently, with caution, as if she wasn't sure she recognized him.

Time passed, said Arn.

And so you forgot about it, said his therapist.

No, said Arn, *I never forgot. Every time I fell asleep I expected to open my eyes and see that door open again, and in its dark opening a darker silhouette standing.*

But it didn't happen again. Not in that house, anyway. Not around his aunt. That was the odd thing, he told his therapist: he'd always thought of hauntings as being bound to a place—a house, a pool in which somebody drowned, the site of a fatal car wreck, that sort of nonsense. He'd wasted a lot of time trying to figure out what it was about his aunt's house that had led to him seeing the silhouette at the threshold of his room. Indian burial ground? Decades-old murder? Previous residence of someone who died alone and neglected? But there was nothing.

So, said his therapist once he fell silent, *you were already thinking of it as a ghost.*

Oh yes, Arn said, *as a haunting. But not yet as* my *haunting.*

"You must have dreamed it," his aunt said as he kept talking, kept quizzing her about the house. "It's just an ordinary house, built just a year or two before you were born. Before that, this was an orange grove."

"But there must—" he started.

"Sometimes dreams can be so vivid they seem real," his aunt said firmly. "You dreamed it."

...

Your aunt raised you, ventured his therapist. *But I'm afraid I'm confused about what happened to your parents.*

So am I, said Arn.

His therapist tented his fingers, gazing at Arn over them, eyes steady. He waited.

I never knew my mother, Arn finally said. *She died when I was born. My father . . . vanished.*

Vanished?

Arn nodded. *One day my father woke up, and he no longer looked like himself.*

What did he look like if not himself?

I don't know. I remember sitting at the breakfast table with him, looking for something in his face, unsure what. All I knew was it wasn't there. And then I realized he was looking at me too, staring. He was trying to pretend he was reading his paper, but he was staring over it at me. Whatever he was looking for he was finding, and it frightened him.

I left for school, Arn continued. *When I came back that afternoon, he was gone. I never saw him again.*

What do you think happened to him?

I don't want to talk about it, said Arn. *Not today.*

This is a safe place, his therapist began, but Arn rapidly cut him off.

You believe my haunting will tell you something about my relationship with my missing father, he said, *that that's the point of me telling it to you. Maybe so. You can tell me that next time if you'd like. But for now, let my haunting be my haunting.*

But Arn seemed to have lost the thread. For a moment the two of them just sat there, faces blank, expressionless. Then his therapist cleared his throat and spoke.

She thought you were dreaming, he said. *Your aunt, I mean.*

Yes, so she said.

Have you considered she may have been right?

Yes.

And?

Not remotely possible.

How can you be sure?

I'm sure.

But how?

Arn, humming softly under his breath, ignored him.

And the second time? asked his therapist.

Excuse me? said Arn.

There were three times, you said. What about the second?

Ah, said Arn. *Yes.*

2.

Time marched on. Arn grew up. He was admitted to the local college. He moved out of his aunt's house and into a dormitory.

More time passed. He was studying something, working toward a degree. It did not matter what he was studying, he told his therapist; it had no bearing on his haunting. He was a junior in college and suddenly was living alone, his roommate having received academic probation followed by a semester of suspension.

He was lying on his bed trying to sleep. It was perhaps two in the morning. There were still noises coming from the hall despite the time being late enough that quiet was supposedly in effect. His door was closed, the light from the hallway shining through the crack beneath it. Occasionally the light would flicker as someone walked down the hall and past his door.

At some point, he drifted off. Maybe he was asleep for a few minutes, maybe for several hours.

He awoke to the impression something was wrong. He remained in bed, blinking, trying to see. Why couldn't he see? Usually he could, even at night, even if only a little. But now he couldn't. Suddenly he realized why: the light in the hallway was no longer on.

But the light in the hallway was *always* on. There wasn't even a switch to turn it off. All night it seeped beneath the door enough for him to dimly make things out, as if in sleep he remained lodged in a colorless facsimile of the actual world.

There was a light of sorts, but exceptionally low and at a great remove, like a single flickering candle cupped by a hand at the far end of the hall. He could see nothing at all of the room around him. The only thing he could see, barely, was the outline of the doorframe.

Even seeing this, it took his mind some time to register the fact that the door must be open. But once it did, he began to see the silhouette crowded into the doorframe, hunched, almost too large to fit, waiting, immobile, watching him.

How do you know it was watching? interrupted his therapist.

I thought I could see its eyes, he said. *Or not eyes exactly, but a gleam or glister where I knew eyes should be. Which led me to believe its eyes were open and looking steadily at me.*

"Hello?" Arn had said. "Who are you?" Because he did want to know. He was frightened, of course, but above all else, he wanted to know who or what it was.

The figure did not respond. It seemed again, just like that first time years before, not to have heard him.

Carefully, slowly, Arn started out of the bed and crept toward the door. But the door was already closing, and even though he rushed it at the end, he was not quick enough to stop it from slamming shut. Or, rather, he managed to get two of his fingers around the edge of the door before it closed in its frame, but the door closed anyway.

He lifted his hand, showed his therapist the awkwardly crimped ends of his middle and index finger where the last joint of both digits had been sewed back on. He had felt the severing, the brief, sharp pain of each joint being sheared off, followed by the warm throb, enough of a distraction that he almost missed that something had changed: he could see.

The light in the hallway was on again. He tore open the door and looked out onto an ordinary hall: no silhouette in sight, the hall just as it had always been, except for the blood drizzling from his fingers onto the grimy carpet.

The fingers had been reattached, though he could feel nothing in the top joint of either of them—it was as if they were dead. He had thought long and hard about this second time, unsure what to make of it. The only point in common between his aunt's house and his dorm room, at least that he could see, was himself. The ghost, if it was a ghost, must be tied to him.

But why him? For this, he had no answer. Nor did he have an answer for why it would visit him so infrequently, or why both times it was always reduced to that single gesture of standing in a doorway, his doorway, the doorway to his bedroom, in the dark.

3.

Another decade passed, he told his therapist. He graduated, got a job, became a responsible citizen. He met the man who would become his husband, they fell in love, lived together, married once the law allowed it. They bought an apartment together, and he allowed a certain form of existence to crystallize or calcify around him. And yet, all the while he was waiting, wondering when—not if but when—despite his move far away, his haunting would find him again. For it would find him, he was sure of that.

He had a few false alarms. Times when he awoke to find his husband, who tended to come to bed much later than he, standing in the open door, motionless, waiting for his eyes to adjust to the darkness before navigating to the bed. But his husband's silhouette looked nothing like the silhouette of his haunting. Arn was the larger of the two of them by far. His husband, small, could not come close to filling a doorway.

The third incident he thought at first was just that—his husband hesitating in the doorway before coming to bed. He felt a presence and half opened his eyes and groaned, and said, "How late is it? Come to bed already."

When there was no answer, not a sound, he found himself startled fully awake.

The room around him seemed too dark. He turned and could just make out the open doorway.

"What's wrong?" he started to say, but got very little of it out, for he realized the shape in the doorway was so large it could not possibly be his husband. And, in any case, his husband was there already in the bed beside him, breathing heavily, sound asleep.

And then, he told his therapist, *something happened that I didn't expect. You see, I had made the mistake of inviting it, whatever it was, to come to bed.*

The figure was still motionless, still little more than a silhouette, but it was no longer in the doorway. No, it was just inside the room now, as if a bit of film had skipped, or as if he had closed his eyes and it had moved only while it could not be seen. And then it was closer still, and closer still, until it was there, just beside the bed but still motionless, still little more than a silhouette. Arn could see again those dull gleams he thought of as its eyes—but could see now that they were scattered all over its body, as if its entire skin was studded with them, with eyes that couldn't quite be made out. He couldn't move. It came very close until it was touching him, but he couldn't feel anything. And then it came closer still, and he felt very cold. And then it passed slowly through him and across the bed.

Somebody's breath was hissing fast through clenched teeth, and though he rationally understood it must be his teeth, his breath, they still seemed to belong to somebody else. Someone was screaming and it was him screaming, only it wasn't him either. And then his husband was shaking him, and the light was on and shining into his eyes, and the figure in the doorway was again nowhere to be seen.

...

Where do you think it went? his therapist asked, after waiting a long time for Arn to continue.

My husband, he said.

Your husband?

He was the only other one in the bed. It was moving toward him. It moved through me and toward him.

Don't you think that—

Now, sometimes in its least guarded moments, I see something flit across his face, coming to the surface to breathe.

It seems to me—

It's his haunting now. He doesn't know yet, of course. How could he? He won't know until it is his turn to see it in the doorway.

But then where was it before?

Arn looked hard at his therapist. *Can't you guess?* he asked. *Why do you think my father left? What do you think he was looking for in my face? The same thing I was no longer finding in his. It must have been in him before. After it left him, where else could it have been but in me?*

He cracked his neck, then slowly took hold of the arms of the chair and pulled himself to his feet. He looked older, tired somehow, almost a different person.

Next time, he said, *you can ask me the usual questions. Next time we can analyze all this to death.*

We still have a few minutes, his therapist said. *I really think we should talk about this.*

But Arn just shook his head. *Next time,* he repeated, and he made his way to the door. Upon opening it he hesitated a moment, his body nearly filling the frame. Then he turned his shoulders slightly and sidled through.

4.

It was a moment the therapist would think about often, particularly after it became clear he would never see Arn again. After Arn missed the next few appointments and he took steps to try to find him, he would discover, talking to his distraught spouse, that Arn, like his father before him, had simply disappeared.

Which meant the therapist's last real memory of Arn was of the man standing motionless in the open doorway, facing away from him. But the back of his head still, somehow, gave (when the therapist thought about it later, alone, at night in bed, in the dark, struggling to sleep) the impression of looking back in, of noticing him.

Haver

By December, six months into his institutionalization, Festus had begun exclusively to draw his own apartment. Or rather, just one room of his apartment, his studio, nothing but that, over and over again. He had given up painting entirely, was only drawing now. When Haver asked him why, he only shrugged and said, "I must not give in too easily to color."

"Why not?" asked Haver.

For a long time Festus did not respond, which was not unusual for him. Indeed, Haver had come to think of the times when Festus did respond as the exceptions rather than the rule. Festus kept drawing, kept sketching with a nub of charcoal held delicately between thumb and forefinger, as if Haver wasn't there. Which was why Haver was surprised when a minute or two later he actually did speak.

"Black and white give way to me. But color, no. Color does not give in easily."

"But how—" began Haver, but Festus just pressed one charcoal-blackened finger to his lips and shushed him.

...

Haver kept coming back; he wasn't sure why. He spent far more time with Festus than any of his other patients. There was something about the man's drawings that spoke to him—or not spoke exactly: threatened to speak. If he kept coming back, it was in part to try to hear whatever they were saying. Or whatever Festus was saying, he corrected himself—because how could a drawing say anything on its own?

They were always the same, rapidly sketched on cheap butcher paper, and just as rapidly added to the growing stack beside the bed. Haver had instructed the orderlies to leave the stack where it was—the one time they tried to remove it, Festus grew very upset. This despite the fact that once Festus finished a drawing, he, as far as Haver could ascertain, never glanced at it again. But he still wanted them there beside him, in the room.

Haver was allowed to look through them. Often Haver began his visit by thumbing through the drawings, careful not to smear the charcoal or change the ordering. Festus's talent was such that even though he worked at speed, the drawings struck Haver as remarkably vivid and clear. He felt almost as if he knew Festus's studio, almost as if he could imagine himself in it, almost as if he had been there himself. The drawings were all, as far as he could tell, identical, all rendered from precisely the same perspective, with the objects always in the same place. The studio was empty of human or animal presence, the perspective exacting and unvarying. Which meant, Haver came to understand, that there was one full wall, and small parts of two others, that could not be glimpsed, portions of the room that could not be seen.

What could be seen was simple enough: A drafting table set at a slight incline. A stool with what looked like a chrome base—though since it was drawn in charcoal, it was hard to be certain. Metal anyway—the slenderness of the legs and their smoothness precluded it being anything else. A large window, just above the drafting table, that looked out on what Haver guessed was a ventilation shaft. A wastepaper basket, half-full. Walls made of plaster, just enough irregularity and cracking to make Haver believe it must be horsehair plaster instead of mason board or drywall. A portion of floor: what appeared to be soft pine underflooring left exposed and now scarred and irregular. And, in the corner to the left, where the walls met, a stack of paper Haver could only assume was similar to the stack in Festus's room, no doubt depicting a series of images, no doubt repetitions of the same thing, the same place, maybe even this very studio.

What could he not see? That was just it: how could he know since he couldn't see it? He assumed the perspective was that of an individual standing just inside the doorway, but why should he assume this? Perhaps it was from four or five steps into the studio, or perhaps the studio was an old railroad apartment and was quite long.

So, he simultaneously felt as though he knew the room quite well and didn't know it at all. Which, Haver found, was a very strange thing—unless it was two things—to feel.

He kept looking at Festus's drawings, idly picking up the last few each time he came into the room. The stack was nearly as tall as he was now, and always in danger of collapse. He would come in, look at the drawings, chat idly with, or rather at, Festus, and then leave, continuing on his rounds.

Which was precisely what he was doing one day, half-distractedly saying God knows what, when suddenly, almost as if it belonged to someone else, he heard his voice trail off. The picture he was examining, he suddenly realized, was different from the others.

He couldn't place the difference at first. Indeed, it looked at first glance like all the others. But he could sense a difference, could feel it.

"What's this?" he asked Festus. "What's changed?"

Festus, as usual, didn't answer. It took Haver a few moments of staring to grasp what it was: within the frame of the darkened window, there was, half-hidden, the vague suggestion of another shape. Round or ovular, its edges eaten away by the darkness around it.

But the shape was a little more deliberate, a little darker, than the rest of the shaded frame.

"What's this?" he asked, thrusting the drawing at Festus and pointing to the shape.

Festus glanced at it briefly. "He's new," he said.

"I know it's new," Haver said. "What is it? What is it doing there?"

"He seems to be looking in," said Festus.

A head then, a human figure, the first one he knew of that Festus had drawn. Haver looked at the oval more closely. It was barely there. It was impossible to say anything of substance about it.

He scrutinized the drawing Festus had done just before it. The shape wasn't there. He waited impatiently for Festus to finish his current drawing and once he did almost snatched it away. He pored over it. Everything that had been in the drawings all along was still present, but the window was uniformly shaded again, no suggestion of a head.

"I was waiting for you to draw it again," Haver said. "Why didn't you?"

"What?" asked Festus, confused.

"It's not there," said Haver. "The head's not there."

"No," said Festus.

"Why?"

"Because he's gone."

"No longer in the drawing, you mean."

"That too."

Over the next few weeks Haver found no variations in Festus's drawings, or only variations so slight they were all but unnoticeable. No more heads, nothing out of the ordinary. Which, perhaps, was what made Haver continue to press his patient about the head. *Why in that drawing and not in the next?* he asked. *Because it was there,* Festus responded, implacably, when he bothered to respond at all. But bit by bit, Haver squeezed enough out of him to be certain, or almost so, that Festus genuinely believed he was drawing the studio as it was, actually, at that very moment. He had drawn a head because, at that moment, a head had been peering into the studio.

"Which is strange," said Festus, "since the studio is at the top of the building."

"But how can you see the studio from here?" Haver asked.

Festus, seemingly confused by this question, did not respond.

It was not a good sign, Haver felt. Perhaps he had been wrong to encourage Festus artistically. The man certainly hadn't gotten any better since having been institutionalized, and perhaps had even gotten worse.

He spoke to the supervising clinician.

"I wonder if we shouldn't change Festus's medication," he said.

"Festus?" said the woman, and frowned. She got out his file and skimmed through it while Haver awkwardly waited, standing beside her window, unsure what to do with himself.

"According to this, it seems as though he's doing fine," she said.

"It's subtle," Haver claimed.

She looked at him for a moment, then shrugged. "Fine," she said. "I'll defer to you."

The new medication had a different shape from the old medication, a different color, too. He worried Festus would notice and refuse to take it. But Festus swallowed them as usual.

He continued to draw, the same picture of the studio. Even a few days into the new medication, nothing had changed.

And then something did change. Perhaps two weeks had passed when, suddenly, plucking up the latest drawings, Haver noticed something: a strand of red, subdued, nearly buried in the black of the charcoal, a slender ribbon threaded insidiously through the drawing, increasingly visible the more he looked for it.

"What's this?" he asked. And then, when Festus didn't answer, "I thought you weren't to give in to color."

"Not easily," said Festus. "Give in, but not easily."

Only then did Haver notice the dressings wrapped around Festus's hand. He reached out and took hold of the man's wrist. Suddenly Festus fell inert, as if powered off. The charcoal slipped out of the other hand, the undamaged one. Haver unwrapped the dressings and saw the deep gash in the palm beneath them, still suppurating.

"That's no way to get color," said Haver. "Do you need color?"

"Red," said Festus. "I have red."

"But wouldn't you like an easier way? Chalk maybe? Pastels? Not only red, but blue, green?"

Festus thought for a moment. "Yes," he finally said.

"I can buy some," said Haver.

"No need," said Festus.

"No need?"

"I have some."

"You do?"

"In my studio," said Festus. "They are waiting for you in my studio."

Which was why, a few days later, Haver found himself, during his day off, knocking on Festus's landlord's door. The door opened and revealed the landlord, toadlike and inscrutable. Once Haver explained what he wanted, the landlord, without saying a word, turned and padded deeper into the gloom of his apartment, returning a moment later with a key.

"Apartment's on the third floor," said the landlord. "Studio's the floor above it."

Haver trudged up, step by step, until he finally gained the top floor. It was musty there, the air close. There was a single door, exactly his height. He inserted the key, jiggled it until tumblers turned and the door opened.

Inside, the room was just as Festus had depicted it. Exactly. Not an object out of place. If he stood right there in the doorway and held one of the drawings in front of his eyes, and then lowered it, Haver would see the exact same thing.

Where were they? There, on the drafting table, a box of pastels, lid off—just like in the drawings. Where was the lid? It had fallen there, on the floor, just behind one of the legs of the table, which explained why it was not depicted in the drawings. Lid on now, box tucked into his coat pocket, time to go back out the door, lock it, and leave.

Only he didn't leave, not yet. Instead, he approached the stack of papers. Yes, he saw, there were drawings on all of them, and these drawings were all identical. But they were not drawings of the studio. Instead, they depicted a simple room containing an empty bed. An ordinary room, he thought, standard design, plain, could be anywhere, part of any hospital, any institution. But it was, he suspected, not any room but one particular room: the room in the hospital that Festus now occupied. As he flipped further back through the drawings he became sure, for now the bed wasn't empty but occupied: a figure within it that he recognized as the patient who had occupied the room before Festus.

He was at the door without quite understanding how he had gotten there. The stack of papers had collapsed, was more of a heap now, drawings spilling everywhere. He hesitated, his sense of order encouraging him to go back and pick them up, to rearrange the room to be just as he had found it. But he couldn't bring himself to reenter the room.

And then, as he watched, the stool before the table slid slowly to one side. Or not slid exactly, since it was both where it had been before and where it was now, and every place in between. Where there had been a chair there was now a smear. He was looking at something that was no longer an object, but what it was exactly he would have been hard-pressed to say. He couldn't move. He found he couldn't move. Then the drafting table slid too, and the whole room took on that smeared and insubstantial quality, and Haver, afraid he was beginning to take it on as well, suddenly found he could move again and fled.

By the time he returned to the institution the next day, he had gathered himself. What he had experienced, he told himself, was a momentary lapse, a hallucination, brought on by fatigue. He was working too hard. It all could be explained away.

He gave Festus the pastels, just as he had promised. Festus did not thank him, his work on a drawing continuing at the same pace.

Will he draw the same room? Haver wondered. *Will color change anything?*

Waiting for Festus to finish the current drawing, Haver leafed through the latest ones Festus had added to the stack. *Same, same, same,* he thought, and then, suddenly stunned, didn't think anything at all, just looked.

It was a drawing that was, in a sense, like all the others, though in another sense not like any of them. It was the studio, still the studio, true, but this time a human figure was in it. He could tell, even though the figure was facing away, that it was meant to be him, Haver, standing just where he had stood.

But Festus knew he was there in the studio, he reassured himself, there were only a few places in the room he'd be likely to stand, so it didn't mean anything. It couldn't.

Except that the stack of drawings in the corner, usually so tidy, had collapsed into a heap, just as it had in the room itself after Haver had looked at the drawings. But still, Haver told himself, it meant nothing. It could have been a guess on Festus's part, just a guess.

He took a deep breath and turned to the next drawing. When he saw it, he thought, *Dear God, help me.*

This too was a drawing that was, in a sense, like all the others, though also not. It was still the studio, but here everything was smeared, the drafting table a smear, the stool a smear. It was just as he, Haver, had seen it from the doorway. He was not depicted in it, since he was standing in the doorway. It was as if Festus had seen the scene through his eyes.

He had the orderlies take the stack of drawings away. Festus protested, screamed, shouted, but Haver ignored him. He had the charcoal taken away too, as well as the barely used pastels.

"Letting you draw wasn't helping you," he told Festus once he was straitjacketed. "It was only making things worse." Though inside he knew that what mattered to him was not Festus's health but his own. He needed to believe the world was a stable, solid place, not a place that could be manipulated by a gnarled, blackened hand grasping a nub of charcoal.

For a time all went well. Festus, sedated, stopped protesting. He shuffled around the ward slowly, as if in his own world. Haver deliberately spent less time with the man, saw him hardly more than his other patients. *Everything is okay,* Haver told himself, *everything is back to normal.* Though what constituted normal he would have been hard-pressed to say. He did his rounds, updated the patient records, went home, slept. He awoke, showered, breakfasted, drove to the hospital, did his rounds, updated records, and so on. He knew who he was: Haver. The world held no surprises for him. That was how he liked it.

"Doctor Haver," said an orderly from the hall behind him. "Doctor Haver, please wait."

His shift was done. He was heading toward the outer door, ready to go home, but he waited. The orderly hustled up to him, still panting, then took his arm and began to drag him back the other way.

"What is it?" asked Haver.

"Festus," said the orderly.

"What's happened? Has he hurt himself?"

The orderly shook his head. "Better if you just see," he said.

...

From the doorway, he saw Festus, straitjacketed, immobile on his bed. But other than that and a general disorder in the room, no doubt caused when the orderlies restrained him, there was nothing out of the ordinary.

"What is it?" asked Haver of the orderly. "What am I supposed to see?"

"Go in," said the orderly.

And so he did. He took two steps in, but even then, didn't see anything. It was only when he took another step and turned slightly that he caught it out of the corner of his eye, and then he turned and stared back at the wall behind him. Even knowing there would be something, that something had rattled the orderly, he was not prepared for what he saw.

Festus had used the entire wall to one side of the door. He had drawn there, life-size or a little larger, a picture of his studio, the condition just as Haver had left it. What was it drawn in? Charcoal, it seemed.

"Where did he get charcoal?" asked Haver, not looking away from the drawing.

"He burned something," said the orderly. "He made his own."

"What did he burn?"

"We don't know."

"Where did he get matches?"

The orderly shrugged. "We don't know that either," he said.

The drawing was not finished, Haver realized. And there was one variation to the charcoal depiction of the studio: from a light fixture was suspended a rope. The space directly below it was untouched, the only part of the wall not drawn on. If he looked at it closely, he could see that the untouched space was the size and shape of a human being, though if a human being was actually there, he would be suspended in midair, his feet not touching the ground.

Haver stared. "Why haven't you finished it?" he heard his voice asking. He had to ask a second time before Festus responded.

"I can't," he said.

"Why not?"

"Because you haven't gone back yet."

Haver stared. When Festus put it that way, he could see that the drawing seemed to be inviting him in. The unfinished space was just his size. He couldn't take his eyes away from it.

He would, whether he wanted to or not, he somehow knew, go back. It was just a matter of time, he feared. Just a matter of time. And then Festus's drawing would be complete.

The Extrication

In the early days of this world, lifeforms were not as distinct as they are today. There were no separate species but only a single fecund mire of creatures indiscriminately breeding, changing and striating with each new generation. With every blind coupling, new forms of creature came into existence.

Mere speculation, you might say, were you free to speak. Yes, speculation. Perhaps the truth, perhaps not. And yet the idea struck me as offering a compelling map for the future.

Which is why you are here.

How are you? Are you comfortable? Can I get you anything? A cup of water perhaps? A crust of bread?

No, I shouldn't needle you. We both know your needs are being provided for, being dripped slowly into your body by way of a central venous catheter. To allow you to feed yourself I would have to undo the straps that keep you immobilized. I am not sure that is such a good idea. Not until I have convinced you of the necessity of what we are trying to accomplish.

But don't worry. I am a patient man. I will not give up on you. I will convince you.

As the world sickens further, as the air grows poisonous, as the oceans die, so too must we shift and change if we care to survive. We must extricate ourselves from humanity and become something other than ourselves. Something that can adapt to the harshness of this new world. We must loosen the strands that differentiate us from other creatures, unravel our coding—loosen it just enough that our bodies are free to become more than what they are.

By *us,* I mean of course you.

You see these suspended bags? If you tip your head back and crane your neck and look behind you, there they are. These ones to the left, the ones bloated with clear fluid, need not concern us; they are simply meant to keep you nourished and hydrated, to keep you alive. They contain, as well, a painkiller. Nothing too addictive. Or, rather, yes, quite addictive, but the treatment plan I have developed for you allows me to taper you off slowly. Withdrawal will not be pleasant, but you will survive it. I have learned from past mistakes.

It is this other bag that matters, the one to the right, the one filled with an absinthe-colored fluid. This will enter your body much more slowly. In the time it takes for the entire bag to enter your system, we will go through a dozen bags of clear fluid. But this, my friend, is the bag that matters.

I claimed these bags of clear fluid need not concern us, but of course they do. Think of them as a sort of clock. By the time the first bag is empty, you will sense something beginning to happen to you. By the time you reach the fourth, your skin will feel as if it is on fire, despite the painkillers. By the sixth, you will begin to transform.

How you will change exactly, I cannot predict. It is different for everyone and depends on what sort of choices your body makes.

Some—most, if I am being honest—dissolve into a kind of muck. They writhe and fold inward and expire sometime in the course of the seventh bag. I hose what remains of them off the table. A few, a very select few, have made it all the way to the final bag, the twelfth. By that time, they have become something else. Something at least theoretically more suited to live in this new world. They are more resistant to cold or heat, their skin becomes scaled or slimy or photo-sensitive, they lose or gain a limb or two or three.

I have chosen you very carefully. I have faith that you will be one of those select few.

Perhaps if I were to remove your gag you would have questions for me. Perhaps, instead, you would just shriek and scream. Those who came before you have done sometimes one, sometimes the other. There have even been those who, gag removed, remained stubbornly silent. I am, I admit, tempted to remove your gag, if only to see if my guess about what you in particular would do is correct.

But the screams in the past have been too shrill to be anything but a distraction, and the questions asked are always the wrong ones. The silence I find even worse. Whatever you choose to do, it will only make me think less of you.

No, it is a waste of time. Better never to loosen the gag.

Have I been clear enough? The world is dying, is in fact already well on its way to being dead. Were it not, you would never have wandered in here. You never would have had occasion to think, *What is this? An unoccupied bunker in which I can shelter myself? What luck!* and then have fallen into my trap. You would, instead, have a job in a small town as an accountant, say, or a data entry specialist. But there are no real towns anymore, small or otherwise. And that I am alive here, in this bunker, is due only to my foresight. I could see the collapse coming, and I said to myself I needed to prepare. The world was changing. We had ruined it. Things had gone too far to change them back. And so, I told myself, it is *we* who must change to meet the world.

Or you, rather. By *we*, I meant and still mean you.

Don't worry, friend. We're in this together. I want humanity to survive. I have done my best to calibrate the formula exactly right this time. I will stay beside you. I will observe the change.

True enough, I couldn't save the others, but that is no reason to think I won't be able to save you. The one just before you made it through all twelve bags and still lived, gasping, for thirty-eight minutes after that. His skin had begun to extrude a slick, mucosal layer, and I suspect he no longer belonged in air but in water. I learned so much from him, and I will use all I learned to save you.

Even if I do not succeed, perhaps we will learn enough so that the individual who comes after you will survive. Or perhaps the individual after him. And, once the procedure has been perfected, it will be ready for me.

When will we begin? your eyes seem to be asking.

But can't you see we have already begun? Look at how much less clear fluid there is in the first bag than in the bags that will succeed it. Yes, we have already begun.

I will do what I can for you. I am rooting for you. Whether you survive the change or perish, I will be here with you, I swear, until the bitter end.

A Bad Patch

In January, I began to have difficulties with my stomach and intes-
tines. I could hardly keep any food down, but despite this my belly
began to bloat and swell. It was sore, tender to the touch, and soon
I could no longer wear any of my pants; the pressure of the waist-
line against my belly caused cramps and acute pain and made it
impossible for me to walk. Instead, I began to wear the housedresses my wife left behind when she died. These were billowing
and voluminous and put no pressure on my belly at all.

The first week, unsure of what was happening, I called in sick
to work. In retrospect, I should have gone to see a doctor, but I
kept thinking it would pass. As the second week began, I found
my thoughts sufficiently muddled and confused that I somehow
no longer even thought of a doctor as a possibility. I was not, in a
manner of speaking, myself. I didn't leave the house, did very little
beyond sit on the couch, staring down, watching my stomach ripple
gently beneath my wife's housedress.

I still had enough presence of mind to call in each morning
and report myself ill to the Corporation. But as the third week
began, I was told by the Corporation's health auditor that I needed

a certification from a medical professional if this was to continue. If I did not submit one in four days, he regretted to inform me, I would be terminated.

And so, the morning of the fourth day, I put on my favorite of my wife's housedresses—which, by now, I had begun to think of as *my* housedresses—and put a trench coat over it. I found a pair of my wife's leggings and snipped the legs off midthigh with a pair of shears. These snipped-off leggings I slid over my own legs, affixing the top of them to the inside of the dress with safety pins to keep them in place. I pinned up the hem of the dress too so it wouldn't show below the trench coat. When I regarded myself in the mirror, forcibly holding the trench coat closed with my hands since my belly was too distended for me to belt it, I approved of what I saw. From a distance, it looked like I was wearing pants, like there was nothing wrong with me beyond the fact that I was wearing a trench coat in summer. With my protruding belly I looked a little strange, perhaps, but I did not judge myself to be alarming.

My wife's brother was a pathologist. He was, technically speaking, a medical professional, though he was currently employed as a coroner by the police. Since the Corporation had not specified that I must see a particular kind of medical professional, I decided he would do.

My belly roiled as I walked. Several times my stomach clenched hard, and I had to hold to a light pole or lean against a building wall or a parked car until the pain passed, sweat beading on my forehead. Something, I realized briefly, was very wrong with me, but almost as soon as I thought this, the thought swirled away and was gone. As long as I had stayed at home, in my wife's housedresses, moving little, I could pretend I was experiencing a transient illness, that it would soon pass, but now, out and walking, there was no denying how ill I was. I was almost tempted to see an actual doctor, but since I had nearly reached the police station, I simply continued as planned.

My brother-in-law was not at his desk. "Has he perhaps taken a very late lunch?" I wondered aloud. One of his colleagues was looking at me with a certain amount of what I interpreted to be anxiety. I asked him if he knew where my brother-in-law was.

"Morgue," he said, and turned away, a look of disgust creasing his face.

And so I thanked him and made my way to the morgue.

He had a body laid out on the table. It looked fresh, but perhaps it was not all that fresh and had merely been kept cold in a refrigerated drawer. It was very pale, no doubt exsanguinated. He had cut open the breastbone and spread the ribs. He appeared to be removing and examining the organs one by one, occasionally speaking into a portable tape recorder. He was wearing a mask and gloves, a smock. After a few moments he noticed me out of the corner of his eye.

"You can't be in here, miss," he said. And then, "Oh, it's you, Peter." And then, "Is that Helen's dress?"

"Hello, Magnus," I said, and tugged the trench coat closed again.

"Hello," he said warily.

"It's nice to see you," I said.

"It's nice to see you too," he claimed, but he sounded less than certain of this. "You look awful. What's wrong with you?"

"That's what I came to see you about," I said. "I need a doctor's note."

"A doctor's note?"

"Saying I'm ill. To give to the Corporation. Otherwise, I'll be terminated."

"You want me to recommend a doctor?"

"No," I said patiently. "I want you to write the note for me."

"I'm not that kind of doctor. I only deal with corpses."

"It doesn't matter," I said. "You're a medical professional. They'll accept a note from you."

He stripped off his gloves and deposited them in a bin. He kept his mask and smock on. He came closer. His brow furrowed.

"What's the matter with your stomach?" he asked. He reached out to open my trench coat, then thought better of it. Instead he went over to the dispenser and took out a new set of nitrile gloves, wriggled them on. Only then did he coax my hands away and pull the trench coat open.

"Jesus," he said.

When he pushed against my belly, I groaned. I had to grab hold of a table to keep from collapsing.

"You've got to get to the hospital, Peter," he said. "Right away."

"It'll go away," I said. "I'm just going through a bad patch." Even as I said this I realized I mostly didn't believe it, but something compelled me to say it anyway.

"Remember what happened to Helen," he said. "You need to go to the hospital. I'll call an ambulance."

"I can make it," I said. "I'll walk there."

He looked at me a long moment, then shook his head. "No," he said.

"No?"

"You'll die on the way. Come on. I'll drive you. We're going now."

He turned and picked up his tape recorder, slipping it into the pocket of his smock. While he was turned, I pocketed the scalpel he had been using. *You never know when you are going to need a good scalpel*, a part of my mind thought. The rest of my mind was puzzled as to what I was doing stealing a scalpel, though not sufficiently to stop myself from doing it.

He wore his mask and gloves as he drove. He kept glancing over at me nervously. The funny thing was that on the way to the hospital, I realized I *didn't* remember what had happened to my wife, to Helen. It was at that moment that I began to suspect my mind was not entirely my own. I knew she was dead, but the specifics of her death had grown vague. It was as if there was a curtain in my mind, gray and fibrous, and behind it were things I was not allowed to remember. What else was to be found behind it?

"You should have gone to the hospital days ago," my brother-in-law was saying. "Lord knows how advanced you are."

"Like Helen did," I said, trying to get some information from him.

"Like Helen should have," he said. "It's the same damned thing all over again."

"It was terrible what happened to Helen," I claimed.

"Yes," he said, keeping his eyes on the road. "Terrible. But you look even worse."

When we pulled up to the emergency entrance, my brother-in-law said, "Stay here. I'll go get help. Don't move."

"All right," I said.

He ran inside. Then he ran back out and removed the key from the ignition, and ran back in again.

You should leave, a part of my mind told me. I have since come to understand that it was not part of my mind at all, but something quite different. *You can't stay here.*

I need to stay here, I told myself. *My brother-in-law told me to stay here. He's getting me help.* But even as I thought this, I felt my body getting out of the car. It was like I was watching it, riding in a little chamber behind the eyes as it moved, jerky and swaying, across the drive and over the curb and through a stretch of ground strewn with woodchips, finally pushing its way into the bushes before collapsing there. Someone was groaning. With surprise, I realized it was me.

From where I was, I could see Magnus's car. After a moment two men wearing protective suits came out of the hospital, my brother-in-law following them. They stopped at the open door of the car, looked around.

"He can't have gotten far," my brother-in-law said, and they began to search for me.

Quickly, my mind that was not my mind said, *you don't have much time.*

...

I did not know what this meant. But as the men in protective suits ran to the far end of the drive searching for me, my hand fumbled in my pocket until it closed on the scalpel. In a moment I had cut open the dress over my belly. I could see my brother-in-law's legs; they weren't far from me. He would find me soon. And then I felt a prickling and looked down to see my hand push the scalpel into my belly and draw the blade quickly down.

There was a kind of whoosh of fetid air and an uprush of yellow fluid. The smell was awful, as of something dead. There was very little blood, but yes, there was some blood too. There was little pain, or rather what pain there was seemed to be muffled, as if hidden behind the gray curtain and beating its wings against it.

I reached in and let my fingers travel over the slick dampness within myself. I did not know what I was looking for or why I was doing it. After a moment, something slid through my fingers and wrapped around my wrist. I tried to withdraw my hand but could not. I tugged hard, then harder still, until, with a sudden pop, it came free.

Pain came roaring over me and I cried out. Suddenly the gray curtain parted and I remembered how my wife had died of the same bloating, and how in the emergency room, short staffed, they had needed me to immobilize her hands as, with an insanely long needle, they had injected her belly, or rather the thing within her belly, with poison. But since the thing was attached to her spine, the poison took her along with it. And in her struggle to break away as I held her, she had managed to bite me and had broken the skin.

Around my hand was something that seemed like a lamprey, slick and dark, strangely ridged along its spine.

"Jesus," said my brother-in-law.

The thing released my hand and flowed quickly toward him and up his boot. He cried out and shook it off. This time it flowed instead the other way, away from him, wriggling into the bushes. He followed it, stomping, trying to crush it. I was in so much pain that all I could do was lie there and wait to die. The two men in protective suits suddenly appeared, peering down at me. Somewhere out of sight my brother-in-law was screaming, screaming. I passed out.

When I came to days later, I was not the same person. I was in an isolation chamber, lying in a hospital bed. I could not move my legs. A nurse was there, beside me. At least I assume it was a nurse; she was in a protective suit with a mirrored faceplate. In it, I could see reflected an image of an emaciated man on the verge of death. It took me some time to realize this was me.

The person in the suit could have been a doctor, I suppose. To be honest, I'm not even sure if the suit contained a man or a woman.

"How are you feeling?" a voice asked. It came from a box on the neck of the suit and was electronically processed, flat.

"I . . . ," I said. "Am I going to be okay?"

"No," said the box. "You are going to die. We would like permission to study you, both before and after your death."

"Study me?"

"We want to understand what happened to you. So we can keep it from happening to other people."

"I . . . Where's Magnus? My brother-in-law? Did he kill it?"

"He killed it, but not in time."

"Not in time for what?"

Instead of answering, the faceless figure pressed a button on the side of my bed. Slowly the head of the bed lifted until I was sitting upright. At that height, I could see through the window into the isolation chamber next to mine. There was a bed in it, and in this bed was my brother-in-law. His belly was swollen, though not to the extent mine had been. A respirator was strapped over his face.

"Will he die too?" I asked.

"We are seeing what we can do," the box on the neck of the suit said. "We might be able to save him. We have refined our procedure since your wife underwent it."

I leaned back. I closed my eyes.

"Do we have your permission to study you?" asked the box.

"No," I said.

I opened my eyes. The suited figure remained motionless. I did not, I realized, have any idea who was in it at all.

"To clarify," said the box, "technically we do not need your permission. We ask only as a courtesy."

I chose not to respond. After a time, the being in the protective suit left and entered an adjacent decontamination chamber. Later, I saw both a doctor and a nurse on the outside of the wall, looking in through the glass at me and my brother-in-law. I do not know which one of them, if either, had been in the suit.

I do not know how much time I have left. I am weak, and the way the creature was separated from my spine left me paralyzed from the waist down. My belly, now flat and crisscrossed with stitches, feels empty. My stomach no longer functions as a stomach, and I take my nourishment by drip. They will study me whether I want them to or not.

All I can do is elevate the head of my bed slightly and sit there, waiting, looking through the glass at my brother-in-law. Despite the distance I can see his belly roiling. It swells bigger every day. At first, from what the box on the neck of the suit said, I thought they had plans to try to remove the creature, but I have come to believe that their plans have changed. They are more interested in studying it, in seeing what happens once the creature is allowed to mature. There are individuals in protective suits with Magnus day and night now, two at a time, monitoring him, measuring him. Sometimes he struggles or resists, but so far the straps have held him in place.

That could be me, I sometimes think. I know the creature convinced me not to go to the hospital for its own purposes, but, still, had I gone, what good would it have done? I would have spent the rest of my brief life in isolation under bright lights as a group of individuals in protective suits watched my creature kill me.

Soon, it will burst out of its own accord. These suits think they have the situation under control, but I know better. It was part of me for long enough that I can still sense it, its impulses, behind the tattered gray curtain within my mind. From this, I know that we have seen nothing yet. The suits have never seen one that is full-grown, one that leaves the host not prematurely out of fear but because, simply, it is ready to unfurl.

I watch. I wait. When it finally happens, the creature opening and spreading redly in the window before me like a movie on a screen, the suits disposed of quickly one by one, I will not look away.

Hospice

In late July, suddenly and without warning, Buhl found himself incapable of drawing a breath. He crawled from his study to the head of the stairs, and there he beat on the wall, trying to signal his girlfriend. By the time she arrived, he had lost consciousness and had tumbled to the foot of the stairs.

He awoke sore, confused. Something had been strapped over his face to help him breathe. He couldn't swallow. His girlfriend was speaking to a woman in white who it took him much longer than it should have to realize was a nurse.

He tried to speak, but nothing came out. They didn't notice him. It still hurt to breathe.

The nurse explained to his girlfriend that they would have to make a hole through his ribs and force a tube in. It would be painful, she told her, probably the worst pain Buhl had ever felt. Buhl, she told her, placing a hand on her shoulder, needed to be told this.

His girlfriend nodded as if she understood, and then the nurse left.

...

Buhl closed his eyes, pretended to sleep. He could hear his girl-friend breathing beside him. For a while he just listened to that. Then he heard her step away from the bed, dial her phone, and speak in a hushed voice.

At first he thought she was speaking to his parents, telling them what had happened. But, though he couldn't quite hear the words, he heard in her tone, in her cadence, a different kind of intimacy. He opened his eyes and stared at her. When she realized she was being observed, the look that came over her face convinced him she had been talking to a lover.

When he told the story later, he often claimed this was the last time he saw his girlfriend. This was false—though it was true that after that he could no longer think of her as his girlfriend. He said noth-ing about the phone call. He had no interest in knowing who her lover was. He only wanted her to leave him alone.

And yet she kept coming, day after day, despite being clearly uncomfortable being there. She felt perhaps some obligation, or simply was afraid of being judged by others: his nurse, say. He watched her, tried to read her, waited for her to say something. In another act of betrayal, she had said nothing about the tube that would be thrust through his ribs, how painful it would be, and he had done his level best not to let on that he had some inkling, that he'd heard anything. But yes, it turned out to be as pain-ful as the nurse had promised his girlfriend it would be. The way his girlfriend watched him through the procedure, the careful, unblinking attention she paid to his pain, made him very nervous indeed.

Look who's here, the nurse would say. *Look who's come to visit.* And then his girlfriend would appear, pretending to be happy to see him until the nurse left the room.

...

Why was she torturing him? Why wouldn't she go? And why couldn't he say anything?

If he had the strength, he began to feel, he would strangle her.

In a way, he told himself, thinking again of how she'd looked at him, it could be called self-defense.

Do you need anything? the nurse asked, late at night. *Can I bring you anything?*

He shook his head. Beneath the sheets he tensed his hands into fists and released them, tensed and released them, building his strength, thinking of the woman still pretending to be his girlfriend the whole time.

Soon, he told himself. It wouldn't be long now.

The Glassy, Burning Floor of Hell

It began with Hekla's sister, who had always been, so she liked to style herself, a *seeker*. There was a workshop she was dying to attend, with a guru of sorts, concerning attunement. But it was taking place some distance away, far outside the city. Would Hekla accompany her? It was a long way to go, and she didn't want to make the drive alone.

"Not really my thing," said Hekla.

"I'll pay your way," said her sister. "You'll share my room and I'll cover the workshop fee. It's in a place called Verglas lodge, out in the middle of nowhere: birds, cows, trees, probably. Come on, it'll be fun."

Initially Hekla resisted. She didn't have a believing bone in her body. But when her sister continued to pester her, she began to think, *Why not?* It would be a vacation, a chance to get out of the city. The workshop would do nothing for her—none of the events her sister convinced her to attend ever did—but she'd tune it out, just as she always did, and enjoy spending time with her sister.

When the day came and she arrived at her sister's place with her bag, she found her hunched over the toilet, vomiting. "I can't go," her sister said between bouts. "Too sick. Something I ate."

"We'll skip it then," said Hekla. "Or go late."

Her sister groaned. "We can't go late. It isn't done. But you go."

"I'd rather skip. I was only going for you."

"It's nonrefundable," said her exhausted sister. "Take my car. I need you to go so I won't feel like I lost all my money."

Hekla, as much to avoid seeing her sister vomit again as anything else, reluctantly assented.

She arrived at Verglas lodge quite late, hours after the other participants. She had no excuse. Her sister's car had not broken down, nor had she been unavoidably detained. It was simply that, outside the confines of the city for the first time in a decade, she had allowed herself to meander. She had stopped in a gravel pull-out beside a river and watched the eddy and flow of the water below, finally picking her way down the slope. She waded in up to her knees, and then, instead of climbing back straightaway, wandered along the bank. Only once she saw the sun setting did she realize how much time she had lost and how far she still had to go.

She arrived at an hour that, in the city, would have been considered merely uncomfortably late, still within the range of acceptability. Apparently, country etiquette was different. The chest-high gate at the bottom of the property was chained closed.

She parked the car on the road's shoulder, heaved her bag over the gate, then clambered over as well. The gravel of the drive was coarse enough that her bag's wheels wouldn't turn. She was forced to carry it.

She followed the road up through the trees until it opened into a weedy parking area, Verglas lodge looming above it. Tired from lugging the bag, she set it down and stretched, taking a moment to catch her breath. Above, the lights of Verglas lodge, both inside and out, had been extinguished.

She picked up her bag and crossed the lot. There was a set of steps cut in the hill at the far end of the lot, hard to make out until she drew close. She climbed them and followed a stone path at the top until she reached the lodge's porch.

The door was massive, stained dark. It had a scene carved on it: she could see a fleeing creature, perhaps a stylized deer, surrounded by a profusion of curves. Flames, maybe?

She looked for a doorbell but saw none. She rapped on the head of the deer, if it was in fact a deer, but nobody came to the door.

Leaving her bag, she followed the wraparound porch to the back. There were no lights on there either, and the only door she found, a battered metal one out of character with the rest of the lodge, proved firmly locked.

She returned to the front door and rapped again. "Hello?" she called, then listened. Still no answer.

She tried to call her sister for advice on what to do, but her phone had no signal. She spent some minutes knocking before she thought to try the handle. It was unlocked.

Had it always been unlocked? Perhaps she had simply foolishly forgotten to try the door handle when she first arrived, had begun by knocking. After all, the gate had been chained closed, the lights off: was there any reason to think the lodge door would be open? True, she was a meticulous person, the kind of person who almost certainly would have thought to check the door when she first arrived. But she found it preferable to think she had forgotten to check it rather than that someone had unlocked it while she was behind the lodge, and yet hadn't turned on any lights.

She pushed her way in, then stood just inside the doorframe, waiting for her eyes to adjust. She could smell something sharp and also the smell of pine—a cleaning product perhaps. She let her hand run along the wall just beside the doorway until it found the blunt stubs of light switches. She flicked up one then the other, but nothing happened.

For a moment she had the distinct impression she was somewhere other than she was meant to be. That she had taken a wrong turn and was now entering a long-deserted place. Surrounded by darkness, it took her some effort to stop from backing out the door. She closed her eyes and held still, trying to master herself.

...

After a while she calmed down again. She was not certain how long she had held still. Probably just a minute or two, though it felt much longer. Perhaps it had been.

There are cars in the lot, she told herself. *This must be the right place.* Probably it was just a matter of a broken switch, or perhaps these switches were turning on lights elsewhere, where she couldn't see. Perhaps the power was out, or perhaps the lodge wasn't connected to the grid, was running off a generator that had been shut down for the night. *There are many plausible explanations,* she told herself, *and very little to worry about.*

"Hello?" she called. Her voice vanished into the darkness.

She got out her phone, turned its flashlight on. In the light, it became an ordinary entrance hall: bare wood floors, gleaming where the light struck them; wood-paneled walls; a ponderous hanging light fixture made of a metal painted dull black; the head of a deer, turned slightly, as if surprised. To her left was a reception counter, a bell on it, a rack of hooks on the wall behind.

She approached the counter and rang the bell, waited. After a while, she rang it a second time. She looked for a door, a room the clerk might be sleeping in, but there was nothing, only the rack of hooks, a number burnt into the wood below each one. None of the hooks held anything, save for one at the very bottom, from which a key hung. Number nine.

It was obvious, then: they had left the door unlocked for her and here was the key to her room. It had to be hers—there was only one key.

She went behind the counter and took the key. Number nine. Carrying her bag so as to make less noise, she made her way down a nearby hallway and deeper into the lodge.

She guided herself using the flashlight on her phone, shining it on each door in turn. As with the hook board, the number of each room had been burned directly into the wood, somewhat crudely. The odd numbers were on the left and the even numbers on the right, until she reached room number five, where, suddenly, the sides reversed. The numbering ended at room eight. At the very end of the hall was a final, narrower door without a number on it. A supply closet, perhaps.

She backtracked and looked for other hallways leading off the entrance hall. There was one other. It led her to a dining room, where she saw a table laid for breakfast. She found a meeting room, a kitchen, and a storeroom farther down the hallway, but no door marked with a nine.

Puzzled, she returned to the entrance hall. Was there an upstairs? Didn't seem to be; no stairway she could see. When she turned her phone light upward, she saw only exposed beams and the slant of the roof.

She could sleep in her car, but that was hardly safe—anyone could come along. Maybe there was a separate cabin somewhere on the property with a nine on its door?

But instead of going outside to see, she returned to the first hallway, counting her way past each room in numerical order. She stared at the unnumbered door at the hall's extreme, then reached out and grasped the knob.

It turned.

She pulled the door open. Beyond was a cramped passageway, walls and floor and ceiling all encased in cedar. She had the vague impression of stepping into a defunct sauna. She moved down the passageway and there, at the end, there it was: a door with a shaky 9 burned into it at the level of her forehead.

She dropped her bag beside the bed and tried the light switch. It made a clicking sound, but no lights came on. She set her phone on the dresser with the light shining up at the ceiling. It didn't light the room well, but it was enough.

The bed was unmade, the sheets and blankets folded in a pile on top of it, as if the maid had forgotten to make it. And the bed was a twin—it wouldn't have been big enough for both her and her sister.

She made it quickly and sloppily, all the while thinking, absurdly, *You've made your bed, now lie in it.*

There was no bathroom, only a half wall near the back wall of the room, behind which was a commode. A mirror hung beside it, though it had been turned to face the wall. She turned it around and found it foxed, almost useless. In it, her face seemed covered with flowers of mold. She hesitated, momentarily transfixed, then shook her head and turned the mirror to face the wall again.

Her phone was almost dead. There seemed no place to plug it in, no outlet. She sighed, then quickly undressed, climbed into bed, and turned out the light.

It was very dark—so dark that when she waved her fingers in front of her face she saw nothing at all. She lay in bed, staring into the darkness. After a while she began to see little vague flashes of light, her eyes misfiring as they attempted to see. Closing her eyes, she turned on her side and tried to sleep.

She dreamt she was in another place, all plastic and steel, far in the future or perhaps simply elsewhere, another world. She was in charge, or not quite, not exactly. She was missing her leg, and the prosthetic she wore was a living thing, a strange creature that knew how to look just like an artificial leg. Nobody except her knew it was anything other than an artificial leg. Once removed, it could unfurl itself and become more or less human. Less, she would have said, rather than more, but then one day she unstrapped the leg in preparation for sleep and it unfurled and took its customary place beside her bed, conversing with her in its soft, soothing voice as she slowly drifted off to sleep, the voice humming gently in the background. What was this creature? How had it come to be beholden to her? How had it come to take the place of her leg? In the dream she did not know the answer to these questions, but found herself wondering as she slowly drifted off, falling asleep within the dream.

But then the creature's gentle humming changed in pitch and register and became strangely familiar. She was abruptly awake again, listening, her eyes still closed. She looked through the slits of her eyelids and saw that the creature beside the bed was staring intently at her, eyes gleaming. As she watched, its face shifted, then shifted again to slowly resemble her own face. Another shift and it looked exactly like her, and the voice it now had was exactly her voice.

She awoke in the darkness with the distinct impression that something was in the room with her. She thought she heard a snuffling sound, felt something brush her arm. She tried to move, to reach for her phone, but she couldn't. She heard a ragged wheezing, which it took her more than a moment to realize was her own frightened breathing.

Shhh, she heard a voice say, or maybe it was the air hissing through her clenched teeth.

Suddenly it felt as if a heavy blanket had been placed on top of her. She was very afraid. The heavy blanket, if that was what it was, made it impossible for her to breathe. Slowly, painfully, she lost consciousness.

She awoke gasping. She could move again. She felt around beside her in the dim light and found her phone, turned it on. Already 9 a.m. She was late for breakfast.

She opened the curtain and soon had enough light to get dressed by. Hurriedly, she brushed her hair, and, limping slightly, left the room.

The lights were on in the entrance hall, and a man with curly black hair stood behind the reception counter. He nodded to her as she hurried past, and she nodded back, moving past him and toward the other hallway.

"Miss?" he called from behind her. "Miss? Over here?"

She slowed. She'd never checked in: of course he needed to talk to her.

She returned to the counter.

"You must be one of the Misses Rognund." He had an accent she couldn't place. Somewhere in Eastern Europe, maybe.

She nodded.

"And where is the other Miss Rognund?" he asked.

"Sick," he said. "She can't come."

"I see," he said. "No bags?" he said. "Perhaps they are in the car?"

"They're in my room," she said.

He looked mildly affronted. "But I have given you no room."

"I came late. There was only the one key. I figured it must be for me."

He frowned, held up an envelope with her name on it.

"I . . . ," she started to say, then stopped.

"Did you not follow the procedure for late arrival that was emailed to you with your confirmation?" he asked. And then, almost as if to himself, "No, you must not have. Where, might I ask, did you spend last night?"

"In number nine."

A strange look crossed his face before being quickly mastered and hidden away. He held out a hand. "Give me the key," he said. She fumbled it out of her pocket. He took it. He started to hand over the envelope, then drew it back.

"How did you find it?" he asked.

"It was just behind the small door," she said. "Not exactly hidden."

"No," he said, "you misunderstand. How did you find your stay?"

"My stay?"

"In nine."

"I . . . it was fine," she said. And then added, "Any reason it shouldn't have been?"

Instead of answering he gave her the envelope. "Here is your key," he said. "Room five."

"But my things," she said. "They're in the other room."

"I will move your things from room number nine," he said.

"I need to repack them," she said.

He shook his head firmly. "I will move them. I will note where they are placed and will do my best to replicate their placement in the proper room, the room you should have been in all along."

"But—" she said.

"You must go. You are late for your workshop."

"But—" she said again.

"Go," he said, shooing her with the tips of his fingers. "Go now. They await."

But they did not await, or at least they had not awaited for her. They were already nearly done with breakfast, the dishes on the table in disarray, the food in the chafing dishes all but gone.

There was no plate left for her: someone had taken two. It was a florid-faced man with watery eyes, wheezingly overweight, with a beard that seemed to have spread too far up his cheeks, as if threatening to consume his entire face. When he saw her take in the two dirtied plates before him, he gave a half shrug of indifference.

She removed two cups from their saucers and then loaded the saucers with the bits and scraps she could find in the chafing dishes— overcooked hunks of scrambled eggs, limp and greasy ends of bacon, hash browns whose latticework had become mush, a soggy toast point. She poured a cup of tepid coffee and then juggled the two saucers and the cup over to an unoccupied corner of the table.

"And you are?" said the florid-faced man, once she was seated.

She introduced herself, apologized for being late.

"You missed yesterday evening's session as well," noted the man, apparently the workshop leader. "A critical session. You are already so far behind," he said, shaking his head. "I am not sure you will manage to catch up." And then, shrugging, he added, "But since the workshop fee is nonrefundable, you might as well stay."

She felt a dull, irrational rage rising bile-like within her, but swallowed it back down. Instead she slightly inclined her head toward him.

For a long time there was silence, and then the man gave a wheeze and spoke.

"As I was saying before I was interrupted," he began, "the quality most needed is a peculiar attentiveness, an ability to tune the soul to a frequency where its vibrations fall slightly below the surface of appearances. A whole world lies beneath this world, comprised of the unheard, the unseen. With attentiveness, you shall begin to learn to hear this world, to see it."

Hekla glanced around the room. Everyone except her seemed to pay this man rapt attention. There was a woman with limp blond hair, obviously and poorly dyed; a man whose face so resembled that of a bulldog that he must own one; a woman, obviously wealthy, wrapped in the tie-dyed scarves of a seeker (Hekla's sister had an array of similar scarves); and four seemingly interchangeable men wearing red ties and white shirts.

"How does one do so?" the leader asked. "How does one go from seeing merely the surface of things to seeing what lies beneath? It is a long and arduous process, full of missteps. In a workshop like this one, we can only accomplish so much, but still perhaps we can lead you there quicker than you might arrive on your own . . ."

She stopped listening. This, she suspected, was a sign that she was on the surface of things, but how could she see this gasping fat man who had stolen her plate and her share of breakfast as a spiritual guru? Listening to her sister read to her the vague description of the workshop over the phone, as she sat in her cubicle surrounded by accountants and actuaries and with her awful middle manager lurking nearby, she had felt that the workshop was probably harmless and worth tolerating for her sister's sake, and to get a vacation. But now, sitting among the participants, it felt like the same set of people as in her office, with an even more awful middle manager.

And then, abruptly, people were standing, breaking into groups of two, leaving her on her own. She approached the leader, who had paired up with the scarved seeker.

"Mr. . . . ," she said.

"Szabo," the leader said.

"I don't have a group, Mr. Szabo," said Hekla.

The leader sighed. "Just Szabo will do. You'll have to join one of the other groups. One group will have to have three."

"All right," said Hekla, and sat down next to the leader.

"One of the *other* groups," said Szabo. "Not ours." He pointed to the two suited men closest to them, who looked startled to be singled out. "That one."

She pulled up a chair beside the two men, who involuntarily drew closer together, as if slightly afraid of her. Eventually they gave her a partial explanation of what they were meant to be doing. *Tuning,* one of them described it as. It involved, so she gathered, exchanging a series of maxims and then interrogating them and thereby puncturing the surface of the world and catching a glimpse of the other world hidden beneath. What was meant by *interrogating* was initially unclear, and remained so. She sighed. It was, she supposed, one way of passing the morning.

By lunch the group had grudgingly accepted her, or at the very least the leader had. Though he had claimed his name was Szabo, she suspected he had been christened something like Rupert or Stephen. By *accepted* she meant that he did not steal her lunch plate, though the way he glumly stared at his now-empty plate suggested he probably would if she left the room. Licking his lips, he delivered a lecture, the same sort of meandering obscurantist mysticism as at breakfast. She secretly checked her phone under the table, hoping to text her sister, but she still had no signal.

Attunement, he told them, was, in a manner of speaking, *at-one-ment,* the state of being at one with the world. *Wouldn't that be atonement?* wondered Hekla. It was a question, Szabo told them, of seeping through the world's surface to permeate its entire being. And then, perhaps because it was clear that she, Hekla, was the one paying the least attention, he turned to face her and looked at her in a different way than before. For the first time, he fixed her in the spotlight of his attention, his *attunement,* and she began to glimpse what it might be that the others found so intriguing about him.

"Hekla," he said. "Curious name. It means *cloak,* does it not?" And before she could bring herself to respond, "What is it you are cloaking, cloak? What do you hide?" And then his gaze left her and he turned away, and her skepticism was free to rise again.

After lunch, Szabo said, "For the afternoon we shall do something different." He stood. "Have you wondered why I hold this workshop here and no place else?" he asked.

He moved toward the door and went out.

For a moment they all sat there, and then with a great scraping of chair legs the four interchangeable men stood and rushed after him. The two other women were close behind, then the man who resembled a bulldog, and finally Hekla. *Does my name really mean cloak?* she wondered. If so, why had her parents named her that? And more important, why hadn't her sister, who scrutinized the names of everyone around her, searching for meaning, ever informed her?

She turned it over in her head, half-distracted as she followed the others into the entrance hall. She was still considering her name, what it said about her, when Szabo turned down the other hall. But she stopped thinking about it entirely as soon as she realized where he was going.

He halted at the narrow door at the end of the hall. "When they were modernizing Verglas lodge," Szabo said, "there was one room they left just as it was. Behind this door lies a fragment of the lodge that used to be."

Hekla felt her arms grow suddenly heavy.

"Is it haunted?" asked the bulldog.

"Haunted?" said Szabo. "What does *haunted* mean? Shall we say rather that this is a special place, a passage back in time?" He turned the handle and entered the narrow passageway behind it, the others filing after him until the narrow space was too full to contain anyone else. Hekla was tempted to turn on her heel and leave, but when Szabo opened the door marked with a nine and entered, and the others trickled in after him, she found herself powerless to do anything but follow.

...

"What do you see?" asked Szabo, his voice hushed. "What do you feel?" He paused, his gaze sweeping slowly around the circle. "Breathe in the air. This is the air of the past. Be attuned. Something happened in this room that made them leave it as it was when the rest of the house was remodeled. What happened here?"

"Someone killed himself!" said the woman with limp hair excitedly.

"A ceremony took place," whispered one of the identical men. "A dark one."

A flicker of irritation passed over Szabo's face. "No," he said. He slapped his hands together sharply. "No! Do not guess! Feel!"

The people around Hekla closed their eyes, breathed in deeply. Hekla kept her eyes wide open.

"Reach," Szabo was saying, sonorously. His eyes, she noticed, were not closed either. He was staring at her, curious. Her effort to make her face reveal nothing made it feel stiff, almost dead. *Does he notice?* she wondered.

"Let the words come to you from the room itself," he said. "Then inhale them, hold them within your lungs, and let them slip through your lips."

He waited, staring at Hekla. She was not going to speak. There was no fucking way she was going to speak.

"No one?" Szabo said. "Then be attuned to me as a start. Watch and learn."

He held his face in one hand, extending the other hand before him, almost brushing the shirts of the interchangeable men.

"A woman came here," he said. "She hoped to escape her life, but she found someone waiting for her—or something, rather. Here in this room. We know from what was pieced together by doctors later that she awoke in the middle of the night, the room deeply dark around her, and felt someone there with her. Or perhaps something. She could not move, she could hardly breathe. She felt as if something heavy had been placed atop her, a great weight, so heavy that she found herself unable to get enough air. Eventually she lost consciousness.

"When she awoke, it was with a start, gasping, as if coming back to life." Szabo lifted his face from his hand. "She went about her day, a perfectly ordinary day, then packed her things and drove back home. Only later did she realize that part of her had been taken by whatever had come in the night. That part of her remained in this very room, and she had no way to get it back."

He was silent, letting his gaze wander from face to face. "Attunement," he said. "I feel the vibrations the events have left. You will too once you are properly attuned."

Perhaps I knew about this woman, thought Hekla. *Perhaps I glimpsed the story years ago in some newspaper or other and subconsciously remembered when I came to the lodge, and then I dreamed it.*

She hoped that was it. She told herself that it was but didn't completely believe it.

And then a spasm flickered across Szabo's face, as if he were in pain.

"Something else," he said. "Something . . ." Abruptly he fell silent. His eyes moved frantically, his gaze refusing to settle anywhere. A spasm rippled over his face again.

A good performance, thought Hekla. *An impressive—*

"Strange," Szabo said, and his voice was different now, less theatrical. "My attunement seems to have shifted to a deeper level. I am being told that the woman in question was missing her leg, though I know for a fact that she was *not* missing a leg. And, even stranger, they tell me the prosthetic she wore looked just like an artificial leg but was also something else. Or, rather, *someone* else. What can this mean? Perhaps this is a metaphor for something real, the room telling us what it can with the language it has at its disposal? It is up to us to properly interpret what it means to say . . .

"And now I see this 'leg' . . . unfurling? Yes, unfurling, and becoming a being of glass and steel. It stands beside her bed staring down at her. Slowly it takes on her form and her appearance— catch her!"

But nobody was quick enough to stop Hekla's fall before she struck the floor.

She woke up lying on the bed. For a moment she panicked, thinking she was still in nine. But no, it was a different room, the furnishings upgraded, with an actual bathroom instead of a commode behind an odd half wall. Number five, her new room. A glass of water stood on the bedside table in a puddle of condensation. The clerk from reception was stationed a few steps from the bed, his hands clasped in front of him like a funeral director. The door of the room had been left ajar.

"Here you are, then," said the clerk. "Back among us."

"What happened?" she asked.

"According to Szabo, you fainted. I took charge of you so the workshop could proceed."

"Thank you," she said. She tried to sit up, found herself dizzy.

He moved forward and pushed her shoulders gently back down. "Perhaps you shouldn't go back to the workshop," he said. "At least not until they are finished with what they are doing in that room."

"Why?"

But the clerk did not respond.

"I don't want to go back," she told him. "I want to leave."

"Leave?" the clerk said. He shook his head. "Miss Rognund, it is a little late for that."

After a while the clerk left, and she was alone. She tried to stand but the dizziness was still strong, and one of her legs refused to support her. She fell onto the floor, had to claw her way panting back onto the bed. She could not leave, not yet. But she would stay here and rest until she could.

She closed her eyes. Even though it was still early afternoon, she soon fell asleep.

...

Her dreams, the few she had, were at first vague and indistinct, as if being glimpsed from too great a distance. They seemed vaguely familiar and not at the same time: more like someone was telling her about their dream than experiencing a dream herself. There were bits and pieces of the lodge in it—a version of the clerk with a different accent, the stag's head now topped with a profusion of antlers instead of the two it had, a much longer and more meandering gravel path leading to the lodge—but all as if seen through a dirty pane of glass.

And then, suddenly, it all came into focus. She imagined herself walking down the hall, a hitch in her step. She came to the door with the number five burned into it, tried the knob, found it unlocked. She opened it and looked inside.

The room was empty. She stayed, hesitating for a long moment, then went out and continued down the hall.

She walked past room six, then seven, then eight, then opened the door at the very end of the hall, then the door beyond that, the one with a *9* burned at the level of her forehead.

Inside, lying on the bed, was a woman who looked exactly like her. She approached slowly, careful not to wake her. She bent over the bed and stared down, but no matter how closely she scrutinized the woman she was unable to say which one of them was the real her.

When she awoke, she was in a different place. Someone was shaking her. It took her more time than it should have to realize that that someone was Szabo, and that he was sitting beside the bed, staring at her.

"What are you doing here?" she asked. Szabo ignored this. "Where am I?" she asked, and when Szabo ignored this as well, she suddenly knew she was in number nine.

But how had she gotten here? Had he carried her? Had she, asleep, wandered back here herself? Why would she ever want to come back here?

"I knew you would come," said Szabo. "I suspected when you fainted, and so I kept vigil and now I know for certain. I hardly dared hope for this. I sat and watched the bed and for a long, long while there was nothing, and then I watched you slowly come into existence here. I have been waiting for you, for someone like you, for years!"

"What are you talking about?" she asked.

"Don't you see?" he said. "You have been chosen. You are attuned, not just your mind but your body too. You belong to this room. You belong to *her*." He groped for her hand, squeezed it too hard. "Together we will accomplish so much!"

She fled. Szabo hurried after her, at first cajoling and then, when it became clear she wasn't going to stop, pleading and threatening. He grabbed her by the arm and she shook him off. When he grabbed her again she shoved him, got him sufficiently off balance that she could yank her arm free.

She rushed to her room—five, not nine—and managed to unlock the door, step inside, and shut it again before Szabo could get his foot in.

"Hekla!" he yelled, pounding on the door. "You owe me this! You owe this to everybody!"

She shuddered. Rapidly she thrust her things into her bag and zipped it shut. Szabo was still pounding on the door, desperate now, back to pleading again.

She came close to the door and considered what to do. Beneath her feet, the floorboards creaked. Szabo stopped shouting, stood silent instead, listening. Hekla listened back.

"Hekla, are you there?" he finally said.

"I'm here," she said.

"Come out, Hekla," he said. "I want to make you famous."

She didn't say anything.

"I will make it worth your while," he said through the door. "I'll pay. Just to be around you. Later, once you understand, we'll be partners."

"Okay," said Hekla.

"Okay?" he said, surprised, and she realized she should have resisted more before giving in. "Then open the door."

"I'm going to take a shower," said Hekla. "I need to gather my thoughts. I'll be out in a minute."

He was saying something else through the door, but she paid no attention. She moved into the bathroom, turned on the faucet, switched it over to the shower. As steam began to fill the bathroom, she walked to the far side of the room, opened the window, dropped her bag through, and clambered out after it.

The car was where she had left it, though the gate was open now and there was a note under the windshield wiper written on lodge stationery asking her to kindly move it into the lot. She opened the trunk and threw her bag inside. She had just unlocked the front door and was climbing in when she heard a shout and saw Szabo rushing down the drive, his cheeks puffing desperately for air, his entourage scurrying all around him. Quickly she started the car, drove.

She didn't stop at all on the way back to the city. The whole trip she kept glancing in the rearview mirror, expecting Szabo's car. But she didn't know what sort of car he drove; how would she possibly recognize him?

She arrived quite late, too late to go to her sister's house and return her car, so instead she drove back to her apartment. In any case, her sister didn't expect to see her until the next day. She was exhausted. She left the bag in the trunk; she could get it out in the morning. She climbed the four flights of stairs, opened the door to her apartment, stepped inside, and fell onto the bed. Almost immediately she was asleep.

Did she dream? Yes, she dreamed. At first it seemed vague and indistinct, but in the dream she warned herself that she should not be fooled by this. And indeed, when everything sprang into focus and she saw herself walking through the paneled entrance hall and past the stag's head, whose antlers now were so vast and ramified they spread like a tree up the wall and into the rafters, she was braced for what she knew would happen next. There she was, walking down a hall that seemed longer than the hall should be, stopping to open a door, looking into the empty passageway behind it, continuing down the passageway to its very end, then past that end and into a room marked with a blackened number nine, and to the side of a bed in which she saw, sleeping, unaware, herself.

When she awoke, she knew something was wrong. She could not hear the noises of the city she usually heard, and the light through her eyelids was too dim. She could hear, if she listened closely, the distant crowing of a man's voice, excited, triumphant. She felt something brush her arm. Or no, that wasn't quite right—it brushed *through* her arm, leaving it tingling.

Hekla, she heard him say, barely a whisper. *Focus. We begin to glimpse you. You are nearly here!*

She stayed, eyelids clenched shut, willing the noises of the city to rise up around her. They wouldn't come. *Don't open your eyes,* she told herself. *Don't open your eyes.*

But, eventually, she did.

Acknowledgments

The title of this book (and of the final story in it) is taken from Marguerite Young's massive and wonderful experimental novel, *Miss MacIntosh, My Darling*. It is a book that I deeply admire, and that manages the confusion of what is real and what is imagined in a way that I find truly remarkable. I owe a debt of gratitude to Steven Shaviro, who encouraged me to read it and helped lead many of us through it with his careful notes and commentary. I could not have written this book without Young, Robert Aickman, and Algernon Blackwood. They, and so many other writers, taught me so much as I read them, and made my work better.

I want to thank Sarah Evenson for continuing to so ably remake the beast and to expand the concept with the covers she does for each new book.

I owe a great deal to the editors of the many journals and anthologies that published these stories. The stories are better for the careful attention they paid them.

Thank you to my agent, Matt McGowan, and to my publisher, Chris Fischbach, and to all the amazing people at Coffee House Press who helped bring this book into the world. And above all, to all those readers who continue to support my work.

Publication History

"Leg": Lincoln Michel and Nadxieli Nieto, Eds., *Tiny Nightmares*

"In Dreams": *Conjunctions*

"Myling Kommer": Tim Jarvis, Ed., *Uncertainties*

"Come Up": Alessandro Manzetti and Jodi Renée Lester, Eds., *The Beauty of Death II: Death by Water*

"Palisade": *The Silent Garden: A Journal of Esoteric Fabulism*

"Curator": *Conjunctions*

"To Breathe the Air": *McSweeney's*

"The Barrow-Men": *UNSAID*

"The Shimmering Wall": Darren Speegle and Michael Bailey, Eds., *Prisms*

"Grauer in the Snow": Jordan Krall, Ed., *In Stefan's House: A Weird Fiction Tribute to Stefan Grabinski*

"Justle": *Alienocene: Journal of the First Outernational*

"The Devil's Hand": Ben Thomas, Ed., *The Willows Magazine*

"Nameless Citizen": Darren Speegle and Michael Bailey, Eds., *Adam's Ladder*

"The Coldness of His Eye": Christopher M. Jones, Ed., *The Porcupine Boy and Other Anthological Oddities*

"Elo Havel": *Nightmare Magazine*

"His Haunting": Ellen Datlow, Ed., *Echoes: The Saga Anthology of Ghost Stories*

"Haver": *Strange Aeons*

"The Extrication": *Conjunctions*

"A Bad Patch": Brendan Vidito and Sam Richard, Eds., *The New Flesh: A Literary Tribute to David Cronenberg*

"Hospice": *UNSAID*

"The Glassy, Burning Floor of Hell": Michael Kelly, Ed., *Shadows and Tall Trees*

Funder Acknowledgments

Coffee House Press is an internationally renowned independent book publisher and arts nonprofit based in Minneapolis, MN; through its literary publications and *Books in Action* program, Coffee House acts as a catalyst and connector—between authors and readers, ideas and resources, creativity and community, inspiration and action.

Coffee House Press books are made possible through the generous support of grants and donations from corporations, state and federal grant programs, family foundations, and the many individuals who believe in the transformational power of literature. This activity is made possible by the voters of Minnesota through a Minnesota State Arts Board Operating Support grant, thanks to the legislative appropriation from the Arts and Cultural Heritage Fund. Coffee House also receives major operating support from the Amazon Literary Partnership, Jerome Foundation, McKnight Foundation, Target Foundation, and the National Endowment for the Arts (NEA). To find out more about how NEA grants impact individuals and communities, visit www.arts.gov.

Coffee House Press receives additional support from Bookmobile; Dorsey & Whitney LLP; Fredrikson & Byron, P.A.; Kenneth Koch Literary Estate; the Matching Grant Program Fund of the Minneapolis Foundation; Mr. Pancks' Fund in memory of Graham Kimpton; the Schwab Charitable Fund; and the U.S. Bank Foundation.

The Publisher's Circle of Coffee House Press

Publisher's Circle members make significant contributions to Coffee House Press's annual giving campaign. Understanding that a strong financial base is necessary for the press to meet the challenges and opportunities that arise each year, this group plays a crucial part in the success of Coffee House's mission.

Recent Publisher's Circle members include many anonymous donors, Patricia A. Beithon, Anitra Budd, Andrew Brantingham, Dave & Kelli Cloutier, Mary Ebert & Paul Stembler, Chris Fischbach & Katie Dublinski, Jocelyn Hale & Glenn Miller, the Rehael Fund-Roger Hale/Nor Hall of the Minneapolis Foundation, Randy Hartten & Ron Lotz, Dylan Hicks & Nina Hale, William Hardacker, Kenneth & Susan Kahn, Stephen & Isabel Keating, the Kenneth Koch Literary Estate, Cinda Kornblum, Jennifer Kwon Dobbs & Stefan Liess, the Lambert Family Foundation, the Lenfestey Family Foundation, Sarah Lutman & Rob Rudolph, the Carol & Aaron Mack Charitable Fund of the Minneapolis Foundation, Gillian McCain, Malcolm S. McDermid & Katie Windle, Mary & Malcolm McDermid, Daniel N. Smith III & Maureen Millea Smith, Peter Nelson & Jennifer Swenson, Enrique & Jennifer Olivarez, Alan Polsky, Robin Preble, Jeffrey Sugerman & Sarah Schultz, Nan G. Swid, Grant Wood, and Margaret Wurtele.

For more information about the Publisher's Circle and other ways to support Coffee House Press books, authors, and activities, please visit www.coffeehousepress.org/pages/donate or contact us at info@coffeehousepress.org.

BRIAN EVENSON is the author of over a dozen works of fiction. He has received three O. Henry Prizes for his fiction. His most recent book, *Song for the Unraveling of the World*, won a World Fantasy Award and a Shirley Jackson Award and was a finalist for both the Los Angeles Times Ray Bradbury Prize for Science Fiction, Fantasy, and Speculative Fiction and the Balcones Fiction Prize. He lives in Los Angeles and teaches at CalArts.

The Glassy, Burning Floor of Hell was designed by
Bookmobile Design & Digital Publisher Services.
Text is set in Adobe Caslon Pro.